MW00987434

Meet the Meat Man

Richard Morgen

To Therese

CHAPTER 1

Even You Can Haiku

2012 – San Francisco, California

How does one summarize the past 35 years of his life for an old friend that suddenly reappears via the Internet?

Richard took another sip from his Manhattan. It dawned on him that a Haiku would be the perfect vehicle to mock the ludicrous nature of his dilemma. Five minutes later he looked at his laptop screen, smiled, and read it to his reluctant muse Terrie.

> *Into the wilderness I went,*
> *can't remember shit,*
> *women keep taking my money.*

Richard felt an elbow jab into his ribs. "Ow! Mercy! Mercy!"

"Mercy? Mercy? We don't give no stinking mercy!" Terrie replied.

Richard said, "It took me two days to write that thing!"

"Anyway," Terrie said, "First try fixing your malfunctioning mouth! Then maybe I'll talk mercy with you."

She migrated back to her dinner preparations in the kitchen, while Richard's eyes followed her fifty-year-old body trapped in a younger movie star figure.

Richard unruffled his feathers and mumbled to himself, "Well, that about covers everything." He downed the last sip of his drink. "I wonder if there's a market for this Haiku stuff?" he called out to Terrie, who was now busily constructing a pasta sauce in the kitchen for dinner.

"I think about five-hundred years ago in Japan you could have made a pretty shitty living doing that," she called back while rummaging through the spice cabinet. "But don't quit your day job," she said. "Oh yeah, you don't have one, do you?"

"Thanks for your sensitivity," Richard replied as he pushed himself up from his desk. "I should make one up about your life."

"Yeah, you should," she responded. "I could use a good lawsuit to jumpstart my new career."

"What career are you talking about?" Richard said, stretching his back.

"Suing assholes. It's a growth industry. Anybody can do it." She was losing interest in the chatter and went into her office since her sauce was now on autopilot, simmering.

Richard called out to her across the small apartment. "Sewing assholes or suing assholes?" He was just getting warmed up. He ignored the deafening silence and walked into her office. "I bet that you are dying to hear the only asshole joke that I know."

"Get out of my office," she said without looking up.

Richard continued his joke undaunted, "An apprentice at a mortuary named Jenkins, was working graveyard shift, preserving bodies. His boss had instructed Jenkins to call him at home only if there was an emergency but otherwise just do his job and let him sleep. As you can imagine, it was a bit spooky being in a room full of corpses late at night, but Jenkins had been doing this job for some time and up until now there had been no emergencies of any kind. But on this night, Jenkins was working away on a corpse when, from out of its asshole, clear as a bell, came the sound of the classic song 'Moon River.' Not the whole song, mind you, just the two words, 'Moon River,' sung exquisitely by a choir.

Well, the first couple of times, Jenkins pinched himself in disbelief but every few minutes this kept repeating and a bit louder each time. Finally, not at all sure what to do, Jenkins decides he better call his boss. It's 2 A.M. and the phone wakes up the boss from a deep sleep. Jenkins explains the problem and then holds the phone up in the air when the singing starts up again, this time the loudest yet.

'I thought I better call you. I'm out of my league. I really don't know what to do.'

There's a twenty-second pause, and the boss finally says loudly and slowly, 'Jenkins, it's two in the morning. I cannot for the life of me believe that you would feel compelled to wake me up at two in the morning, just to listen to some asshole sing Moon River!'"

Terrie slowly looked up from her computer screen and said, "Richard, get out of my office."

CHAPTER 2

Breaking into Canada

1973 – Blaine, Washington (US-Canada Border)

The four woebegone hitchhikers brought to mind Dorothy and her entourage from The Wizard of Oz as they set their eyes on the Emerald City, in this case, a nondescript Canadian Customs border checkpoint "glistening" in the distance.

"Gentlemen, I guess this is the moment we've all been waiting for." Richard said, stating the obvious. "Ahead lies the land of milk and honey."

"You sure that wasn't supposed to be the land of whale blubber and doughnuts?" Kenny inquired.

"Lordy, Lordy! Dey sez da watamelons grows as big as trees daire, dey shurly doos!" David marveled. David had a habit of reverting to the voice of an escaped slave looking for a better life.

The four of them had been hitching-hiking together for over one month, during which time they'd begun adopting alter egos, and would intermittently switch back and forth initially as a means to keep each other's spirits up, but now just out of habit. And the list of identities was growing. Strangers overhearing snippets of these conversations tended to leave a wide berth between themselves and this group primarily out of concern for their own safety.

By now, the inane humor no longer quelled the group's anxiety. They were starting to feel the pain of poverty, and filled with gear that they looked like they were planning to create a new civilization.

After having hiked a half mile or so, a pickup truck came flying toward them, dust billowing. A red truck emerged from the dust and ground to a halt amongst the four weary travelers.

"Get in, get in," shouted several voices from inside the truck. The four threw their packs into the back of the pickup truck and they crammed inside. "So, where you fellas off to today."

"Well man," David said, "at the moment we have a little problem. We are heading up to Alaska, but we can't cross the border at Blaine 'cause we don't have enough bread to get through the checkpoint. So, unless we can go around it, we're screwed."

The three teens in the truck wriggled with excitement. The driver turned his head back to the travelers and said, "You fellas are in luck! We can help you! Our parents are all border guards."

The third one interrupted, "We'll take you to exactly where you need to go! It's easy. You just wait until dark, and you follow the border road right back towards Blaine for about two miles, but about a quarter mile before you get to it, you cut through the big cattle pasture until you get to the highway in Canada."

The driver tipped his hand. "They already got something like half a million of us getting shot at by North Vietnamese, the Draft Board won't even notice that you forgot to show up to get killed." Within ten minutes they were standing on the border road, having been pointed in the correct direction by the traitorous border patrol teenagers.

Just say "eh" a lot and you'll be fine. It apparently was going to be that simple. It all seemed that perfect. Once again, loaded down with their gigantic backpacks, they headed down the dark and dusty road, talking in whispers. Euphoric whispers. The four trudged through the darkness

CHAPTER 2

Breaking into Canada

1973 – Blaine, Washington (US-Canada Border)

The four woebegone hitchhikers brought to mind Dorothy and her entourage from The Wizard of Oz as they set their eyes on the Emerald City, in this case, a nondescript Canadian Customs border checkpoint "glistening" in the distance.

"Gentlemen, I guess this is the moment we've all been waiting for." Richard said, stating the obvious. "Ahead lies the land of milk and honey."

"You sure that wasn't supposed to be the land of whale blubber and doughnuts?" Kenny inquired.

"Lordy, Lordy! Dey sez da watamelons grows as big as trees daire, dey shurly doos!" David marveled. David had a habit of reverting to the voice of an escaped slave looking for a better life.

The four of them had been hitching-hiking together for over one month, during which time they'd begun adopting alter egos, and would intermittently switch back and forth initially as a means to keep each other's spirits up, but now just out of habit. And the list of identities was growing. Strangers overhearing snippets of these conversations tended to leave a wide berth between themselves and this group primarily out of concern for their own safety.

By now, the inane humor no longer quelled the group's anxiety. They were starting to feel the pain of poverty, and the possibility of conscription to fight in the Vietnam War. Among the four of them they now had only $74.23, way below the minimum $200 per person required by Canada in 1973. Without at least that much scratch, you were unceremoniously turned away at the border crossing.

To complicate matters, not only did all four have tenuous status with the U.S. draft board but also, potentially, with the Canadian immigration authorities.

"Okay," Kenny said in his most authoritative voice. "Time for Plan B." Kenny liked to act like the leader, but he was delusional. It was a futile effort, nevertheless he gravitated to the thankless job of Chief Cat Herder. With his long, black, pony tail, half-way down his back, tattered t-shirt and holes in his jeans, his outward appearance certainly wasn't the problem, as this was the uniform of the times. The fact that he seemed to always need to be in charge created a constant source of friction with his fellow travelers.

"Yeah, Plan B, Plan B." Brad said with his mouth full, spreading a copious quantity of butter onto a hunk of bread. Brad spoke in short sentences since his mouth was usually full and he didn't have a whole lot to say. He seemed to survive almost completely on butter with a little bread. Unlike their endlessly pontificating fearless "leader," Kenny, who was often seen striking a pose that replicated the famous oil painting of General George Washington crossing the Delaware River, Brad was comfortable sitting by the side of the road in the dirt with the others.

"The way I see it," General Kenny continued, "the border's over there." He pointed over there.

"Yeah, over there, like he said." Brad repeated without looking up. Like the others, Brad had long hair but his bushy black beard was his distinguishing feature. Covering his baby face, it made him look closer to forty years of age rather than his actual twenty.

"Yeah, I was thinkin' the same thing exactly, yeah." David added slowly, now slipping into his village idiot persona. Richard wondered if David was brain damaged since he was such a convincing moron sometimes. He found this thought frightening since David was probably the smartest of the four. What did that make the rest of them?

Undaunted by his useless companions, the General continued, "And since we are going to have to use the back entrance door into Canada, we need to go over there," this time pointing parallel to the border. "Okay!" he concluded enthusiastically, as if he had just given the Gettysburg Address, "It's agreed. As chairperson of this loose association of mentally deficient losers and deadbeats, by unanimous acclamation transmitted to me psychically and as endorsed by Robert's Rules of Order, I, Ken Weisman of New York, New York, hereby declare that the resolution to sneak across the Canadian border via Washington State, on this day of... Does anyone know the date?" He looked around.

Greeted by silence as the others drew figures in the roadside dust, he heard Richard speak, not looking up. "I lost you after the part about Plan B." A few different sized sticks were neatly piled around him as if this was his livelihood.

This startled Brad and David out of their own dust worlds, and they started babbling, "Yeah Plan B! Plan B!" again.

"Okay, fuck it then" Kenny said. "We go that way for a mile, turn north, then go that way into Canada, and Brad gets the first bite of da watamelon! The ayes have it!" They all mumbled "here, here" in their best British accents, something they would often do to acknowledge general agreement amongst themselves and gradually began to reassemble their packs. Soon they were trudging down a dirt farm road, each of them carrying a huge backpack so filled with gear that they looked like they were planning to create a new civilization.

After having hiked a half mile or so, a pickup truck came flying toward them, dust billowing. A red truck emerged from the dust and ground to a halt amongst the four weary travelers.

"Get in, get in," shouted several voices from inside the truck. The four threw their packs into the back of the pickup truck and they crammed inside. "So, where you fellas off to today."

"Well man," David said, "at the moment we have a little problem. We are heading up to Alaska, but we can't cross the border at Blaine 'cause we don't have enough bread to get through the checkpoint. So, unless we can go around it, we're screwed."

The three teens in the truck wriggled with excitement. The driver turned his head back to the travelers and said, "You fellas are in luck! We can help you! Our parents are all border guards."

The third one interrupted, "We'll take you to exactly where you need to go! It's easy. You just wait until dark, and you follow the border road right back towards Blaine for about two miles, but about a quarter mile before you get to it, you cut through the big cattle pasture until you get to the highway in Canada."

The driver tipped his hand. "They already got something like half a million of us getting shot at by North Vietnamese, the Draft Board won't even notice that you forgot to show up to get killed." Within ten minutes they were standing on the border road, having been pointed in the correct direction by the traitorous border patrol teenagers.

Just say "eh" a lot and you'll be fine. It apparently was going to be that simple. It all seemed that perfect. Once again, loaded down with their gigantic backpacks, they headed down the dark and dusty road, talking in whispers. Euphoric whispers. The four trudged through the darkness for about a mile, when a U.S. Border Patrol four-wheel drive pickup truck came flying over a knoll. Terrified, someone blurted out, "Abort! Abort!" In a split second, all four dove face first, backpacks and all, into a ditch. To their amazement, the patrol truck zoomed by the travelers without incident but the ditch was not merely a ditch but an ancient blackberry patch. Slowly the moaning began, as the travelers found themselves completely stuck in the brambles.

Richard was the first to extricate himself. His eyes, now adjusted to the darkness, evaluated the carnage as he picked thorns out of his body. "You guys look like a bunch of tar babies," he said.

David, who was face down in the thicket about 3 feet up in the air, whimpered pitifully. "Fuck a duck. I can't move. Can anybody hear me?"

Kenny, who had chosen a sideways lunge into the abyss, was virtually unsalvageable. "Somebody help me!" he commanded.

Brad sputtered pitifully, "What... I don't... guys... hey," incapable of finishing a sentence. It appeared that his mouth only worked when the rest of his body was in an upright position.

Having now assumed the role of God, Richard considered the triage priorities and concluded, "I might need to just shoot a couple of you poor fools and put you out of your misery. I really think that you're beyond saving." He was starting to enjoy their predicaments; they were so absurd. None of the blackberry patch prisoners appreciated his attempt at levity but their fifty-pound packs, in combination with gravity, put them in poor negotiating position. "Okay, Tar Baby Number One, I'll cut you free first," he said to David, "then Tar Baby Number Two, then Tar Baby Number Three."

"Just hurry up!" ordered General Weisman.

"Or maybe I'll leave one in the bramble bush for Mr. Fox to eat," Richard reflected as he began to consider a deranged version of Beatrix Potter's story. "Now, which one might it be?" he said, standing over Kenny.

"I swear I am going to strangle you with my bare hands if you don't hurry up!" General Tar Baby growled "All right, all right, you pathetic little tar babies," Richard relented. His Buck knife cut David and Kenny free in no time. It virtually took the Jaws of Life to extract Brad, who not only was completely tangled but also weighed 40 pounds more than the others. "You've been eating too much butter, Br'er Brad," Richard scolded.

It took nearly a half hour before all of the thorn damage was mitigated to levels allowing the illegal crossing mission to continue. The General punctuated his strides with a mantra of obscenities but since he was a renowned whiner nobody sympathized.

David seemed possessed, his voice dropping a full octave to become growly and mega-macho as he constantly produced and spat some sort of imaginary toxic waste from his mouth. He took a more stoic injured-soldier view of things, matter-of-factly commenting, "Listen up girls and don't take this as a complaint, 'cause we all have to keep our minds on the mission but I believe my pecker might have taken a thorn for the cause and that just may mean that, after we win this darn war, this G.I. Joe might be out of the procreation business." His matter of fact speculating about his future fertility being compromised was no doubt an inspiration to the rest of the platoon.

Richard knew that David was feeling better whenever his multiple personality disorder kicked in. This particular manifestation was known as "Sergeant Rock," who feared nothing and along with his subordinate, "Ice-Cream Soldier," who periodically inhabited Richard's body, would make morbid jokes about any atrocity yet still be the go-to-guy you wanted in your corner when the going got rough. He always liked to finish on an upbeat note. "Just some fun and games. Maybe the world wasn't ready for a bunch of Baby Rocks anyhow."

"Right you are!" concurred his subordinate, Ice Cream Soldier, the quintessential yes-man.

Brad, who had applied some butter to his wounds to kill the pain, said, "This stuff really works!" like he was making a TV commercial.

They soldiered on into the darkness. Kenny inspired by his earlier border-crossing vision. After about a half-hour the Blaine border crossing shone bright, having morphed from the Emerald City to the Canadian version of the Statue of Liberty (in this case, a statue of an enormous Beaver with a sword held up to the sky). Kenny spoke as if the others could see his vision which was weird, since most people don't feel particularly inspired when they are tromping across a cow pasture immersed in manure. Kenny continued his mantra, "Bring me your stoned. Bring me your dysfunctional." They came to a barbed wire fence and, with no end of suffering in sight, made it through with only a few more puncture wounds. In the darkness they made their way as Kenny continued "Bring me your blackberry bush ravaged." They headed in the direction of a gas station a half mile past the crossing site. Despite the lights in the distance, the four young travelers could barely see the ground in front of them, and since the farm turned out to be a dairy farm, it soon became apparent that the field was just one enormous cow pie. Unable to determine where the next land mine was placed, they just hiked as fast as they could. "Bring me your cow dung encrusted hippies." Eventually, they came to another taut barbed wire fence. At this point it wouldn't have stopped them even if it had been electrified and manned with machine gun nests. "Bring me your thorn riddled, barb-wire punctured, cow-pie encrusted hippies..."

Thanks to all the indignities that they had just endured, the young men had descended into such a low level of sanitation that they were virtually self-contained human hazardous-waste sites. They unceremoniously endured the final humiliation in the border-crossing saga by getting hung up in barbed wire by the side of the highway. They took turns tearing themselves free from the wire, shredding their clothes and puncturing their skin.

The four climbed up to the busy highway. It started to sink in. They had made it!

"I had no idea that Canada was made completely out of shit," Ice Cream Soldier reflected.

"I might not of come if I had known," General Kenny muttered to himself.

Looking back at the border crossing in the distance, Sergeant Rock said quietly, "You just try and keep us out, you Canadian mothers."

Brad, having now returned from his own private world of fantasy dairy products, observed, "You know that butter really was effective. I feel great!"

They remained silent for a couple of minutes. The sky was clear and the stars were out in full force. Ice-Cream Soldier pronounced, "Well boys, welcome to Canada, eh."

"Mission Accomplished," the Rock said, issuing his stamp of approval. "I just feel sorry for the poor blockheads that pick us up next. Their car's gonna be a total write-off. But war is Hell." He spit out some more toxic waste as if to punctuate his point.

CHAPTER 3

Motion Picture Madness

1969 – Marin County, California

"What's the name of your movie?" Richard asked the two fifteen-year-old directors, his next door neighbor, David, and David's jovial friend Rex. He could hardly believe that his eccentric neighbor was also a movie director of sorts. Richard was one grade younger than the two directors and, as was the custom, had rarely interacted with them until now, due to their one-year grade difference.

"We call it Meet the Meat Man, David said proudly, his wire-rim glasses slightly steamed up in excitement. The lights went out and the projector started making its distinctive clicking sound. Immediately the title, made up entirely of sausages and cold cuts, lit up the screen. Following the opening credits, culminating in link sausages dancing, using the latest in technological advances (in this case, string threaded through each individual sausage link), the main character made his initial entrance.

The butcher, portrayed by a butcher, is seen chopping up meat in a manner suggestive of a criminal enterprise of some sort. In conjunction with the choice of music, the maniacal war song "Mars, the Bringer of War" by Gustav Holst, the audience was filled with the desire to invade something.

In any event, the influence of Alfred Hitchcock and Ingmar Bergman, as interpreted by the minds of two unique fifteen-year-olds, was fresh and original and the first four minutes of the film showed great promise. In particular, the butcher's acting was flawless, because he wasn't so much acting as just doing his job.

The second scene, which conveyed an impending catastrophe, had the butcher revealing his inner rage to a customer (played by Rex, who wore a pin-striped suit and fedora). Rex made a special request for a pastrami sandwich, totally ignoring the sign on the wall that stated in bold print:

THIS IS NOT A DELI!! THIS IS A BUTCHER SHOP!!!!

This set off the butcher's hair-trigger temper and he flung an expensive handful of liverwurst at the wall so violently it stuck. The scene closed focused on the liverwurst as it slowly succumbed to gravity.

The film had not been edited, so it wasn't fair for Richard to draw any conclusions but he did see a couple of slightly disjointed clips that exhibited moments of genius, one with the butcher driving away in his personal vehicle making angry gestures toward the filmmakers, that indicated this filming wasn't part of their original agreement. When the tape fell off the reel, David said; "That's as far as we got. We are having funding issues, until our next allowances we can't afford any more film." But he went on to share that the butcher's obscene gestures would be softened with some upbeat music. Something like "California Dreamin'" by The Mamas and the Papas. Then the film could easily segue into a dramatic shift whereby the butcher hooks up with a baker and a candlestick maker and they have a ménage à trois during which all three would catch on fire during a tryst. The moral of the story being—maybe don't smoke in bed. Or never have a sexual relationship with more than one highly combustible tradesman at the same time. With their critical funding problems and all, art was going to have to take a back seat to the constraints of the almighty dollar.

Rex nevertheless had given a lot of thought to this part of the film. "Maybe the candlestick maker, maybe he was a she, and she intentionally lit the fire? Maybe she was a pyromaniac, or a nymphomaniac-pyromaniac candlestick maker. If we can just get the plot right, I think we're talking blockbuster."

Richard couldn't argue with his logic but that was because he didn't know the definitions of half of the words Rex had just used. Plus, Rex wore a cool red and white checkered bandana around his neck, which added to his mystique.

"Listen up, Kid," Rex said as he anointed Richard with a nickname. "David and I have some really good mescaline that you might want to try out with us."

"Yeah," David said, suddenly excited. "We could go backpacking in Bear Valley this weekend and try it out. It's supposed to be really fun. And it's not addictive or anything. I've read up on it. It's mellower than LSD. According to Aldous Huxley, anyways."

The Kid didn't know anything on this subject; his mind was usually on baseball or girls. "Sure, sounds like fun," he said, as if he had the faintest idea what they were talking about.

Parenting skills at that moment in history were not even close to keeping up with the situation on the ground, which was changing rapidly. Looking back at this world with the benefit of what would one day become common parenting knowledge, there would be considerable concern that these three young teenagers might themselves be prime candidates for spontaneous combustion, not unlike the butcher, baker, and candlestick maker.

David pulled open the living room blinds. Richard noticed that across the street his father was patrolling their lawn, his face showing frustration as he examined the dying grass. He had an infamous black thumb, having systematically killed off all of the plants on the property in the two years since they moved in. It was a holocaust. The grass was his grand finale. He walked over to the garage to investigate if he had any type of chemical that might resuscitate the lawn. He loved chemicals.

David looked at Rex and said, "You remind me of Aunt Jemima with that scarf." Rex and The Kid both laughed. They decided to go downstairs into David's bedroom and make a list for the backpacking trip. They made a nice trio.

CHAPTER 4

Drug Deal Gone Awry

2013 – San Francisco, California

Richard had just returned to the City from five months of traveling through Southeast Asia. You really shouldn't smoke pot there; the penalty is death. Then a group of peasants urinate on your remains, then your body is fed to a Komodo dragon. Even alcohol could be surprisingly hard to find in many areas of Indonesia, suffice it to say, by the time he had de-planed, Richard had a hankering for mind-altering substances.

Terrie wanted to go dancing to celebrate his return and suggested they pick up a little weed at the local dispensary in Golden Gate Park—ten dubious characters hanging out in the shadows, looking completely suspicious. It appeared the police had determined this mob was too benign to be any danger to the local citizenry. There were bigger fish to fry—or they were down at the local donut shop. Who knows? Richard did know that he and Terrie were now only half a block away and could just make out the usual suspects in the distance.

Terrie dropped Richard off across the street from the drug lords. He made his way up to a scruffy, furry faced, long-haired, middle-aged man who was standing off from the rest. "Hey!" Richard said. "Do you know where a guy can get twenty dollars of pot around here?"

The dealer looked Richard over, decided that he was harmless, said, "Yeah, I can do that. But I can't take the money on the street. Cops," he looked at the trees around them. Richard followed his eyes into the trees but didn't see any cops. The dealer continued, "Just meet me across the street at McDonald's. Order me a Bacon Habanero Ranch Quarter Pounder meal, with a large fry and a McCafé Frappé Caramel. I will come over in five minutes and sit down with you. While I'm eating, we'll do the deal."

Taken aback, Richard thought this seemed a lot of work for a couple of joints. "You know," he replied, "by the time I cross the street, I will have completely forgotten your order. In fact, I have already completely forgotten your order. Isn't there an easier way?" Richard was just starting to formulate a theory that this guy was an undercover agent. But if he was, he was good. Damn good. To be able to convincingly play the part of such a moron, this would take a bit of talent. But why would they invest such resources into such a trivial crime anyway? Richard decided to go with the assumption that the dealer was just an aspiring criminal who was in slightly over his head. Since Richard hadn't bought pot on a street corner in many years, the dealer was spooking him a bit as well.

Whoever he was, came up with a revised plan. "Okay, okay, get me a medium Caramel Macchiato with whipped cream and sprinkles."

Richard was trying not to laugh when he again changed his line of thought—maybe this asshole is a narc and instead of arresting me, he's toying with me.

Richard repeated the order back to the dealer. His mind swam. He tried to remember. Who approached who? The macchiato is legal and the pot is illegal. Does he want pot in his macchiato? At last Richard had all the ducks in a row and made his next move. "Fuck it. Let's do this puppy."

The dealer looked at him like, "Who talks like that? A narc?" But before he had time to line up his own animals in a row, Richard had turned and was heading straight to Micky-D's to do the puppy.

Richard stood in line calculating exactly what laws he was breaking. Possession of marijuana, was that even a crime anymore? Was there some sort of law that he was breaking that he didn't even know about? Fast-food Fraud? McMealin' dealin'? Macchiato-transport between street lights? But by now, he was in too deep. It was show time. He got to the front of the line. He looked up and saw a camera pointed directly at him. He turned and saw a second camera. This is just great, he thought. He decided if the server asked him to speak a bit louder into the microphone, he would make a run for it.

Remembering Goofy and the Seven Dwarfs, the cops outside eating donuts, waiting to kick his butt and cuff him with; "Book 'em, Danno."—without missing a bite from their donut—Richard could see the headline. "Local Man Arrested, Fast-Food Drug Deal Gone Awry!" with a picture of him holding his hand in front of his face.

"How can I help you, sir?" the server said, snapping Richard out of his thoughts.

Now Richard knew he was dead. This one had to be a cop. Her delivery was just too polished he thought to himself. He figured he was as good as jail bait. Looking at four to ten in a federal penitentiary, squealing like a pig and wearing pig-pink hot pants. "I'll have a medium Caramel Macchiato with whipped cream and sprinkles please," he said with the sound of a prison door slamming in his ears.

"Would you like chocolate chips on your Macchiato?" she asked.

Why is she playing cat and mouse with me? The drug lord had never mentioned anything about chocolate chips being part of the deal. This puppy was spiraling out of control!

"Chocolate chips?" Richard stammered. "Um, yeah, whatever! Let's do the chocolate chips." The server was unfazed. Richard quickly glanced around the room and realized that all the customers were either homeless people, drug dealers or drug addicts. He was the least frightening person in the room, with the unfortunate effect of making him stand out like a sore thumb. He got his drink and change and went to the corner of the room and sat down. He noticed another camera pointed at his table. He was starting to wonder if he had inadvertently walked in on an undercover sting operation, he being the inevitable collateral damage. Had the FBI shared notes with the Department of Homeland Security? Was this an interagency squabble coming to fruition?

After a couple of minutes, Richard's Medellin drug lord connection came in and walked over to the table looking as suspicious as possible. His eyes darted from one camera to the next. He looked at his drink on the table. "Oh no!" he whined as his head flopped against his chest, his arms dangling. "I hate chocolate chips in my macchiato!" He seemed devastated.

Richard looked him directly in the eyes. "Sit down, Serpico!" he whispered as violently as he was capable of. "I don't give a flying fig about your macchiato! Where's my pot? I want to see product." He was starting to scare himself. Their heated exchange didn't seem to arouse any interest from the adjoining tables. Richard did note a slight increase in respect from his business associate as he sat down. They stared at each other warily, mano a mano, as the dealer took a slurp from his drink.

The dealer pulled out a clear plastic container full of pot and plunked it on the table beside his macchiato. "Do you have a bag?" he asked.

Richard was starting to lose it. "Don't drug dealers carry plastic bags anymore?" he asked. The deal was starting to go sideways on him, and he was getting really close to taking back the macchiato and walking out the door.

Richard's new friend shook his head at him like he was talking to the village idiot. "It isn't environmentally OK to use plastic bags unnecessarily, dude. I charge an extra ten cents for the plastic bag. Are you cool with that?"

Richard was speechless. The dealer was grinding him down to his level. "Yeah sure, fine. I'm cool, I'm cool," he said, pacified. The dealer bagged up the product and handed it to him. Richard looked up and flipped the bird at the camera and then put it into his pocket. He handed over the $20.

The dealer looked at it and said, "Okay, now I'll go get your change for the macchiato."

"No!" Richard said, popping up out of his seat. He couldn't handle another transaction no matter what. "I mean no, that's on the house. Thanks."

The dealer looked at Richard like he had won the lottery. "Hey, thanks!"

Richard bolted out the door where Terrie was double-parked. "What took so long?" she asked.

"You wouldn't believe me if I told you," he replied. "I am never buying drugs at this dispensary again."

They drove off down Haight Street towards their next adventure.

CHAPTER 5

The Scrapyard Blues

1973 – Vancouver, British Columbia

Having successfully broken into Canada, the four now encountered a new obstacle. In order to work, it was essential that each one of them acquire what was known as a Social Insurance Number, referred to by the locals as a SIN card. According to the manager of their youth hostel, one could acquire a close replica for $100.00 at a local nightclub called The Dead and the Dying from a fella named Ian, who presumably wasn't dead yet. As none of them had one hundred bucks, they instead availed themselves of the local underground economy most in need of workers, that being the strawberry and raspberry farmers. One week and a couple of million brain cells later, they had collectively amassed enough money to pay Ian in advance for the order of phony ID's.

As it would take approximately two weeks for the ID to get produced, the travelers decided to go camping and live off the rice, beans, dried fruit and granola that they still had in large supply. Whatever else could be scrounged up (clams and mussels) would be added to the pot to break the monotony. But Brad had a different idea, which he revealed to the others the day before their departure. "I've decided that my path is heading in a different direction than yours. I found a yoga ashram on Granville Street that is willing to take me in. This is exactly what I've been wanting for myself spiritually. To have something in my life that helps me grow into a better person."

Richard thought of Brad as growing into a bigger person, rather than a better person, thanks mostly to his obsession with butter but showed his support in spite of being devoid of any spiritual philosophy. "That's great, Brad. We're gonna miss you. What do you do in an ashram? Shoot up smack?"

Brad was immune to Richard's twisted humor. "Lots of meditation. Lots of yoga. Lots of shooting up smack."

Kenny didn't look up as he pondered having a diminished group of minions that never properly listened to him anyway. "Sounds great, Brad. Congratulations. It's not going to be the same without you." He paused, deep in thought, planning their next campaign. "We'll have more to eat now."

Of the three left, David was the least cynical. "I hope that works out for you. If they allow visitors maybe I can pay you a visit sometime and I can get all meditated and yoga-ed up."

Next morning the remaining three, each carrying their trademark enormous and heavy backpacks, set out by bus, hitch-hiking and public ferry. A few hours later they found themselves in the capital of British Columbia, Victoria, on Vancouver Island. It was a charming city but due to lack of finances they continued on toward their final destination, the West Coast Trail, a backpacking trail in an isolated area on the rain-saturated western side of the island. They say sunbathers on the West Coast of Vancouver Island don't tan, they rust.

It was a pleasant enough trip there, except for the two different times when they had to run the gauntlet through logging camps. In both cases numerous loggers were digesting their logger food on the front porch of their feeding stations, commonly referred to as cook shacks. As the three walked by on the dirt road, a steady tirade of trademark redneck observations rained upon them.

"Look over there Bill, looks like the company sent us some new loggers," or the endlessly amusing, "Do you think that one there is a boy or a girl?" This was a particularly interesting observation, as all three travelers had beards. Then a bunch of loggers would laugh raucously, impressed by each other's razor-sharp wit. The temptation to say something back to them was compelling but, having strong survival instincts, the three stoically continued onward.

It is often someone's misfortune that manages to break up the monotony that backpacking has lots of. In this case, it was poor David that metaphorically pulled the short straw less than an hour before arriving at the trailhead. The narrow dirt logging road that had been their compass, gradually became the entrance road only, since logging was no longer allowed near the park itself. The road had been grown over with grass and other plants, and David had started meandering a bit off of it. The silence and tranquility were suddenly interrupted by David.

"Oh no! Logger shit!" David had stepped into a huge Paul Bunyan sized logger turd and was having a hard time extracting his boot to safety. As he began the cleanup stage, his "friends" roared with laughter.

"David, ixnay on the logger shit!" Richard suggested.

"Yeah" Kenny added. "It's not hygienic to hang out in that stuff."

"As much as you'd like to." Richard added. "You sick pervert."

Kenny and Richard were laughing at David's plight while David groused.

"You guys missed your calling. You should have been comedians. The ole logger shit routine. It never fails to bring down the house." Kenny could barely talk he was laughing so hard. "What does he do for an encore?" he choked.

Finally reaching the trailhead at the start of what turned out to be an eight-day trip, they read a brief explanation about how the trail came into being. The primary reason, to reduce casualties from shipwrecks. Until the West Coast Trail was built, the fortunate sailors that managed to make it to shore found such a rugged and inhospitable forest awaiting them that their attempts to hike out to civilization proved to be more challenging than their prior cold-water swim in the ocean. The government of the day built this fifty-mile-long trail replete with over one hundred ladders and bridges, miles of slippery boards and several high-tide surge channels. Cougars, Wolves, and Black Bears patrolled the wilderness area year-round, except during the hibernation season for four months or so.

By modern times, the trail also brought in revenue for the Pacheedaht Indigenous people, who lived along these ocean inlets and could be counted upon to ferry backpackers across to the other side for a reasonable fee, and often would cook up all-you-can-eat delicious fresh crabs for crustacean lovers. David and Richard were reading all this while talking about what a relief it would be to leave the annoying loggers behind, when a van with a Utah license plate pulled into the empty parking lot. Four young fellows, a few years older than they, got out and purposefully strolled to the trailhead. They were dressed conservatively, no blue jeans or long hair, but instead, clean-cut starched pants and shirts. There was an awkward silence. Richard attempted to break the ice, as they might be crossing paths over the next week. "Hi," he said with a smile. Their leader mumbled hello back in an obligatory manner. "We're from San Francisco," Richard tried again. This time a couple of them nodded like this explained everything. Sensing the futility of the cultural divide, he added, "We're hippies." All four of them nodded as though Richard had made a confession.

Before Richard could conclude by saying, "and serial killers," Utah's front man spoke. "We're from Utah. We're Mormons." What does a hippie say to a Mormon? And what does a Mormon say to a hippie? So, they went their separate ways, the three longhairs heading down the trail.

Infamous for heavy rainfall twelve months of the year, they did not experience one drop of rain. That and finding a nice chunk of hashish in the fire pit the first night out made for the ultimate imaginable beach camping experience. Every night saw a blazing bonfire, a rationed supply of hashish and all the mussels you could eat. Once medicated, Kenny would regale the others with stories about his job as a mail sorter in New York City along with his partner in crime, Simon. Their main concern was doing as little work as possible.

Kenny explained, "Our boss's name was Bruno Eichmann and this guy smelled so bad the whole mail sorting room would totally reek when he'd come into the room. I'm serious, he was like a human septic tank. We called him Stinky Eichmann."

It turned out that Stinky Eichmann had some illegal things going on in his department and he was the worst one of the bunch. The heinous crimes committed ranged from various and sundry mail fraud issues, to an institutionalized lack of work ethics. Not to mention the brain numbing monotony of sorting mail. David and Richard found his stories amusing since neither of them had ever had a real job yet in the above the ground economy.

The three finished the hike in the dark and came to the last salt water crossing. They didn't have to yell for long. An indigenous fisherman who lived on the other side came to pick them up. He sold them live crabs that he caught and kept cooking more until they were stuffed.

The three made record time getting back to the hostel in Vancouver and were surprised to find the SIN cards waiting for them at the post office's General Delivery. With no more obstacles preventing them from applying for work, they made their way over to the government Manpower office, which many used to acquire jobs.

"All things in due time," the old wise man at the Manpower office said to Richard, in response to his inquiry about proper protocol. The old geezer was so full of himself that he was unbearable. Richard looked around the room. He went back to his seat and whispered to David, "If I go directly for that prick's jugular vein, I might be able to kill him before they pull me off."

As usual, David, being the voice of reason, took a deep breath and said reflectively, "Breathe deep my son. Try to appreciate our last minutes of freedom before we become answerable to our next slave owner."

What had been perplexing the three since they showed up at the office early, was how they were to interpret the ritualistic process that was unfolding in front of their eyes. What would happen typically was that the wise guy would pull an index card from an envelope, slowly and methodically, and painstakingly jot down a couple of notes. Then he would stand up from his desk and make a pronouncement to the entire room full of job seekers, specifying the pay per hour, the business and address, and the job title. That was the comprehensible part. The potential employees were spread out at tables, many of them smoking and playing cards. But instead of a stampede of bodies throwing themselves to the front of the line, only one, usually an older man, would slowly get up from his chair and nonchalantly glide up to the wise man's desk and take the index card where the details were clarified. The three finally realized that there was an unspoken pecking order, whereby those with seniority could cherry-pick the best jobs. After about twenty minutes of this Chinese water torture, the wise man called out another job description. "The next job is Barnes Scrap Yard on Burnaby Street. Pay is seven dollars per hour. Job starts today." A deadly silence fell over the room. The card players didn't even look up from their hands. Richard nudged David. Kenny, ever the slacker, was busy looking at a magazine and settling in with the crowd at large. David nodded back and Richard stepped forward. "We'll take it," he said.

The room continued expressing indifference, while the wise man looked up with a smirk on his face saying, "We have a couple of scrapyard workers. That's excellent."

"Did you happen to notice that we were the only ones in that room of a hundred people who stepped forward?" David reflected.

"Yeah, but we're down to less than thirty dollars between the three of us," Richard replied. "We're broke man! And those rice and beans are killing me. We need some meat man!" His fear was justifiable, as his wiry frame topped out at 147 pounds, despite being six feet tall. He needed calories and lots of them to prevent himself from blowing away in the wind.

"But I did notice that everybody's favorite postal worker, Mr. New York-New York, has gone AWOL." The two searched for Kenny for a couple of minutes to no avail. They decided to head out, David pointing out that "a bird in hand was better than two in the bush." Just as they opened the door to leave, who do they bump into but none other than the phantom Kenny.

"There you are! We were worried sick about you." Richard said, feigning distress.

Kenny had news. While David and Richard were filling out forms, he got a hot tip from a stranger about unionized sawmill jobs opening up three hundred miles north. Now! Such was the way of labor shortages. And not only that, the stranger asked Kenny if he wanted a ride to the sawmill in exchange for splitting the gas with him. This did have the unfortunate side-effect of wiping out the last of Kenny' share of the cash but there still was a couple of days' worth of rice and beans with his name on it.

As David put it, "The worst that could happen is you'll slowly starve to death writhing in great pain." Before they headed off to work, Richard and David decided that they could give Kenny ten dollars each of their money since they were already employed. This gesture was enough to make the usually cynical Kenny a bit choked up. All he could get out was a heart-felt "Thanks."

Within twenty minutes they found themselves on a city bus heading to work.

The run-down business consisted of the Barnes family, who handled the management and administration, overseeing the entire employee pool of five workers including themselves. The other three consisted of a young man named Caesar, a recent immigrant from Czechoslovakia named Carl, and the crane operator, Dimitri.

Within minutes the new employees were promoted to overseeing a baling machine. The industrial products to be baled consisted of metals in various forms, from aluminum cans to rusty wire and copper equipment parts. All products deemed worthy of recycling needed to be thrown over the five-foot high walls of the crusher before the compacting stage. Once the machine had been filled to the top, it had a lid that was able to crush the contents down to a significantly smaller size. Once crushed, they were baled with metal strapping. One of the four sidewalls could be opened, allowing access for the crane to remove the contents. Only Dimitri was deemed competent enough to operate the enormous crane. The work was perversely satisfying.

The Barnes were a tight-knit Jewish family. The son ran the joint but every day his ancient father would make the rounds, rubbing his hands together the whole time.

Richard remarked to David one day, "You know, he's the kind of Jew who gives the rest of us a bad name. I mean he walks around like Shylock, the way he's always rubbing his hands together."

"Aren't you being a little hard on your people?" David wondered back. "Maybe he has some sort of hand condition or something?"

Richard reflected for a moment, "Maybe he does, but that's my prerogative. Jews can criticize other Jews. It's one of the only fringe benefits of being in our club. That plus all the gefilte fish you can eat."

David grimaced then said, "Just our luck. I think collectively we represent two of the worst cuisines in the world." David was of Swedish descent.

Just then Caesar came over and told them, "Carl's bringing a pile of old wire over, better hop to it before Barnes sees you. You're gonna love this stuff!" he said, laughing to himself. Things like this absolutely made Caesar's day.

The bus ride back to the hostel that night was standing room only but both men had empty seats beside them. The old wire had been so rusty they had worked in a rust cloud all day and now looked like a cross between coal miners returning from the pits, and the dirtiest homeless people on the planet. One prissy middle-aged woman leaned over to David and said, "Really, must you!"

David broke out laughing in her face. It had been a long day in the mines.

CHAPTER 6

Better Living through Chemicals

2012 – San Francisco, California

Richard woke up to the sound of his father's voice outside his bedroom door. "Rick, get up, would you? I have a job for you." He woke up to pretty much the same opening salvo every weekend. His father was the enforcer while his mom provided the sound effects of the outraged parent.

"Millard! Richard has to do his share of the work around here! I feel very strongly about this." His mother, on a roll now, always had been the bad cop. Her specialty was summarizing just how unfair everything was. "I've had it up to here with these kids!" she roared, holding up a hand in front of her eyes, leaving an entire arms-length for more dastardly crimes that would undoubtedly be committed in the future.

His father continued, "Rick, get up, will you? I need you to mow the lawn. Now!" Richard rolled in bed, not quite ready to acknowledge the existence of his parents. He visualized walking in an upright position, eating breakfast and finally having a good whine about the injustice of life, where a fourteen-year-old could be treated like a slave in need of a U.N. tribunal to convict his parents for crimes against humanity. He slowly got out of bed, pulled on some pants, went into the kitchen and poured himself a bowl of cold cereal. His father went outside and poured gasoline into the lawn mower's gas tank. He came back into the house and said, "Rick."

"Yeah?" Richard responded, slurping down his cereal.

"I have to run down to the hardware store. Get the lawn mowed while I'm gone." His father could be relentless when any of his kids resisted.

"You mean quit chewing my Fruit Loops? Or can I finish chewing my Fruitus Loopus and afterwards mow the lawn, which is my preferred choice by the way."

His father wasn't about to get sucked into the vortex of Saturday morning cleanup. Richard's mom was now out of earshot. "Just mow the darn lawn before I get back and cut the crap about the Fruit Loops. It's not a bright idea to make your mother angry this morning."

"Yeah, okay," Richard replied, pacified, concluding that the U.N. tribunal might have to wait until his mom had killed one of her own, holding a smoking gun for all to see. The lawn had been a point of great disappointment for the entire family. Everybody else in the neighborhood seemed to have a green lawn but not the Morgensterns'. His father treated the garden as if it were the enemy. Like something that had to be subdued. In this scenario chemicals, and lots of them, were the only solution, the garden one large test tube. The lawn hadn't died completely but like seeing a beggar with half of his body parts missing, you want to help but it seems futile.

After Richard fired up the lawn mower, he mowed the "lawn" down to within an inch of its life. The neighbor across the street, Mrs. Vincenza, had a white poodle that went by the name of Fifi. Fifi regularly patrolled her quadrant of 10 or so homes. If you had questioned any of the local pets in the neighborhood, they would all have agreed this was Fifi's fiefdom. Usually impeccably quaffed, Fifi wasn't really feeling like her usual self today. She had just had a surgery to take care of a womanly condition and to add indignities to indignities, the vet had put a conical piece of white plastic around her neck, so she wouldn't lick her wound. Basically, treating her like one of the brain-dead mixed breeds on the block that Fifi wouldn't normally have a thing to do with. Before Richard started raking up the dead grass, Fifi came by and rolled in it.

"Hi, Fifi," Richard said as he picked up the rake. "Love your new neck collar." He scratched both of her cheeks.

Fifi thought to herself, "You love my new 'neck collar'? How about fuck you and the horse you rode in on?" She intentionally peed in the dead grass so that Richard could see and daintily trotted away.

"Nice touch, Fifi." Richard called out after her. "You're a class act."

Fifi briefly considered one last visit to the land where plants went to die, in order to take a huge dump but decided to take the high road instead. At her core, Fifi was a lady.

Richard's dad was exuberant upon his return from the hardware store. He claimed to have found a new product that was reputed to be the answer for a lawn that was only moments away from certain death. Their lawn fell squarely into this bracket. But it was somehow ironic that as an act of desperation, a Professor of Jewish History would buy a product called "Final Solution." He pulled the Final Solution out of the bag. It consisted of a paint dispenser and some green paint—for painting lawns.

Richard's mother was the first to ridicule her husband. "Millard, you've had some bad ideas before, but this might be your worst one ever." She paused for effect and continued. "Congratulations."

"Putting in a new lawn is over two hundred dollars. This kit is only eight dollars. Worth a try. What have we got to lose?" Millard replied.

Richard's mom rolled her eyes. "Go ahead. But when this is all over, I think this is going to cost us two hundred and eight dollars."

Thankfully, Richard's Dad decided to apply the paint himself. After threatening to kill any member of the family dumb enough to step onto the grass before it had dried, he had the entire lawn looking like new in only twenty minutes. The entire neighborhood seemed to walk by to check out the advantages of better living through chemicals. They seemed suitably impressed. But later in the afternoon, Hawthorne Avenue witnessed an event that still lives in the folklore of suburbia.

Upon further reflection, Fifi decided that she would, in fact, return to the Morgensterns' dead grass and plant an enormous dog turd in prominent display, as her way of saying, "Thanks for your sensitivity during these difficult times."

In Fifi's defense, hindsight is always twenty-twenty and when you think about it, why should a poodle be knowledgeable about new lawn products? But in any event, it all happened in a minute or two. Fifi quickly did her duty on a prominent location where her symbolic gesture could be viewed by one and all. Feeling good about herself, she rolled on the Morgenstern's freshly rejuvenated lawn. As Fifi rolled, a sensation of oneness with the universe enveloped her. She could hear a choir of angels singing a delightful melody that permeated her pores. She lay flat on her back, paws outstretched to the heavens. Everything was in slow motion, the defecation, the roll, another roll, then Fifi noticed that she was completely green. "Oh my God!!!!!" she barked. "I look like a frickin' Martian!"

Fifi never was the same after this nightmare. People would point at her and laugh. Her self-esteem was shattered. The story about the green poodle from outer space with the matching white collar was an instant favorite amongst gardeners and non-gardeners alike. It seemed that it probably was the single largest contributing factor to lawn paint's demise as the solution to dead grass. Dead grass was here to stay. And somewhere... somewhere the spirit of one green and humiliated space poodle lives on.

CHAPTER 7

Attack of the Winged Baby Jesus

2014 – Florence, Italy

Richard stared up toward the ceiling of the ancient church. The spectacular Roman columns stood at attention on all sides of the building. His eyes drifted over to a huge oil painting. The characters in the painting consisted of numerous bearded men in long robes, dragging a bloody corpse. Winged babies fluttered above the chaos.

Richard spoke in spite of his fear of offending somebody, "These winged babies are kind of creepin' me out. I had no idea that they ever existed. They must have evolved in some remote place like the Galápagos Islands." Terrie ignored him, choosing instead to focus on the building's beauty.

Richard whispered to Terrie with his best Italian accent, "Do you notice how the baby Jesus' little wings flutter much-a faster than the other babies? That is because he has-a the super powers. The other winged babies, they are very sweet but they no have-a the super powers. They just flap-a their wings and pester people. Like-a the mosquitos 'cept-a they sweet like the candy. All of the winged babies, they-a died off during the last ice-a age."

Terrie continued her thoughtful observation and when finished said, "If you don't-a shut-a up-a, I'm-a gonna knock-a your head off. Capisci?"

Richard, knowing when it was best to cut and run, summarized saying, "You can learn-a a thing-a or two from the winged baby Jesus. He was a very wise guy."

Terrie would have no more of this. "You're-a gonna get-a us kicked out of the church-a if you don't make-a your mouth stop-a moving. You might even-a get me exco-friggin'-communicated."

Richard was surprised. "I thought-a you quit-a the church already. Mama mia!"

"They make-a the rulebook, not-a me. If they-a kick-a me outta the church, I think I might-a go straight-a to Hell on the Devil's Express-a bus," she said, concerned about the repercussions.

"No-a pass-a the go?" Richard replied.

"Go-a straight to the jail without having the two hundred dollars," Terrie said, looking straight into Richard's eyes.

Richard pointed to the huge front doors. "Let's-a blow-a this winged-a baby Jesus factory."

They made their way outside and looked around in the bright sun, trying to make their next move. Richard took a deep breath of Tuscan air and looked in the direction of another ancient church. "If I-a so much as see-a one more winged-baby Jesus painting, I might-a start-a the pukin'" Terrie took Richard's hand and they walked down the cobble-stoned street in silence.

CHAPTER 8

Richard and David Get New Shitty Jobs

1974 – Revelstoke, British Columbia

They woke up in a dark forest around 2:30 in the morning, both hung over. Richard and David started to reconstruct what had happened. Early that morning, after having worked one full month at the scrap yard, the two Boy-Palz concluded that a career in crushing metal and metal products wasn't going to bring either of them the full and fruitful lifestyle that they both so desired. They had gotten a ride from two already slightly drunk older loggers, who both drove something called "loaders" for a living. At some point they diverted from the highway, which was a winding two-lane road in the Rocky Mountains and headed down a bumpy and much narrower dirt road. The real purpose for this side trip turned out to be that the two loggers both wanted to fire up their enormous pieces of heavy equipment and do battle. They appeared to be incapable of communicating complex thoughts, or for that matter, simple thoughts, so the travelers had to surmise that this was what loggers did on their days off. The loggers got out of their pickup and fired up their machines. The two loaders raised their huge blades as high up into the sky as they could extend and started some sort of ritualistic phallic pushing contest. This was all happening in the darkness with the machines' enormous headlights lighting the spectacle.

The young men watched the battle act out until one of the machines acknowledged defeat by flashing its headlights. "I wonder if the loaders are going to start mating now," Richard mumbled to himself.

"If that happens I'm making a run for it," David replied.

"Aren't you at all curious which one is the male and which one is the female?" Richard continued.

David looked at Richard incredulously and said, "It's the middle of the night. It's pitch black. We're in an ancient rain forest somewhere in British Columbia with two loggers who apparently can't speak English and we are about to watch two pieces of heavy equipment start breeding. Doesn't this strike you as a bit odd?"

Richard thought about this for a moment and said, "Well, when you put it that way..." He pondered in mid-sentence, then concluded, "...yeah, that is pretty fucked up."

The two loggers, having completed whatever it was that they were doing, came back to their pickup truck and, without explaining, drove back to the main road and the nearest bar. It was full of more drunk loggers but David and Richard and their wild hair were not harassed so long as they sat at the same table with these two strange men. The two loggers continued to use words sparingly but when they did it seemed like every thought was punctuated by saying "piece of cake" and, as they drank more, it became just "cake." Their words were otherwise unintelligible, unless it was a special logger language that the two hitchhikers just didn't understand. After about an hour of drinking, it became obvious that getting into a vehicle with these two guys was no longer a viable option and to make matters worse, Richard was starting to see comic book bubbles coming out of the loggers' mouths with just the word "cake" inside of them. They instead took their packs out of the back of the pickup, walked into the forest darkness, crawled under a tree and passed out.

When the two young men found themselves wide awake in the wee hours of the morning, they made their way back to the road and, mercifully, the light from the now closed pub was still on. David noticed two local native men were passed out and lying on the ground by the front door.

They hadn't been there but a couple of minutes when a Volkswagen van pulled over and picked them up. They were greeted by three long-haired young men in their early twenties named Danny, Tony, and Silvio, all from Los Angeles. They were making a pilgrimage home from a sawmill located in northern Alberta where they had just finished working. They were a lively bunch, naturally high on life along with an assortment of other drugs that they kept pulling out of their daypacks.

Danny seemed to be the brightest of the bunch. He had a habit of zoning out when he listened to you but five minutes later would make a thoughtful reference to what was said earlier. Somehow this unorthodox manner of communication seemed to work for him. "You two need money, right?" he surmised, since people hitch-hiking at 2:30 in the morning typically had hit rock bottom.

David laughed. "That would be nice. We're starting to eye road kill."

"Road kill!" Danny repeated. "Oh my God!"

"Yum, road kill," Silvio added.

Danny laughed in a high-pitched insane way. "No really. You want to avoid road kill at all costs. This is not a pretty picture you're painting. Ahhhahaha!"

"Not a pretty picture." Tony contributed.

Richard was noticing Tony didn't construct sentences, he only repeated them.

"It's not that road kill was our first choice," Richard added. "It's just that, well, the other option is grubs and road kill beats the hell out of grubs."

"Oh my God!" Danny repeated. "We are going to give you the address to the Pryson Brothers Sawmill. They even have bunk houses and cook your meals. No road kill. No grubs. Just meat and potatoes. And they always need workers."

"Ahhhahaha!" Danny laughed at nothing in particular.

With a tangible destination, David and Richard parted ways with Danny and the Angelinos, who turned South toward Los Angeles. As they expected, the hitching was slow and it took five days to cover the seven hundred miles north. The scenery and wildlife helped make up for the mind-numbing boredom that was the major drawback of hitching. They lived in terror of the Big Waits which were sort of the opposite of what surfers live for, the Big Wave. These were waits of over twenty-four hours. Stories of legendary Big Waits were common amongst fellow hitchers. The best stories in hitchhiker lore would invariably be the ones where, after days of being stuck in the same spot, the hitcher would meet his future wife and get married and settle down since it became apparent they were predetermined by some higher power to never leave. David and Richard concluded after one particularly horrible Big Wait, that hitching was essentially a type of Zen practice, referring to it as "the lowest form of meditation."

Finally, they arrived at a tiny town in what could safely be called the middle of nowhere. Enilda was a one-horse town, with that horse being the Pryson Brothers Sawmill. It was alongside an enormous body of water known as the Lesser Slave Lake, which played second fiddle to its larger sister lake, the Great Slave Lake. The two entered the ramshackle office, unaware that the only slaves in these parts were all duly employed by the Pryson clan.

Getting hired by the Pryson's was a real family affair, starring Ma and Pa Pryson, their six grown sons and all the miscellaneous and sundry pubescent and baby Pryson's. And they were easy to spot since, in order to be a genuine Pryson, you apparently needed to be missing a couple of fingers. The older the Pryson, the fewer the digits. Much like counting rings on a tree to determine its age but instead by counting missing Pryson fingers.

The travelers were unceremoniously ordered to get to work by one of the Pryson's. The job took place at the "green-chain" and entailed pulling long pieces of green, heavy, lumber off a chain conveyor and onto a pile. It turned out to be easy work... for about three minutes. It dawned on the terrified new workers that, although they were ostensibly hired by the Pryson family, the green-chain was in charge. All the other green-chain workers looked at the new guys with amusement during this rite of passage. Within a couple of minutes, the inevitable would happen, both new guys would get behind and create a lumber jam. Nobody would offer to help them out. Right out of Charlie Chaplin's Modern Times bad would turn into worse and a world of pain rained down upon them. Boards would crisscross each other as order descended into chaos. In desperation the travelers began pulling boards onto the ground to defer the inevitable cleanup. Eight hours became eight thousand hours. Boards would fly at them "like a bat outta Hell." That was how all the laborers would characterize an onslaught of lumber out of control during a night shift. "Like a bat outta Hell." The world became a purgatory for wayward hippies, this brave new world would become... their new jobs. For a couple of weeks anyhow. But that was no consolation since it felt as if time stood still during each shift. This was living hell and no money or meat and potatoes could compensate for this soul-sucking experience.

As previously advertised, a large spread of beef stew, mashed potatoes, and boiled vegetables awaited our heroes at the cook-house. David was famished, while Richard was close to dead from exhaustion. That, however, did little to stop him from filling up his plate with monumental servings of everything, just as David had. However, halfway through devouring the contents of his trough, Richard realized that he had seriously miscalculated his portion size. He suddenly felt a serious nausea attack from the combination of overeating and overworking. In a desperate attempt to bring order to the universe, Richard took his plate to the dirty dish area, where all of the sawmill savages would scrape their plates. Beside those dishes was a sign stating, "DON'T WASTE FOOD! TAKE ONLY WHAT YOU CAN EAT!" Now you tell me, Richard thought to himself. As he scraped what felt like enough food to feed a small country, he noticed that Ma and Pa Pryson, as well as numerous other miscellaneous Prysons, were sitting at an adjoining table, most likely to make sure that law and order was maintained. The entire room went dead quiet as Richard continued to scrape. He felt like time was running in slow motion, with men shaking their heads at the travesty taking place in front of their eyes. Richard finished his plate scraping, which had become disproportionately loud, more like a shriek than a scrape, and then slunk out the door with eyes burning holes into his back.

Richard went directly into their bunkhouse and lay down, feeling as if death was a distinct possibility. David and Kim came back together. "I thought they was gonna string you up on the porch tonight!" Kim said.

"Man Richard, if looks could kill you'd be a dead man right now" David added. "Do you have a lock on this door, Kim?"

"They'd just kick in the door," Kim replied. "That or cut it open with a chainsaw."

Richard moaned in bed in pain. "The way I'm feeling right now, I wouldn't mind someone putting me out of my misery."

David climbed up to the top bunk above Richard. "Another day another dollar" he said.

Kim turned off the light. Richard moaned to himself, "Like a bat outta Hell" and fell into a deep sleep. He dreamt of piling boards the entire night.

CHAPTER 9

Fun with Hallucinogenic Drugs

1969 – Marin County, California

The list for their camping trip was now complete. Although it could have been mistaken for the plans for an expedition to Mt. Everest, this was the first backpacking trip any of them had ever taken without an adult present. Each food item was scrutinized and re-scrutinized before a vote was made by the Four Voyageurs.

Richard, David, and Rex had decided to include Tom on their trip. His main attributes were that he could be exceedingly funny and he had proven himself to be of industrial stock to weather the slings and arrows that could accompany a hallucinogenic trip, without too many signs of trauma. In their professional experience.

David's Father, having grown up in the Montana outdoors, encouraged David to get out of the house and into the hills in the first place. But like most of the other parents of that time, he was oblivious about the new drug scene and its ramifications.

Their plan was to leave after school on Friday, make a short two-mile hike along the beach to Coast Camp. The next morning, they would continue six miles farther to Sky Camp, leaving themselves an easy two-mile hike to the main trailhead on Sunday. There they would be picked up by

Richard's parents. All the while out of their minds on mescaline.

David's mom and dad dropped them off. After Mr. Miller photographed the four with the Pacific Ocean as a backdrop, the parents drove away. With the ocean breeze blowing in their faces and the sound of the Pacific Ocean's serenade, each of them partook of what was deemed to be an accurate dosage of mescaline.

"I need you guys to pay me back for this on Monday," David announced as they dutifully swallowed their pills.

"Right," Rex replied. He was wearing his red checkered bandana that made him look like Aunt Jemima from the maple syrup bottles. Although he was only fifteen years old, Rex was already the size of a full-grown man and had the stage presence of a vaudevillian performer. He threw on his pack first, saying "Or to quote the great explorer, Marco Polo," Rex, with his arms pointing to the Heavens, suddenly was at a loss for words and concluded, "Let's blow this pancake factory!"

Tom weighed in with some expert advice as they each made last-minute adjustments to their packs. "Both times that I took some acid I was peaking in about an hour. Like super high. So, Aunt Jemima's right. We're on borrowed time before we start peaking. And once we start peaking, we'll be totally useless."

Backpacks were still quite primitive in 1969. They all felt like they were strapping large logs onto their backs. They took turns moaning about their equipment, whose unit was worse, but they reached a consensus that Sherpas would be a necessity on the next backpacking trip. David managed to keep the troops' morale high with an inexhaustible treasure trove of archaic camping expressions that would stop everyone in their tracks. "I've seen enough scenery. Take me to your beanery."

Tom, who was a young man of words, could be heard mumbling to himself, "What's a beanery?"

They got within a half-mile of Coast Camp when the drug kicked in. Rex suddenly stopped hiking to make an announcement. "I'm gonna have to make some pancakes. Right now!" He hiked behind a large sand dune to get out of the wind and set up his small cook stove.

The others followed and marveled at his ability to do what, under the circumstances, was a monumentally complex task. As Rex assembled cookware and began combining ingredients David inquired, "How's the pancakes coming along, Aunt Jemima?"

"I'z just whompin' up a bit of pancake for all you white folk. I think you mos' likely gonna find it mighty good eatin'." Rex seemed possessed by the spirit of Aunt Jemima. He produced an onslaught of Aunt Jemima noises, such as "Um hum, lawdy, lawdy, that's the truth, Ruth." His folksy ways were quickly morphing into those of a drugged-up plantation slave.

Tom called out to Aunt Jemima as she flipped a new cake, "Hey Aunt Jemima. These pancakes are damn good!" He became mesmerized watching the maple syrup dripping from his fork back onto his plate.

Aunt Jemima couldn't keep her secret to herself any longer. "Them there's Aunt Jemima's electric pancakes. They'z surely the best eatin' cake west of the Mississippi. And these ones are chock full of mescaline to help build your body twelve ways. Lawdy, lawdy. Mos' people be hallucinating for a full twenty-four hours on these suckers."

The others were also peaking and too distracted by numerous hallucinations or revelations to focus on Aunt Jemima's world. Although people often had spiritual experiences on psychedelic drugs, this group fell squarely into the type of users that found humor in everything. Rex was unique in that he was also capable of assembling ingredients and cooking on a cook stove while in an altered state.

After a couple of hours, the Aunt Jemima electric pancake episode concluded when David looked at his watch and calculated that it was possible, they had transported themselves back in time by exactly one full year, to the minute. Disregarding this startling revelation, they became fixated upon erecting their campsite prior to darkness, or "all is lost." During their delusional "discussions," the phrase "or all is lost" became their motivating force. Despite the group's inability to focus on the tasks at hand, they managed to erect their two tents. Though they looked like tents erected by people high on mescaline, it was still a major accomplishment. Thanks to David's superior pyromania, they worked toward building a rip-roaring fire. His leadership qualities were impressive as he delegated the work. "Kid, go down the beach and fetch some firewood, or all is lost."

Richard scampered down to the beach into the darkness. "Rex, get some small branches from those bushes over there, or all is lost." David pointed vaguely towards some chaparral that came down to the edge of the beach.

Rex reacted as if he had been specifically called in to defuse a nuclear bomb and charged crashing into the dense chaparral.

Both Richard and Rex took an inordinate amount of time with their tasks. They forgot they had flashlights and wandered in the dark, struggling to see.

But David, in his leadership role as chief fire lighter, waited, hoping—all was not lost. Suddenly from the darkness, Tom arrived towing an enormous dry log and dropped it on the edge of the fire pit. It seemed that mescaline and Tom were an effective partnership. The Kid and Rex laid their wood on. David drenched the works with explosive white gas and the fire roared. The four stared into the flames, hallucinating, proud of their accomplishment.

The six-mile hike the next morning to Sky Camp was uneventful until they took another dose of mescaline. Sky

Camp was a couple of hours hike from the ocean and set in an old-growth forest primarily made up of enormous Douglas firs. After putting up their tents and setting aside enough firewood for the evening, David and Tom began decorating the lower boughs of a few evergreens with homemade Christmas ornaments. They hung curved macaroni on the branches but also inserted the plain ends of wooden matches into the macaroni, so the final product had a red and white tip sticking out. The two must have hung up about two hundred of these things to liven up their campsite.

Richard and Rex came over to inspect the decorated Christmas trees. That evening they watched, mesmerized, as Rex pulled out a couple of boxes of animal crackers and passed them around. The four hungrily chewed up a few animals each when Richard noticed that the others were spitting out the tails. "What are you guys doing?" he asked.

David looked up with a pink lion hanging from his mouth. "You shouldn't eat the tails; they can make you sick!" he said. They continued eating the multi-colored animals, while fastidiously spitting out the tails.

Now alerted to the dangers of animal crackers, Richard asked, "Are the giraffe tails safe?"

"They're safe. I wouldn't trust any of the others though" Tom said and then, realizing that he had stuffed about twelve tail-less cookies into his mouth without swallowing, started laughing and gagging about the scene surrounding him. All four simultaneously broke down into uncontrollable laughter. During the pandemonium that ensued, David, for reasons never explained, was renamed Sheriff Andy or The Sheriff for short.

They woke up at dawn, covered with animal cracker tails. After making breakfast, David insisted they thoroughly clean up their campsite and make sure the coals from the previous evening's campfire were completely out. "The next campers will say many thanks" he said, quoting a recollection from his Boy Scout Handbook.

Rather than walk a way down to the spring to collect water to extinguish their fire, David chose in his wisdom to pee on the coals instead. The resulting cloud of stench inspired the oft repeated slogan amongst these four lads, "Never, ever piss on a fire!"

CHAPTER 10

Dress for Success

2014 – San Francisco, California

The Sixties have been referred to as the "decade that fashion forgot," which is a lousy thing for one decade to say about another. As if any given decade is above ridicule. There is this thing called the test of time and when applied objectively, all decades have something or other that they would have left in the closet if they had only known. Think of all the fashion travesties throughout the twentieth century that have already been given two thumbs down by historians of pop culture, such as the shoe hat, shoulder pads, the Gibson Girl hairdo, the cone bra, and the unspeakable powder-blue polyester leisure suit.

The Sixties and Seventies were Richard's formative years and he certainly made no excuses for the mini skirt (God's gift to men), blue jeans, or hot pants (God's other gift to men). It is not clear how God took care of women's needs, as Nehru jackets, leisure suits and bell bottoms were fairly lame counterbalances. Women's Lib was still new, and God was probably just as stunted in his personal growth as the next supernatural being.

On a personal level, Richard never really "got" fashion anyway. When his girlfriend Terrie, who is a fashion diva, attempted to update his look, it was akin to putting lipstick on a pig. The pig did look better but as they say, you can take the pig out of the country but you can't take the country out of the pig.

Richard found himself trying on some hip clothing at a trendy store with Terrie and he was in the dressing room along with about five hundred different articles of clothing.

"How's it feel?" she asked.

"I feel like a model for a straitjacket company," Richard answered. "But I have to admit, it does look great. I'm just worried—suppose I need to inhale? Shouldn't the label have a warning on it for men over thirty stating that it could be hazardous to their health?"

Terrie laughed. "I guess you've been wearing loose, comfortable clothing for the past few decades so it's hard to switch. But that shirt and pants you're wearing, they totally change your look from a middle-aged fuddy-dud to a sophisticated, hip, fuddy-dud."

"Sarcasm isn't going to win me over at the moment," Richard said, slightly wounded. "All I'm saying is it would be nice to be able to breathe while still looking fashionable."

Terrie rolled her eyes toward the heavens. "I suppose I can look into hooking you up to a stylish oxygen tank, so you don't croak on my watch. Really, Richard, they look fantastic on you. But it's your call. We can always head over to Penny's Department Store instead and find you another pair of da-yuck baggy pants and a matching da-yuck baggy shirt. It would save you some money and I can always date other men for public occasions and just see you when I'm in the mood to hang with a guy that wears sandals with socks."

Richard eyed Terrie faux-menacingly. "Behave. I need your moral support. Every time I go shopping for clothing with you, I practically need to check into a clinic for psychiatric counseling afterwards. Just answer three more questions and I'll decide if I'm gonna pull the trigger. One"!

"Drum-roll please." Terrie said.

"One! Do you think that updating my wardrobe may have the effect of alienating my kids from ever again allowing themselves to be seen with me in public?

Two! Am I going to have to start fending off women like a rock star, which I've heard can become a major bummer?

"Three! Would I be true to my fashion heritage if I just left well enough alone and finished off my days in blue jeans and tee shirts?"

Terrie looked at Richard like he was a lost puppy. "What did your mother do to you when you wet the bed? The answers are No, No and No."

Richard eyed Terrie suspiciously. She kissed him on the forehead and left him to ponder the mysteries of fashion outside the fitting rooms. Barring the possibility that she was involved in a convoluted reality TV show conspiracy to ruin his reputation by way of fashion humiliation, he saw no reason why she couldn't do a credible job of dressing him, considering how good a job she did on herself. Still, after what felt like ten hours of soul searching in the fitting room, he was uncertain. He also felt bad that he was singlehandedly pushing this clothing store into bankruptcy because of all the work he had created for their folding department. It occurred to him that he needed a second opinion.

Fortunately, in San Francisco, in a trendy clothing store, help is only a snap of the fingers away. Yes, if you are a man and want to dress for success, ask the gay salesman for help. Obviously! Look at these guys. They aren't being dressed by anybody else and they look great. Exactly how they know how to do this, Richard never understood. He suspected that it was something about the water. If you aren't a gay man in an Armani suit wearing some good cologne, forget any idea you can dress yourself. You can't. Richard was living proof.

He went over to the sales guy and said, "Is this even in the ballpark or should I just cease and desist?"

The sales guy viewed him critically from all sides with a serious look. "How does it feel?" he asked.

"Like if somebody touches me, I might explode," Richard replied.

"That is an indication that the pants are too tight," the sales guy responded. "But honestly, sometimes there's a time and a place—or girlfriend—for whom you just might want to 'suck it up.'" He tilted his head sideways, looking over in Terrie's direction.

Richard was impressed that this guy can give not only fashion advice but also relationship advice. "Yeah," Richard agreed. "So true." He ended up buying a couple of shirts and pants. Terrie was delighted.

"Thanks for your help," Richard said to her as they walked out of the door. He put on his sunglasses to block the sunlight that was shining directly into his eyes. Richard gasped for air, looking fabulous. He intentionally kept his mouth shut as a new thought crossed his mind. *Were these things still going to shrink?*

CHAPTER 11

Busted!!!

1970 – Marin County, California

"It's going to be so far out!" At least that was the opinion of Chris James, a new friend of David's who had a reputation of sorts. Chris's notoriety hinged upon his fiercely held opinions on all subjects known to mankind. His credibility had recently taken a hit, however. Other equally full-of-themselves high school intellectuals had taken issue with Chris over an important novel. Chris's reputation as an intellectual heavyweight went up in flames when he disclosed that he had read War and Peace in one day and when asked what it was about could only respond, "Russia." But then David wrote a letter to the school newspaper defending Chris, stating that, "Chris's insightful review of Tolstoy's classic was succinct and to the point."

David had organized another backpacking trip to a remote beach in Marin County known as Limantour Beach and subsequently convinced Chris to join the camping group. They were working out the details of the upcoming trip.

David handed him a wad of small bills. "So, you've already tried the mescaline and it's really good for sure, right?" Three dollars per hit was a lot for a sixteen-year-old.

"Real good. Real mellow. I felt like I melted into a puddle." Chris had a way with words.

David wrestled with the puddle analogy for a minute, decided turning into a puddle had its merits and said, "Far out. So, like, if we don't melt into puddles we get a full refund?"

"David, my man, you'll be completely liquefied or your money back. Try to find a better warranty from a different dealer. You can't! And I'm just about giving this stuff away."

Richard, who had been quietly taking in Chris's used car salesman techniques a couple of feet away, tiptoed into the fray. "Everything must go! We got to clear out this year's drugs to make room for next year's drugs!"

"This is The Kid" David announced. Chris looked Richard over.

"The Kiiiid," Chris drawled out. He seemed to have heard about Richard already and indicated that he had been pre-approved. Chris was two grades higher than Richard, so this needed to happen, much like when a new wolf is accepted into a pack.

They were all a bit giddy that Chris had a station wagon to take out to the trailhead.

"So, we got a car all weekend, this is too cool!" Richard said. He liked Chris. Chris had a head of black curly hair and a messy beard. Something about his persona screamed out "Hobbit!" You just knew he grew hair between his toes.

David and Richard had quickly adapted to the camping life and were becoming known amongst their peers as the camping experts, since none of their other friends (except Rex and Tom) had been properly introduced to this world of fun and pain. But it was David, with his lineage going back to Montana days and his father's fanciful recollections, who solidified their combined aptitudes for being out in the woods. His enormous reservoir of outdated camping expressions, sourced from an assortment of Hardy Boys stories, Boy Scout manuals and Montana relatives, contributed to his status as top-dog woodsman.

Also impressive to his friends was his miniature white gas stove, with which he would routinely tempt fate. Only David was comfortable with this virtual time-bomb and would often perform a monologue which he would refer to as "Fun with White Gas," The Grand Finale taking place (in the black of night) when David would set the toes of his hiking boots ablaze with a tablespoon of white gas and do a tap dance.

Having recently been banished from the sporting world due to his non-conforming hair, Richard was looking for a new way to channel his now unharnessed energy.

They sat around a bonfire on the beach late into the evening, smoking pot and swapping stories. As expected, Chris lived up to his reputation of being an opinionated character with a quick wit. He fit in perfectly with the others, not a surprise since you have to be a character to hang out with a Hobbit. Over a jumbo-joint in the wee hours of the morning, an itinerary change was agreed upon, it was unanimously decided the next morning would entail walking out to the original trail-head and driving to a different, presumably better, beach. The station wagon beckoned.

Limantour Beach was off-limits to backpackers and rarely patrolled. It had no road, just a trail that went about half the distance to the end of the Spit. It was a narrow finger of sand dunes with the ocean on one side and a salt-water lagoon on the other. Often, at the end of The Spit, there would be elephant seals. It was idyllic in many ways but not without safety concerns, both natural and as a result of inexperienced backpackers, namely the likes of the Boy-Palz contingent.

One consideration overlooked was tidal safety. The end of The Spit was occasionally surrounded by water. That night happened to be one of those nights. David woke up first while the others slept to the soothing sound of water lapping a couple of feet below their sleeping bags. David summed up the situation they found themselves in when he said, "Other than the fact that we might die tonight, it's otherwise a perfect campsite location."

As if that wasn't enough to worry about, Rex wanted to use an old indigenous practice of spreading out a pile of coals, covering it with sand and laying his down sleeping bag on top of that, thereby creating the equivalent of a heated mattress. Unfortunately, his sleeping bag burst into flame and Rex narrowly averted barbecuing himself. "So much for Day One." Tom said. Their once pristine camp resembled an exploded duck.

The next morning, after breaking camp, they hiked back out to the station wagon, drove about an hour past a series of picturesque beaches, choosing one called Pt. Reyes North. Signs said; "NO CAMPING ALLOWED" in the parking lot. Exempting themselves from this rule, they gathered their packs together and hiked a mile down the beach. Selecting an idyllic campsite among sand dunes that blocked the wind, they threw down their packs and consumed a hit of mescaline each. David, Chris, Tom and Rex decided to hike down to the crashing waves while Richard stayed behind, already feeling a bit puddlish. Richard thought it prudent that he roll a joint but the effects of the mescaline made that impossible. His mind focused on patterns in the sand. He noticed his thoughts swirl in unison with the gently wind-blown sand and soon felt his thoughts were one and the same. He forgot the others, forgot his usual mundane thoughts, forgot everything except the sand around him and the distant ocean noise.

Feeling more at peace than ever in his life, he slowly noticed a presence. A park ranger stood hovering over him. His mouth was moving but Richard had trouble making sense of the sounds emanating from it. The ranger was trying to decide if Richard was insane, drunk, stoned or all the above. "Didn't you see the no camping signs? There must have been ten of them between here and the parking lot. You and I are going to have to go find your friends and you'll all need to leave the park immediately!"

Richard was rapidly losing interest in the Ranger, who was compounding the overall weirdness of the situation by changing colors like a psychedelic chameleon. The situation seemed profoundly insignificant. Richard chose to focus again on the sand but noticed his bag of pot lying open beside him. *I have to hide this from the ranger*, he decided. Trying not to tip his hand he turned his back to the ranger and buried the pot with sand. But unbeknownst to Richard, turning his back to the ranger did not make him invisible.

"What the hell do you got there?" the Ranger said as he pulled the half-buried pot out of the sand. "Why this is marijuana!" he proclaimed, as if it were the crime of the century. "I'm gonna have to arrest you now, son. And this is a federal property, so that makes this is a federal offense."

Chris, the Hobbit, and the rest of the gang of hardened criminals showed up at the scene of the crime. The less stoned others had the presence of mind to keep their mouths shut as Richard continued to dig himself further into a hole.

"We're not doing anything wrong!" Richard blathered. "Why don't you just leave us alone?"

The Ranger, not comprehending the behavior of a teenager peaking on mescaline responded, "Well, I see things a little differently from you. First of all, you were preparing to camp in a no-camping park. Second of all, you are in possession of illegal drugs in a federal park. Now I'm gonna have to issue you a citation and you're going to have to go to federal court and talk to the judge there." Richard was trying to focus but the mescaline was reaching full strength and the ranger's face was twirling into an array of colors. The ranger had Richard pack up his backpack and they walked back to park headquarters in silence, while the lessor criminals brought up the rear. Richard was given a citation and released. The ranger told him they better beat it by the time he got back from making his rounds or else!

They loaded up the station wagon all the while speculating what "or else" might have meant.

"Or else Ranger Dickhead is gonna pee on our sleeping bags?" Chris wondered out loud.

"Oh please, please don't pee on our sleeping bags Ranger Dickhead. Anything but that!" they all said feigning horror.

"Or else he's going to have us stuffed and mounted on the entrance signs as a warning to others!"

"Oh please, please don't have us stuffed Ranger Dickhead!"

This went on for a while until they finished laughing.

When Richard emerged from the Ranger station his friends were waiting for him.

"Kid! What in God's Green Acres was going on in the Ranger station?" Chris James asked.

"I just got busted for possession of marijuana!" The Kid said. They sat down in sand dunes nearby. They passed around his citation as they shook their heads. Chris handed the citation back to The Kid.

"Did The Kid get busted?" Sheriff Andy said to nobody in particular.

"The Kid got busted," Chris James responded soberly.

Sheriff Andy began to slowly shake his head, saying, "The Kid got busted."

Tom examined the citation, unaware that he was holding it upside down. "Ranger Dickhead" he mumbled to himself, trying to make out the officer's name. They all broke out laughing as if it were the funniest joke ever. They stood in silence, the sound of the waves breaking at the shoreline.

Still stoned, they walked back to the station wagon. They sat there chatting for several hours until the effects from the mescaline wore off, then drove home. Richard asked to be dropped off one block from his house. As he pulled his pack out of the back of the vehicle, a roll of toilet paper fell out and rolled down the street for about 10 yards. Everyone laughed except Richard, then he laughed. He walked home dreading the moment he'd have to tell his Dad, "I got busted for pot." but still laughing to himself about the toilet paper roll.

CHAPTER 12

If You Liked that Song,
You Might Like this One

2014 – Marin County, California

Richard stared at his laptop having purchased a song online. Based on this selection the computer suggested a different song. To quote, "If you liked that song, you might like this one too." Since Richard was technophobic he felt intruded upon.

"Terrie?" he called out across the apartment. "Why does the computer think that it knows what music I might want to listen to, based upon one song that I've purchased?"

"Maybe because your mind is completely predictable to the computer. Maybe it has you figured out? Maybe people in general are walking and talking pop culture algorithms that like to think that they are unique. Maybe most people are repeating what they heard somebody else say yesterday, day after day after day. Maybe there hasn't been an original or unique human thought for a couple of thousand years?"

"How come when I ask you a simple question, you reply with a thesis?" Richard replied. "I have to remember to add to my To Do List that I need to slit my wrists today."

Terrie looked up from her computer screen in her office and called out, "If you like the song What I Say by Ray Charles and you also speculated to your girlfriend about your desire to slit your wrists, you might like this song..."

Richard pondered all this for a minute. "First of all, I meant to say slit my risks, not my wrists."

"Thanks for the clarification," Terrie responded. "If you like the song What I Say you might like to buy the book Personal Financial Management for Blind Jazz Musicians."

Richard nodded in agreement. "Right. Exactly. Exactly something. Who started this conversation, anyway? And so, if you liked reading Personal Financial Management for Blind Jazz Musicians, you'd probably like to read Sky Diving for Dummies."

Terrie walked into Richard's Office in the bedroom and said, "If you liked Sky Diving for Dummies, you'd probably like Do Mannequins Have Rights, Feel Pain and Think Complex Thoughts?"

He continued. "If you like Do Mannequins Have Rights, Feel Pain and Think Complex Thoughts? You'd probably like Are Mass Murderers Evil or Are they Just More Confident and Self-Assured?"

Terrie wrung one more book out of their efforts. "If you like that book about mass murderers, you'd probably like Even You Can Be a Mass Murderer by Son of Sam."

Richard felt they had got their money's worth out of this shtick. He went over to Terrie, sat down next to her and snuggled up. "I'm starting to think that we might both need professional help."

Terrie hugged Richard. "You mean like an agent?"

"Terrie?"

"Yeah?" she said quietly as she nuzzled his neck.

"Are you aware of the fact that it was a miracle that we ever met and that at the end of the day, we're probably the only people who can put up with each other?"

"Yeah," she said. She quietly whispered into his ear, "If you like books about Ray Charles, personal finance for blind jazz musicians, mannequins, and mass murderers, then you're my man."

CHAPTER 13

The People of the Raccoons

1975 – Vancouver, British Columbia

"So, let me get this straight. Kenny just sent a letter inviting us to visit him the next time we pass through Vancouver and that he and his disciples, or whatever they are, have built some sort of hobo encampment in a large patch of forest there. Correct?" Richard asked.

David unfolded the letter with a dramatic flourish and cleared his throat as if he were preparing to make an important speech. "And I quote, 'I got quite the magic mushroom factory started up here, six fungiologists in total. If they don't do their jobs properly, they usually poison themselves and die, so, as you can imagine, that weeds out the sick and the diseased employees. The survivors are solid workers though (see Darwin, Survival of the Smartest). Haha! No costs to speak of either, so next time you're passing through, let me know ahead of time so I can make sure the linens are pressed and that all of the vomit gets cleaned up before you arrive. Haha!—Kenny.'"

Richard mulled over the offer. "He said that he's cleaning up all of the vomit, right? I'd say that he's implying a considerable amount of vomit."

David fluffed up the letter again and pulled the paper taut. "To clarify." He cleared his throat. "All of the vomit. He could have just said the vomit. But no, he went and said all of the vomit. I'd have to say he was definitely implying a volume of vomit."

"Yeah, I caught that too." Richard agreed. He pondered a bit. "Well then, I think it could be summarized, things are going swimmingly for Kenny except for the vomit issue."

David folded the letter and put it in his pocket. "I concur" he said. "Frankly, I'd prefer to just forget about the vomit thingy entirely."

"What vomit?"

"Exactly. Sounds like a distinct possibility that by the time we pass through Vancouver when we hitch back home for Christmas, it could be all cleaned up anyway."

"What?"

"I don't know." Thus, it came to pass the two men stopped by the Mushroom-Hobo encampment. The psilocybin mushroom season had abruptly ended just before their arrival and only some final drying, packaging and weighing was required prior to the group's scattering to the four winds. A couple of folding tables and chairs, along with a tiny scale was the extent of the "factory." A majestic old growth cedar forest surrounded their campsite.

It turned out that vomit wasn't the burning issue of the day, but rather an enormous infestation of bothersome raccoons. After spending a week in Vancouver, David anointed Kenny and his entourage as the last living members of The People of the Raccoons.

The lost tribe had been eating magic mushrooms almost daily, prior to David and Richard's arrival. Their behavior was becoming strange, even for the likes of these two, which spoke volumes. It was clear to the two visitors they were witnessing the final days of The Raccoon People empire. Things were spiraling out of control. This once great and proud indigenous nation had now dwindled down to six stoners. At least that was what Richard and David saw as they observed one act of stupidity after another.

In the evening the group would build a large bonfire, odd when you consider their campsite was squarely within Vancouver's city limits. Even odder was their relationship with nature—raccoons in particular.

The Raccoons of Vancouver had adapted from a purely wild state to one of overfed, furry, acrobats. The raccoons knew The People of the Raccoons always had an assortment of delicacies to be plundered and were too high on magic mushrooms to adequately defend their provisions, perpetuating a cycle of further assaults. With shifting tides, the raccoons gained the upper hand in their symbiotic relationship.

Amazed by the Raccoons' antics, David said, "It reminds me of a school for criminal raccoons," as he watched a mob of them stalking the campsite perimeter, probing for weak spots.

The final straw that prematurely shortened their visit was when normally gentle David, having ingested some mushrooms, had to be restrained from attacking the largest and fattest raccoon known as Fatty Fur Ball. Provoked by the animal's blatant thievery, he said, "That Fatty Fur Ball character has become a breaking and entering expert. I mean, what's next? Identity Fraud? Forged credit cards?"

Considering that a few of the Raccoon People had about the same amount of facial hair as Fatty, it really wasn't that much of a stretch to envision Fatty employing some of the more artistically inclined raccoons as forgers.

The last evening with the Raccoon People was sufficiently insane to reassure David and Richard that they were escaping just in time. Four raccoons were wrestling across the campsite with abandon, sometimes crashing into and knocking over camping gear and pots and pans. A couple of the Raccoon People screamed at the creatures in a feeble effort to chase them out of their campsite.

"I'm starting to feel like I'm a prisoner in a Walt Disney movie that never made it to market!" Richard said,

concluding that escape from The People of the Raccoons
was now a necessity.

The two determined they would go hunting for some
of their own psychedelic mushrooms about fifty miles out
of the city. It wasn't as if the lost tribe had been a particularly
inspirational experience. If anything, they were inept, cultish
and incapable of holding off another assault by the superior
army of marauding, pillaging raccoons. Their old friend
Kenny was clearly banging his head against the wall trying
to transform yet another mob of untrainable misfits into, in
this case, an effective group of mushroom harvesters for the
purpose of financial gain.

Richard was commenting to David on the tribe's
itinerary for the day. "Kenny said they are all going hunting
after breakfast."

"For mushrooms?" David asked.

"No. They apparently go dumpster diving for food
behind Safeway. Then they go mushroom hunting."

"That's disgusting" David said. "They should just eat
those trash-slinging fur units. They'd have a chance to return
to the glory days of their traditional way of life. Otherwise,
they stand a good chance of becoming extinct from stupidity.
Like the Dodo birds."

"It wouldn't be too cool if they were to eat the last of
the raccoons from the U.B.C. endowment park," Richard
responded. "I'd say they should just go get a job like
everybody else does."

"We don't have jobs." Richard replied. "But it would
be cool if they were to dress completely in Raccoon fur, I'd
like to see that."

The two men looked around the dysfunctional campsite.
The raccoons had devoured most camp provisions during
the night and food wrappers were everywhere.

David and Richard's motivation to have a last mushroom
experience was less complicated than for the others. They
just wanted to complete their lifetime dream of ingesting

every type of natural psychedelic drug known to mankind.
Even if it killed them.

CHAPTER 14

Tell it Bye-Bye, Baby

1965 – San Francisco, California

"Okay Ricky. We better get going out to the ballpark before all of the hot dogs get eaten." Richard's Grandma Marion joked. She was a true San Francisco character. Going to Candlestick Park to watch the San Francisco Giants play the Los Angeles Dodgers with Grandma and her sister, Richard's Great Aunt Alva, was the most exciting event in his ten-year-old world. The two sisters lived together in the same apartment in the Marina District, toward the Golden Gate Bridge. After each game, win or lose, they would celebrate at one of the Italian restaurants right outside their front door on Chestnut Street.

Grandma Marion wasn't your stereotypical Jewish grandmother. On the one hand, she did talk in a loud voice and had absolutely no understanding of confidentiality, an infamous trait shared by many of her tribe. She would never, for example, grasp the sensitivity that others had about yelling across the department store that she had found the correct size of underwear for one of her seven grandchildren. "Ricky!" she'd call out. "These underwear look terrific! Come have a look. Do you like them?" Only his relatives referred to him as Ricky, so combined with including the word "underwear" in the same sentence, there really couldn't have been a more efficient way to publicly humiliate him. But since Richard adored her, he learned to cope with these incidents, thereby negating the need to take his own life to stop the pain. Anyway, he was ten years old now and Marion made up for her lack of sensitivity in so many other ways. Primarily with her sense of humor.

When she was around her brother and sisters, it was like you were hanging out with the Marx Brothers. Always well-dressed, each holding a tinkly drink, with painted finger-nails and quaffed hairdos, they would gossip about each other as if the other couldn't hear.

"Your Aunt Dorothy was the most gorgeous girl at our high school."

"The boys were crazy about her."

"Now look at her."

"Some of us just take longer to ripen I suppose."

"I'm afraid Dorothy's starting to ferment. Being the oldest child can really age a woman."

"Sad really. She has no friends now."

"No, she has one. Tommy Kaufman."

"Tommy's dead!"

"That's right! That's right! I'd forgotten. I don't think he spoke one word in the last couple of years."

"Might as well be dead if you can't talk."

Richard's younger sister, Kathleen, sat the whole time on her Aunt Dot's (Dorothy's) lap, mesmerized, listening to every word, until Dorothy said, "Kathleen darling, don't listen to a single word these two say. They've always been jealous of me because well, just look at them! But I always say, take the high road. Just because I got the beauty and the brains, that doesn't mean that they can't be loved."

Her brother, Uncle Bob, the only male sibling of the bunch, chimed in, "You shouldn't keep lying to our niece, Dorothy. Nobody can love those two trouble-makers and you know it."

"Well, I suppose you're right" Dorothy relented.

Marion seemed to know every person in the city. As they traveled by bus across town to Candlestick Park, home of the San Francisco Giants, it seemed like she had the whole bus laughing at her irreverent style of humor. On one bus ride to see their beloved Giants, Marion could be heard explaining, to the entire bus, just how valuable it was to the team to have a player named Jesus Alou on our side (this time pronouncing his name phonetically).

"I'm Jewish, so this isn't my story, but I have a few Catholic girlfriends and one of them, Debbie Long I believe..."

"That's right" Richard's Great Aunt Alva interjected. "It was Debbie Long"

"Yes. Debbie Long." Marion continued. "Debbie came with us to see the Giants beat the Cincinnati Reds, and she kept saying, whenever Jesus Alou came up to bat, 'We can't lose with Jesus on our side.'"

Once the Giants had an important afternoon game against the Los Angeles Dodgers and Grandma Marion and Alva bought three tickets, which was extravagant for them. It would be a classic matchup, with the team's aces, Juan Marichal and Sandy Koufax, in an expected pitcher's duel. And, truth be known, any baseball fan worth his salt had to love watching Koufax pitch. His dominance was just too impressive to be obscured by petty baseball feuds. If it weren't for Koufax, the Giants' Marichal would have been considered the best pitcher of that time. If they gave pitchers style points for best wind-up, Marichal would have won that trophy hands-down, with his foot higher than his head technique.

The Giants had the better hitting though, with their two sluggers, Willie Mays and Willie McCovey, terrorizing opposing pitchers. Even the Giants' pitching was excellent, with the great Juan Marichal and the infamous spitball pitcher Gaylord Perry. But the Dodgers' pitching was otherworldly, with Don Drysdale, Claude Osteen and possibly the best pitcher in baseball history, Sandy Koufax. Their rivalry carried back in time to the turn of the previous century, way before the 1950s when the San Francisco Giants were the New York Giants and the Los Angeles Dodgers were the Brooklyn Dodgers.

Although Richard was a skinny boy, if the food offerings were to his satisfaction, he would consume vast quantities and the food at the ballpark definitely spoke to him. His grandmother would constantly ask him if he required more sustenance as if he were a concentration camp survivor.

Richard, ecstatic, listened on his transistor radio to the two golden-throated Giants sportscasters, Lon Simmons and Russ Hodges, legends in their field, chatting on his local radio sports station. Today's winning team would finish the game with the National League lead.

And these two teams genuinely hated each other. The age-old retribution of communicating unhappiness via throwing the ball at their opponents' heads and body was alive and well. In fact, during the first two innings, both Marichal and Koufax each knocked down a couple of batters.

Richard and his aunt and grandma joined the crowd of fifty-thousand spectators in roundly booing Koufax for his actions but gave Marichal the home-field benefit of the doubt. It was the bottom of the third inning and the Giants were batting. Marichal was up at the plate and that's when a near riot took place. A routine pitch was thrown back to Koufax but in a non-routine way. The catcher, an All-Star player named Johnny Roseboro, threw the ball back to Koufax so close to Marichal's head that it nicked his ear.

What took place over the next eighteen minutes was confusing and frightening. Marichal, known as the Dominican Dandy, went unhinged and, to be fair to him, Roseboro didn't behave like a Cub Scout himself. Words were exchanged. Roseboro went straight at Marichal with his mask in his hand. And Marichal did what anyone else would have done, he cracked Roseboro over the head with his bat. At least from a Giants fan's perspective. Needless to say, the good folks of Los Angeles didn't see it that way, watching the event on their TV screens back home in the City of Angels. Nor did the Dodger players, who came flying out of their dugout like a swarm of killer bees, quickly followed by the Giants players from their hive. Even the fans seemed to Richard to be on the verge of coming down to the field to help out.

Chaos ensued, as Dodgers went straight for Marichal while Giants prevented this from happening. Marichal and his still dangerous bat were subdued by, of all people, the home plate umpire, Shag Crawford, who wrestled Marichal to the ground. The other hero was Willie Mays, who was the first to get to the bleeding Roseboro and walk him through the chaos to the Dodgers' dugout like a saint. Roseboro later got eighteen, count 'em, eighteen stitches.

The whole time this ruckus ensued, baseball historians, normally obsessed with statistics, totally overlooked the fact that this meant Marichal inflicted one stitch per minute. Also missed was that Richard had consumed enough peanuts and Cracker Jacks to feed a small city, while his Grandma Marion and Aunt Alva, never at a loss for words, could only punctuate the home plate extravaganza with "Oh my God!"

Since Richard always had his transistor radio firmly planted against his ear, he was probably the most informed spectator in the stadium as the announcer excitedly broadcasted the brawl like a boxing match.

To no one's surprise, Marichal was kicked out of the game, which remained tied at one run apiece. Koufax, first to intervene in Marichal's rampage, was still in and got the next two Giants batters out but then allowed the following two to get on base, bringing Willie Mays up to bat. The crowd was electrified as Mays stepped up to the plate. Richard was so immersed in the radio version of the game that he was looking at his feet instead of the field, as perhaps baseball's two finest players ever to have played the game stared at each other, ninety feet apart. Koufax fired in one of his trademark fastballs and Mays crushed it deep into left field. The announcer shouted into Richard's ear, "There's a drive to deep left field, Barnes is back, back, to the wall, he leaps, and you can tell it bye-bye, baby! Willie Mays hits a Koufax fastball out of here for a three-run homer and the Giants lead 4 to 1!" It was pandemonium in the stands.

Richard pressed his transistor radio to his head when he heard his Grandma screaming, "You were looking at the ground the whole time! I saw you! You didn't even see the home run!"

Richard wasn't going to crack and confess to fifty-thousand people. His grandmother's voice sounded louder than the P.A. system. The crowd was going nuts as Richard regained his composure by telling himself it was less than two-thousand spectators within earshot. "We spend all this money for tickets, Willie Mays hits a home run off of Sandy Koufax and the whole time he's staring at his feet with his radio stuck in his ear!" Marion slapped him good-naturedly on the head with a baseball program and Alva started hitting him with her program until the people around them started yelling at them to "Leave the kid alone," and "This is America, he can listen to his radio if he wants, it's his constitutional right." One older woman two rows back did point out to the court of public opinion that, "At least she's not hitting him over the head with a bat!" which got a big laugh. The two ladies pretended to fluff Richard up while getting in one or two last slaps, as Richard laughed at his tormentors.

The Giants won the game 4 to 1, finishing the day in first place. "Well Ricky, I guess we taught those Dodgers a thing or two," Marion said after the last out.

"You never doubted them for a minute, did you?" Alva asked.

"Not for a second," she replied.
"You liar," Alva laughed to herself.

CHAPTER 15

Mario Andretti Syndrome

2014 – Dolomite Mountains, Northern Italy

"I'm just keeping up with the flow of traffic!" Terrie said in her defense.

Richard, having broken the cardinal rule of copiloting, namely accusing the pilot of driving too fast, tried to backtrack. "Sorry, sorry. I'm still getting used to Italian highways." To Richard, the little Fiat sounded more like the space shuttle Challenger than an automobile. More specifically, a Fiat space shuttle with a standard transmission.

Terrie shifted gears for what seemed to be the seventeenth time in the last minute, cornering above a cliff that descended to Hell. "And it's not called a highway, it's called the Autostrada." Terrie said.

Richard braced himself in terror until the road straightened out. "It makes me more stressed when you use that name."

"Autostrada?" Terrie said, perking up.

"Yeah. Don't say that." Richard was deep breathing, trying to regain his composure. "It freaks me out."

"Okay. I won't say that word and you be a good little copilot and help with directions. And quit telling me I'm going too fast. Anyway, too fast is a relative term."

Richard looked up from the map he had been studying. "You mean like Einstein's theory concerning the speed of light, that kind of relativity? Anyway, when I was getting all scientific on you, before you hit Mach 3—about two light years ago—I was simply pointing out that if you drove any faster, it was scientifically possible that, by the time we got to Milano, I could be younger than my children. But I wasn't saying you were driving too fast."

"I guess that was different. Thanks for bringing that distinction to my attention," Terrie said as she slammed the stick shift into what sounded like a recently discovered new gear. "But when you started losing it on the straightaway outside of Brescia about how you felt that your molecular structure was starting to change form, I didn't appreciate that. It's hard enough driving here without that kind of pressure."

Richard squirmed in his seat and said, "It won't happen again. I'm sorry. Sorry."

They drove in silence for a few minutes.

"Terrie," Richard said sheepishly.

The pilot casually negotiated a hairpin corner by downshifting the spacecraft from warp speed to earthling 90 m.p.h. "Yes, copilot Spock?" she said.

"I was just thinking about that movie Apollo 13, when the astronaut called to report, 'Houston, we have a problem.' And later the dude in charge back on Earth said, 'Failure is not an option.' Do you remember those scenes?"

Terrie was massaging her head. She mumbled to herself. "Why am I getting this terrible headache? Yes Richard. I do remember those scenes and I can't wait to know how you're planning on equating that movie to a drive through the mountains of Italy. Please continue but if I happen to suddenly fall asleep, would you mind grabbing the steering wheel?"

Richard ignored her sarcasm and continued. "Well, what I'm thinking is that our situation is analogous to theirs.

You're like the captain of the Apollo 13, except better looking, who's trying to simultaneously deal with a multitude of problems that could have been prevented if you had just done a better pre-rental inspection at Hertz Car Rentals and I am like Mission Control, trying to safely land this rusty tin can of a spacecraft against all odds. You still with me?"

Terrie downshifted from 100 m.p.h. to 80 m.p.h., causing the Fiat to shake violently. Richard thought he saw something fly by the window. "Do Fiats use heat tiles for re-entry into the Earth's atmosphere?"

Terrie looked straight ahead. Without taking her eyes off the road, she said, "You're fired. As the Pilot, I now order you not to speak."

Richard closed his eyes, folded his arms and prepared himself for sleep. "Terrie," he said.

"What did I just say?" she snapped.

"I love you."

"I love you too. Now deactivate your voice box." She shifted into a faster gear as she passed a truck, with just the suggestion of a smile on her face.

CHAPTER 16

Down the Looking Hole

1974 – Vancouver, British Columbia

Next morning, they bid adieu to Kenny and his minions in order to hunt down the one remaining mushroom that had thus far eluded them. They had read that an orange mushroom with white flakes, known as Amanita muscaria, had been used by indigenous people far back in time, give or take a couple of thousand years. The literature on its psychedelic properties ranged from "a really unique high" to "are you out of your mind," to "are you a complete moron?" Also, David had heard through the fungi-line that this mushroom was growing in abundance around a small mountain community close to Vancouver named Pemberton Meadows.

They whipped out their thumbs, doing their ritualistic thumb warming up exercises and began hitching in earnest.

It was now late October, and the conditions in this area were ideal for growing amanita. The brilliant gold and red leaves of poplars, birches, and maples contrasted with the evergreens. Eventually, a small Toyota pickup pulled over and they squeezed into the front. The driver was a tall, thin fellow with a blond ponytail halfway down his back. His name was John Baker but, "My friends call me Baker." At first the two hitchhikers were perplexed by his accent. It turned out he was from New Orleans. He had a friendly and witty personality and before you could say "overdose," he had agreed to accompany them on their amanita mushroom adventure. The two-hour drive there was breathtakingly beautiful and in short order the three found themselves hunting for the elusive orange and white spotted mushrooms. It turned out that these mushrooms weren't so elusive after all. In fact, within a half an hour's time, their quotas had been picked. David had researched the potential risks with amanita and had somehow reached the conclusion that, essentially, it was safe as long as it didn't kill you.

This somewhat sketchy logic was sufficient for David and Richard but didn't cut it for the more skeptical Baker. "It says right here in your mushroom guide that it can be an extremely poisonous mushroom. Why push your luck? Drano is safer. And a lot easier to find, too."

David replied, "Everything is poisonous if you ingest too much. Indians have been getting loaded since Adam and Eve invented the Caesar salad."

"Hell, since Jesus sold his first vacuum cleaner," Richard added.

David continued, "And apparently, enough indians must have died during the trials that they figured out the correct dosage. The work's been done."

Baker rolled his eyes towards the heavens. "First of all, if you are going to use Adam and Eve as points of reference, I think it's safe to assume that the two of them predated Jesus. But what I really want to know is, can I keep your tent if it turns out there was a flaw in your methodology?"

"Yes, you can keep the tent," David said. "But you have to tell my parents that I loved them. And that the time that I set their closet on fire... that it was on purpose. I'm still not sure what got into me that day."

With Baker voting nay, the yeas, on a 2-to-1 vote, pushed through the Ingestion of a Moderate Quantity of Amanita Muscaria Act, which commenced immediately with both men eating one half of one mushroom. Baker was also voted in as the designated ambulance driver.

Within a half hour, David was laughing uproariously about the inevitability of world dominance by cows. Richard was seemingly in a catatonic state. Eight hours passed when he suddenly rejoined his tribe. "How long was I asleep?" he asked in an exhausted voice. He was completely shocked to find out that it had been so long. "That's so weird because it only felt like five minutes. I distinctly remember being led into a kingdom through some gates by somebody in a long robe. It was very mystical. Like I was in some far distant land—like a Tibetan monastery."

The other two were deeply impressed. "I was starting to worry about you, Richard," Baker said. "You were so limp and quiet."

David was still recollecting. "It is definitely a more cerebral high than I ever had. Except for the part about the cows taking over the planet. After that I remember there being a conference for foreign businessmen. I was the only one who wasn't an accredited businessman, but they let me stay because my mom's side of my family was Swedish." He rambled on for a bit, slowly coming to the realization that the foundations of his being had not been altered by this nonsensical gibberish.

Richard, on the other hand, recalled being led back out through the same monastery gates after sitting for tea with the monk. He stared at the campfire.

Baker said, "That's a whole lotta time for just going through some gates."

The next morning they made breakfast and Baker, who was holding the ultimate determiner of their futures in the form of a key to his truck, said, "I need to head down to my place in California, 'cause on the way there I want to try to find some oak wine barrels for the berry wines I'm making." He enlightened them about the small cabin and avocado orchard that he rented overlooking the Pacific

Ocean in the Santa Barbara hills. He also went into detail about how he made a living photographing naked women, photos that he allegedly sold on their merits.

When he invited them down to visit sometime, recognizing providence, Richard immediately accepted. "I'm heading down to the Bay Area for Christmas after I go backpacking in the Olympic Peninsula," he said trying not to appear overeager. "I've heard that the ocean is warm down there."

David was planning on heading back to a sawmill in British Columbia to increase his net worth. I'll send you a letter when I get all gainfully employed and respectable." David said.

They set off in three different directions. However, this time a bear did not eat all of Richard's food, as it had the last time he backpacked across the Olympic National Park.

That bit of good news was offset by spending two weeks backpacking in the pouring rain, complete with daily battles building sub-par campfires in an otherwise majestic rain forest. It was a bleak trip. When he finally bid farewell to the Park, he felt like an amphibious creature that carried heavy objects on his back.

He set his coordinates to his parents' home, ready for a break. California was looking pretty good now and the thought of reuniting with his family excited him. However, hitch-hiking was going at an unbearably slow pace, and he still hadn't reached the Washington-Oregon border after a twenty-four hour stretch.

It was almost dark and pouring rain as he found himself walking onto an on-ramp to Highway 5. In the distance he saw what appeared to be another hitchhiker coming toward him. He was a black man, in his early twenties, with a small shoulder bag, an afro and an intensely serious face. After finding out that he also was heading to Portland, Richard asked his name. "I'm Leroy Jones from Milwaukee,

Wisconsin. Do you take Jesus Christ into your heart as your Lord and Savior?"

Richard stared at this stranger for a few seconds, deciding whether he was a little bit crazy or totally crazy. He knew that the best answer would be some sort of placating lie but he replied in a more direct way, "Jesus Christ as my Lord and Savior? Hell no! I'm not religious at all. What did you say your name was?"

"Leroy Jones from Milwaukee, Wisconsin. All persons that don't take Jesus Christ into their heart as their Lord and Savior will burn in Hell for perpetuity, sir!" It rained harder as darkness overtook the light.

Richard thought that if there was a God, the pouring rain after Leroy's warning speech was a nice touch. No cars appeared for a long minute. He looked over at Leroy. "Do you want to hitch with me, I'm heading to California?"

"Yeah, sure." The odd couple miraculously got a ride in a pickup driven by a man who appeared to be in his sixties. "Hi, thanks for picking us up," Richard said. "Thought we were gonna drown out there." The two took off their rain jackets and set them on the floor.

"Where you gentlemen off to?" the driver asked.

"Saaan Fraaancisco" Richard answered, dragging the name out to make it sound comically dramatic.

"Well," the driver said, "I'm sure as heck not going that far but I can get you as far as Eugene."

"My name is Leroy James from Milwaukee, Wisconsin," Leroy blurted out. "Do you take Jesus Christ into your heart as your Lord and Savior?"

The driver was only a bit taken aback. "Well, son, yes I do, yes I do."

"Praise the Lord," Leroy said, somewhat satisfied. "I'm going to Portland to my sister's apartment, sir." The driver turned out to be a local salt-of-the-earth farmer. Richard quickly steered the conversation to more mundane issues before Leroy was able to go crazy with his shtick again. The ride only lasted an hour, but they now found themselves on a well-lit on-ramp, the rain had stopped, and they were one hour closer to their final destinations. It was now around eight o'clock p.m. and with two men hitching in the darkness, especially when one was a black man and the other a long-haired hippie, the probability of somebody stopping was remote. They were both about ready to crawl into the ditch when a VW van pulled over.

A long-haired, scruffy, unshaven hipster offered them a ride another sixty miles south. They gladly accepted. Before Richard could get settled in, Leroy got the drop on him with his patented taking-Jesus-into-your-heart routine. Richard, feeling peeved and ignoring all hitchhiker's etiquette manuals concerning arguing amongst yourselves while in a client's vehicle, let Leroy finish and then said, "Leroy, are you going to try and convert every single person that we get a ride from? 'Cause we only just got introduced to each other and this is the third time. Can't you space it out a little? Like say only two per day while we are together? You already know that I am planning on burning in Hell, so don't wreck my experience on Earth. It's all I got."

Leroy pouted for a few long seconds, then said, "I'm just doing the work of God, Richard. God has called on me and I think I'm gonna listen to him, not you."

Richard writhed in his seat. "Well, maybe you got a hotline directly into God's office, maybe you don't. Maybe you're a prophet, maybe you're nuts. But we're partners for now and I should get one vote just like you do. How would you like it if I tried to convince every driver that he should become an atheist? You wouldn't like that, would you?"

The driver was amused at this interaction and saved the day by answering the original question, "Let's see. Well, Leroy, I do believe in God. And I believe that Jesus was a very wise man and so I do take many of his teachings into my heart. Or try to anyway. But as my lord and savior? I'd have to think about that for a moment."

Leroy was now the one squirming in his seat. He preferred yes or no answers. But compared to Richard, the driver was at least salvageable. When Leroy started to lead the conversation along his flowchart to burning in Hell, the driver changed the subject by proposing, "If you two need a place to crash tonight, we have room."

The two eagerly accepted the kind offer. The driver's name was Mark and his wife's name was Carla. They lived on a small farm 20 miles outside of the city of Medford. Carla was a gracious host. "Have you two been traveling together long?" she inquired.

"No!!" they both said simultaneously, Richard shaking his head back and forth and Leroy with fire in his eyes.

She served them all a beef stew the two transients consumed ravenously. Richard offered to do the dishes but once he started, Carla noticed that he was falling asleep with a dish in his hands and his chin on his chest. She took the dish away, led him to a room with a bed and laid him down. She removed his shoes and socks and covered him with a blanket. The only thing Richard remembered was she kissed him on his forehead and turned out the light.

The two got back on the road early the next morning and got a ride after two hours of thumbing, this time from two middle-aged black men. "Take Jesus as my Lord and Savior? Sheeit man. If I didn't, my mother would rise up from her grave and wring my neck." Leroy took that as a yes and settled into the ride. They were both dropped off in Portland, where they parted ways.

"You're a good man Leroy, take care of yourself," Richard said, putting his pack on.

"Richard Morgenstern, you're okay for an atheist. Don't forget, it's not too late for you to accept Jesus into your heart as..." Richard interrupted by putting his fingers in his ears and yelling out, "I can't hear you!" as he walked away.

Dropped off at the Oregon-California border, at Grants Pass, Richard walked over the highway on-ramp and saw a fellow with a mane of long, blond, matted hair who was wearing a leather jacket down to his feet. Animal fur puffed out from around the collar. They chatted for a few minutes and it turned out that he was also from British Columbia.

"Moses Burns," he said, shaking Richard's hand. They were both heading to the Bay Area, Moses to visit his grandmother who lived in Santa Rosa. He had a presence that couldn't be missed. Most vehicles would swerve away from him since, other than missing a musket over his shoulder, he otherwise looked like a mountain man from the days of the Wild West.

They had only been standing together for a short time when a tractor-trailer pulled over for them, a surprise since tractor-trailers only rarely picked up hitchhikers unless they were female. The driver introduced himself as Ray Buford. Ray had a wiry build, greasy hair and a face that screamed out "IDIOT." He was happy to have some "compnee." He also "'spected to be arriving to Frisco as fast as the Good Lord was willin'." Ray's tractor-trailer must have been close to 3,000 years old. He could barely make it up a hill and he was double clutching and triple clutching and quadruple clutching in order to keep the beast moving. Ray was "gettin' mighty ticked off" about the slow speed he was traveling, as low as 20 miles per hour, prompting Moses to quip, "Hey Ray, do you want us to go outside and push?" causing Richard to laugh in spite of his best effort not to. Ray scowled his disapproval.

Ray appeared to have a screw loose. They mumbled to each other about him when he made his first diesel stop.

"This guy's a piece of work," Moses said. "That tractor is reserved for whomever is the company loser! Ray probably gets all the good-for-nothing equipment because he's always at the bottom of the company totem pole."

Richard hadn't really given today's soap opera any thought; it was starting to feel normal to him. They planned on driving through the night but around 2:00 A.M. the engine blew up. Ray managed to quintuple clutch the smoking monstrosity over to the highway edge and ground to a halt. The good news for the moment was that Ray had an emergency flashlight and flares, which they set up and lit. The better news was that they really had no reason to stick with him anymore.

The engine wasn't the only thing that was blown, as Ray became unhinged. "This compney has the worst sorry-assed big rigs running on black-top that I've ever seen running in my entire career. I'm gonna tell them guys to stick this job where the sun never shines, cause I ain't gonna be part of amateur hour anymore!

"You tell 'em, Ray!" Richard said supportively. He felt like he had somehow been transported through time into an X-rated version of "The Beverly Hillbillies" in which Jethro had become a foul-mouthed truck driver.

"You'll straighten them out, Ray!" Moses added. "That much is for sure. Well, Ray, your phone should still be humming off of your auxiliary battery now, so we best stick our thumbs out while you're waiting for the tow truck."

Ray didn't look up. A litany of vitriol continued to spew from his mouth as the two hitchhikers walked just enough in front of the flares in hopes that a good Samaritan might pick them up.

The ploy worked, as within 20 minutes Ray was just a foul-mouthed memory. A good Samaritan in the form of a cowboy party animal and his cowgirl friend drove them to the next town, which, considering their condition, was courting disaster. Besides being a bit tipsy, Slutsy the Cowgirl was putting her hands a little too close to Cowboy Bert's thing, which was more excitement than the two travelers bargained for. But since all four of them were crammed into the front of a pickup truck, there was no escaping the evening's porn show. Luckily, it was a short ride and when they stopped at a diner south of the California border, the two couldn't get out of the truck fast enough.

They were let off in front of a large shopping complex beside an onramp to I-5 and they wandered over to a grocery store that also was a 24/7 arcade. Richard went to buy a coke and chips while Moses hit the bathroom. By now it was around 3:00 A.M. and he was feeling punchy. He paid an East Indian gentleman (who had watched his every move for signs of shoplifting) for his stuff and looked around for Moses. He heard an arcade machine making quite a racket—fighter jets emitting dog-fight sounds—and spotted Moses in his full-length leather jacket and dead animal fur hat. His hands on the plane's machine gun, he shot wildly in all directions as his hair flailed from side to side. Is this what I have sunk to? thought Richard as he watched his companion massacring evil doers. So immersed was Moses in the game that Richard went outside, sat down on the cement, and finished off his coke and chips.

Finally, Moses came outside, saying exuberantly, "I got so many bonus points I don't think I'll ever have to work again."

By now it was close to 4 A.M. Punch drunk from sleep deprivation, they staggered over to the on-ramp and followed it close to the highway, which was cheating a bit. The cops never liked it but at this hour the odds were definitely in their favor that the law enforcement community was dreaming about donuts jumping over a fence rather than proactively hassling vagrant hippies. Moses seemed possessed as he danced around, his long jacket flapping, trying to win someone over with his charm. Life was flowing into one big freak show.

CHAPTER 17

The Age of Aquarius

1970 – San Francisco, California

Early in his first year of high school Richard felt pressured to throw off the shackles of virginity. There were historical advantages to being a Marin freshman in 1969, living near the epicenter of the Free Love movement in San Francisco's Haight-Ashbury district. But getting across the Golden Gate bridge to the City by the Bay at fourteen meant figuring out which bus to take—a daunting task.

Richard once heard a comedian on TV comment about his sex life—he had done relatively little to relatively few. This sounded like a realistic goal, having thus far done absolutely nothing to absolutely nobody.

Until high school, he had been competitive in sports. A few weeks into ninth grade he made the baseball team as a starting pitcher. But prior to the first official practice, the coach informed him he had to either cut his long hair or choose a different American pastime. In his wisdom Richard chose to keep his hair and his dignity and quietly move on. He did feel some anguish when he heard that, on the opening day double-header, the team's two starting pitchers managed to throw a no-hitter and a one-hitter, thereby sealing Richard's early retirement. The fact that this team didn't lose a game the entire season added even more insult to injury.

Instead he applied himself to girls, drugs, and camping. But his natural aptitude for sports was of little use in these new arenas. Other than some philosophical slogans like, "wait until next year" and "getting to first base," let alone second, third, or the ever elusive home, the rest of his hard-learned skills were non-transferable.

His friends, mostly one grade higher than him, occasionally gave him some beginner's advice. "Kid," Rex said as they all sat outside on the football field during lunch one day, "girls love it when you pay attention to them." Rex had just started a lustful friendship with a girl named Liz who always had her hand placed on his ass, which in their little circle made Rex a certifiable expert on the subject of sex.

"Like, say hi to them? That sort of thing?"

"Well, yeah, but then have some follow-up lines. You're funny, just say something funny."

"Oh, like... how about... what's a nice girl like you doing in a place like this?"

"Okay, okay, that's good. No points for originality but still good," Rex said optimistically. "Maybe after hi and what's a nice girl doing blah blah blah, you could then make a comment about how cute she is. Nothing real personal yet, you might spook her. Just say, "I love your dress, it's really cool.""

"This is good Rex! Thanks for your help."

"Well, I'm still working on this myself, to be honest," Rex confided. "I haven't gotten to home base yet, but I got real close to third. It was kind of like, I slid into third base and I was going to be out, but the third baseman dropped the ball, kicked it into foul territory and I'm like, get up and run home, you idiot." He plucked some grass out of the field nervously. "I'll let you know this weekend if I beat the throw to the plate."

"Wow! Yeah let me know what happens. It helps when you explain this stuff in baseball terms for me." Finally, his love for baseball minutiae was paying off.

Richard didn't hear from Rex until the following Wednesday, but he did see the two lovebirds walking around with Liz's hand still on his ass but now inside his blue jeans, which told him all he needed to know. "Yeah, I made it around the bases," Rex told him later. "But don't get me started about how hard it was to put a rubber on. It's like, who invented those things? A nun or somebody like that. Believe me, if you can put one of those things on, you deserve to get laid."

Richard hadn't even considered the mechanics of the whole enterprise, let alone what equipment lurked under a woman's hood. He just took it on faith that it had to be a straightforward process, otherwise all this talk about "don't get her pregnant" wouldn't have been necessary. But since he didn't even know what questions to ask Rex, the conversation moved in a different direction.

Life as a 14-year-old boy carried on in an uneventful way for the next month or so. Rex had now moved on to girlfriend number two and their good friend Tom had moved on to girlfriend number one, leaving David and Richard as the remainder of the Boy-Palz trio who still carried around the flashing neon VIRGIN sign on their forehead.

Richard had a stroke of luck when identical twin sisters happened upon him during a party. One of them sidled up to show him her latest obsession. A Pet Rock. Trying to be polite, he agreed with her this rock was, in fact, a special rock indeed. She was wearing blue jeans with holes in them, so he couldn't bring himself to refer to them as being cool. If anything, she was a bit on the intellectual side, so it hadn't entered his mind that she was girlfriend material. As days passed, he received phone calls from her until it became apparent, she had become the hunter and he, the hunted.

At her invitation, they went on a couple of walks. Beyond her infatuation with all things avant-garde, she turned out to be a friendly, soft-spoken, highly intelligent type, with a witty, irreverent sense of humor. But Richard, essentially ignorant of the goings on between the sexes, not only never made a move on her, he never even thought about it. One day, bored of their stilted relationship, she gave him a phone call. After a bit of small talk, she asked, "I know this is forward of me but later this afternoon, would baby, perchance, like to come over to my house and ball?" Richard was speechless. Within a split second he considered that she might have actually meant "bowl," then concluded that this was unlikely since she clearly said, "come over to my house and ball" and besides, he seriously doubted that she had a bowling alley somewhere in her home. Blood rushing from his head down to his loins, he stammered out something to the affirmative.

Although it was a half-hour walk to her home, it seemed to take weeks to get there. Sheila, it turned out, was not a virgin and had taken precautions with birth control using something called an IUD, which looked like a miniature television antenna. She guided him from her front door through a side door and into an empty garage. At the front of the garage, where her Mother's car was usually parked, was a barrier of boxes. On the other side of these boxes was a large, fully functional bed stored under a large sheet of plastic. "My mom won't be home for another hour," she said. They both quickly helped each other undress and were instantly transported into a lustful entwinement. Richard, who had been unaware of what he had been missing until now, was soon making up for lost time, when suddenly the garage door flew open, and her mom's car flew into its usual resting spot on the other side of the boxes. Sheila emitted a shrieking whisper into Richard's ear, "Fuck! It's my mom! The two terrified lovers, still hidden from view, remained motionless in a state of negative sound. Sheila's mom, in what felt like eternity, removed her belongings from the car, walked by the boxes and into the house. In testimony to nature's need for procreation, the two lovers quietly finished up the business at hand. Richard slipped out the side door and walked home alone in the glorious sunshine, feeling light as a feather.

Home-run! he thought as he glided along. Home-run!

CHAPTER 18

The Jeff Grey Way

2014 – Marin County, California

Richard emptied his two bags of pills onto his dining room table. He stared at the pile, mesmerized. His brother Robert sat across the table, eyes glued to his Apple laptop, analyzing a business presentation he was preparing for a large insurance company. He usually stayed at Richard and Terrie's place whenever he came to San Francisco during holidays from his home in London. This was equivalent to being visited by a food factory. Every day Robert would make fresh bread and three gourmet meals, followed by some type of incredible dessert. In short, he appeared to be involved in some sort of international conspiracy to fatten the world up for market. His family and friends anticipated his arrival with dread and excitement as they speculated how to cope with the inevitable weight gain and health risks associated with his lifestyle. As his culinary delights cooked in the oven, he would turn into Super Businessman, closing deals, speaking with CEOs and basically making Richard wonder how this person somehow emerged from the same genetic pool as he had.

After a while, Richard looked up from his pill pile, breaking the trance. "Robby, don't you ever just veg out? It's challenging enough for me just to sort out my thousands of medications into the correct pillboxes without having to listen to your never ending negotiations for voice-recognition contracts. What do you call it? Artificial intelligence?"

Robert took a swig from his ever-present bourbon on the rocks with a mere suggestion of sweet vermouth, also known as a manhattan, then grimaced as his mind recalibrated to moron-mode, his preferred setting for most of humanity with few exceptions. "Think of it this way," he said. "Artificial intelligence is the opposite of what you specialize in, which is natural stupidity." He continued typing as he spoke. "Anyhow, I meant to tell you, I was watching Jeff Grey sorting out his pile of pills and he has a faster system than yours. Do you want to know what he does?"

"Not really," Richard replied. Pill sorting efficiencies weren't on his To Do list for this incarnation.

Jeff and Sharon were old family friends who, for some reason, liked Robert. Perhaps it was because they were at least as smart as he, what with their doctorates in nuclear physics but they also had similar world visions and a dry New York City Jewish sense of humor that was impervious to Robert's sarcasm.

As usual, Robert ignored Richard's answer. "You sort your pills weekly, don't you?"

Richard regrouped from having his weekly pill-sorting technique assaulted and said, "Yes, weekly." Robert was only one year older than his brother, but he wielded this powerful psychological tool deftly. "I really look forward to it. It adds meaning to my otherwise thankless life."

As usual, Robert heard what he wanted to hear, in this case "Yes," and continued. "You see, what Jeff Grey does is to pour at least a one-month supply onto a large surface area, while being careful to keep each medication separated. This way he can quickly load up his large assortment of pill boxes in a fraction of the time you take using your "system." He held up his fat little fingers to emphasize the quotation marks. "Based upon a time/benefit analysis that I've recently completed..."

"When did you do a time/benefit analysis?" Richard interrupted.

"Just now while we were speaking," Robert said calmly as he continued. "Based upon my analysis, you'd save approximately one week per year. So, you're welcome. You now have the opportunity to squander another week of your life every year that you're alive. The bill will be in the mail."

"That's madness!" Richard shouted. "What Jeff Grey doesn't understand and what you also fail to appreciate, is that for me, the time I spend with my pills is a deeply reflective moment when I can be at one with the pharmaceutical industry and my disease."

"Which disease are you referring to? Natural stupidity is a condition, not a disease." The gloves had come off and Robert knew he was at an advantage in spats like this, what with his being the older brother. Not to mention, since his days in diapers he had been convinced that he understood all topics better than any other human being on the planet.

"Robby," Richard said as he crawled down into the rhetorical gutter to challenge his brother's authority, "you piece of human garbage. As you know, I am afflicted with Parkinson's disease. Don't forget that in spite of this, I can still whoop your Rubenesque ass. If you have such a great memory, do you remember back in the late 1950's when Dad used to orchestrate wrestling matches between us, and do you remember who would always prevail? Moi. In fact, I suspect that's maybe why you became a homosexual. Life is strange, isn't it?"

Robert didn't take the bait. "Well, we aren't going to settle this little impasse in one conversation, are we? But let me conclude by saying that you are really milking your Parkinson's card too often."

Richard sputtered sounds to indicate that he was offended.

Robert continued. "That certainly was the case when you blamed Parkinson's that time your car ran out of gas. And when you burned the barbecued squid. I mean, I'm starting to see a pattern. Terrie said you even blamed it once when the Giants lost a night game to the Dodgers."

Just then the phone rang. Richard answered it. It was Sharon, Jeff Grey's wife, calling to find out when they would "have" to take "Bob" to stay at their house as was typically the tradition. "Yes, he is available to be removed from my property. When? Oh, let's just say if you don't come over and get him really fucking soon, he may die a terrible, bloody death. But don't rush or anything."

Robert pulled the phone away from Richard. "Richard's hallucinating again, I think he got confused with his color-coding pill system. I'd stay but since he is threatening to kill me... anyway, my work is done here."

Richard took the phone back. Sharon said, "Do you want me to make him disappear? And are you still maintaining that we are somehow obligated to keep him for half the time based upon—what was that based upon?"

"I was having a bad day at that time. That was just the Parkinson's talking," Richard said, looking directly at Robert who was shaking his head

Terrie arrived home shortly before Sharon and Jeff took Robert away. "We're going to miss you," she said. "What am I going to do without the extra two thousand calories a day?"

The brothers gave each other air kisses. "I'd give you a real kiss, but I don't want you to catch my Parkinson's," Richard said.

"Get a life," Robert said sweetly.

As they walked down the stairs Richard could hear Jeff say to Sharon, "This is going to be fun."

CHAPTER 19

The Rock Gang

1975 – Northern British Columbia

David and Richard felt like multimillionaires. They each had managed to save over two thousand dollars, which was good, but it was the end of September and they both wanted to increase their nest eggs prior to winter. Richard decided to head off to somewhere in northern British Columbia, with a vague idea of living in the wilderness, not certain what that entailed. David would head home to his parents' in California for a month or so, to research going to medical school in British Columbia. They heard about a town up north called Prince George, where railway jobs in remote wilderness areas were rumored to be available. They hitched four hundred miles to Prince George, arriving toward dusk. After seeking directions to the Canadian National Railway office, they headed to their destination. Their plan was first to locate the railway office, then find a forested spot nearby to camp for the night. Staying in a hotel never crossed their minds. They found the office using a flashlight. Mission temporarily accomplished, they continued walking for a half mile parallel to the railroad tracks and spotted their home for the next two days—a stand of cottonwood trees beside the Fraser River. The trees were enormous and beautiful, benefitting from the silt deposited each spring.

That evening they walked back into downtown Prince George to grab a beer at one of the local watering holes. They were struck by the outdoor signage in all the drinking establishments. Each had two separate entrances, one labeled "Gents" and the other "Ladies with Escorts." Once they peeped into the inner sanctums of several bars on George Street, they realized the premises were devoid of "gents" and that the alleged "ladies" didn't fare much better. As far as "Ladies with Escorts" were concerned, this was obviously a cruel hoax from yesteryear. In northern British Columbia, yesteryear was only about one year ago. Time was doing a good job of standing still in these parts. In front of each of these bars, an assortment of drunk loggers and the local indigenous crowd lingered in a variety of Wild West stupor positions. Random fights broke out. "I know I've seen this movie before, but I just can't place it," Richard said to himself out loud.

"Dodge City after the cattle drive," David responded.

The two picked what they perceived as the least dangerous of the bars and walked in dubiously. A few drunks sized them up and, having determined they didn't look like a threat to their women, children, or way of life, continued to drink beer, play pool and throw darts. The newcomers' long hair didn't seem to be an issue for the regulars, although there was a general atmosphere of intolerance in the air.

The two walked up to the bar and ordered a couple of cold ones. No ID was requested because nobody cared. They met a couple of guys, Ralph and Albert, who already worked for the railroad and assured the travelers the railway was perpetually short of workers and jobs could be had if they showed up first thing in the morning. They all had several more drinks, got hammered and saw two fights break out. Both ended in technical knock-outs, with the losers receiving broken noses to show for their efforts. Toward closing time, it became clear that Ralph was a full-fledged asshole who became surlier and surlier the more he drank or perhaps the harder he thought. Albert was more of a follower and Ralph acted as his surrogate older brother. They were working with a squadron of railroad laborers known as the Rock Gang. Their outfit was in town for two nights after having been "out in the bush" for a full two-month stint. Although their actual job description was blowing stuff up with dynamite, they had grudgingly been changing railroad ties lately. They were not happy about this. They spent a lot of the evening grumbling. Ralph a crew leader of sorts, intermittently optimistic about the Rock Gang's future, would wax nostalgic about the glory years when the Rock Gang was "where the action was." Although he hadn't been part of that era, Albert would nod in agreement about how things had nowhere to go but up. Albert had "pyromaniac" written all over his face.

Next morning found them waiting at the doors of the railroad office a full hour before opening time. Their goal was to work at any job available, but God forbid it was the Rock Gang. They were given application forms specifically made for people who had problems scrawling out the letter X for signatures. They interviewed together, with the one skill testing question being, "How are your backs?"

They apparently answered that question correctly, as Office Guy called across the room to Office Lady, "Doesn't the Rock Gang need a couple of fellas?"

She yelled back, even though they were only six feet apart, "You betcha! They want to pull out of town later this morning."

With no choice and mixed emotions, Richard and David headed to the closest store and picked up a couple novels, some chocolate, envelopes and stamps—unsure exactly how they would be able to mail anything out. Their unit consisted of four converted boxcars made into a cookhouse, two bunkhouses for the laborers (eight men in each) and a third for the managers and foremen, divided by levels of importance. An engine and caboose were added to these cars and after five hours of waiting, they lumbered off into the bush. Following two hundred seventy-five miles of banging and clanging, they pulled off onto a siding that would accommodate a work crew for one to two months. Their encampment was nowhere close to any roads and the scenic mountains. It provided world-class views and wildlife galore which soothed the souls of this rowdy crew. The only other task that brought them harmony with nature was when they got to dynamite a rock cliff. The sidings were simply parallel sets of tracks that were used as either turnoffs for slower trains to get out of the way of the faster trains or as a dedicated track for work crews like Richard and David's. The closest town was forty-five miles farther West but that was academic since there were no roads anywhere nearby. David and Richard introduced themselves to their future bunkhouse mates and all, but Ralph, seemed friendly enough, although not exactly Canada's best and brightest. It was midnight before they settled into their bunk beds. Being lowest in seniority, they were both given top bunks. Within ten minutes they were all asleep. Richard was dreaming about discovering a hidden territory, when a ninety-car-freight-train came roaring by on the main track, its headlights only six feet from his head and its horn blasting. He woke up in a cold sweat, terrified. Nobody else in the room had so much as flinched.

The first day out, the two green railroad workers got a taste of what was in store for them. As they had heard previously, the current job description was exclusively changing railroad ties. To do this, one man would first remove the spikes that held the old ties in place, a different man would clamp a special tool onto the wooden tie and pull and pull until he had freed it. The old tie got dragged away and kicked into the ditch. At this point a new tie was carried up and the operation was repeated in reverse. Once the new tie was installed, several workers would grab lining bars, heavy iron bars with a point at the end, and tamp the gravel with the pointed end until the tie was seated firmly. All the while an older Italian foreman would serenade the lower castes with inane advice. "Give 'er shit!" was for the grand finale. Ralph would pound a few spikes to connect the rails to the tracks themselves, ritualistically removing his shirt so that his muscles were on display. He seemed to believe that this would enhance his reputation as the toughest guy in the room. Ralph was clearly a moron with a disproportionate level of confidence. As he worked, he would comment about his legendary sexual abilities. "Strong like ox! Make love like bull!"

Out of earshot, Richard mumbled to David, "What's Ralph sharing with us now? His insights into having sex with farm animals?" But Ralph's routine never seemed to get old with the rest of the crew. This work continued for ten hours a day, six days a week. There was nowhere to spend your money, so it was a good short-term job as brainless jobs went.

Crew boss, Foreman Capurro, was a nice enough guy if you enjoyed being subservient to a 5'6" Italian tyrant. He had a huge neck and his head was considerably larger yet. To top it off, his teeth were disproportionately large, even in relation to his enormous head. He appeared to be some type of hybrid tyrannosaurus rex straight out of a Fellini movie, with an Italian accent and a bad temper. Capurro's orders were passed to the crew by way of the older Italian foremen. When he did speak, it was unintelligible and terrifying. He ran his Rock Gang with an iron fist. Adding to his mystique was his voice, a ferocious Italian growling noise. But most of his communication was through his eyes, which emitted a telltale homicidal twinkle that dared any man to trifle with him. In short, he was a psychopath.

Needless to say, the productivity rate was high on this crew. About eight men, also Italian, appeared to be related in some fashion to Foreman Capurro. This group constantly berated the balance of the crew in pidgin English.

Capurro only rarely "communicated" to anyone but his minions, which came as a relief to the other workers. Generally, the only time you would hear him talk was when he was on his walkie-talkie and the only thing David and Richard could make out was "Foreman Capurro" followed by static. The remaining workers in the railway caste system, by order of prestige, were Ralph, the insanely strong idiot, Bill from Powell River, just as strong as Ralph and dumb as a post, Gino, the friendly Italian who was not part of the mafioso management, Ben George, a Cree Indian fresh out of prison, Albert, because he was Ralph's sidekick, Richard and David, not only were they new but they were obviously hippies, and last but not least, Benny the Newfie, banished to the bottom of the list because he was from Newfoundland. Anyone from Newfoundland went to the bottom of the list being preordained to reside there in Canada, with the possible exception of Pakistani's and East Indians, whose primary perceived problem was their skin color.

Not included in any group, Mario seemed to be in Canada on a hunting expedition rather than working at a job. He was always shooting at something before and after work. Fortunately for the wildlife in the area, he was known as a terrible shot and always missed.

Suffice it to say, that racism and or intolerance was alive and well in British Columbia.

The first day of changing railroad ties was a trial by fire for our heroes. The working Italians would unleash a tirade of berating and unintelligible comments at them, like "Give 'er shit," "Piece of cake," "Vaffanculo" and "Che cazzo fai?" For the first couple of hours this was demoralizing but as they both got the swing of it, the insults and jibes flowed off them like water off a duck and this was more a hazing process that, if you passed, would morph into a railroad worker's equivalent of white noise. Most of the men on the crew used shovels like toothpicks, deftly manipulating them with ease and grace. The two would shortly grow to appreciate their grumpy, matter-of-fact demeanors. But initially, both shared the same fantasy of lining them all up against a wall and shooting them one by one.

The major fringe benefit of this job—actually the only fringe benefit of this job—was the food. While it wasn't gourmet, it was good in a Betty Crocker comfort food way. Stews, mashed potatoes and gravy and berry pies were daily occurrences. The quantity seemed to be limitless. What Richard and David may have lacked in the skills associated with the labor world, they more than made up for with their innately prolific appetites. Lunch was problematic since it only lasted thirty minutes... exactly thirty minutes. For those that shoveled food down their gullets for the entire time, the challenges placed on their digestive system exacted a heavy toll. But after a couple of unpleasant days, they both learned to pace themselves during lunch and eat a large supper later, without any time constraints. For the first time in his life, Richard put on a small amount of weight, while David, who had a larger frame, talked about one day becoming a two hundred pounder.

The two Californians were representative of the garden-variety San Francisco, politically left-wing, young hippie of their day. One of their regular rituals was a daily twenty-minute transcendental meditation, which had been popularized by the Beatles during the Sixties. One of the controversial aspects of it was that the "customized" mantra that you were given was sold to you for twenty dollars. Instead he "borrowed" his mantra by getting one at no charge from a previous disciple who had become disillusioned. The first evening, after working a ten-hour day, both men did a short yoga session and followed it with meditation. A few minutes into their silence, Ralph could be heard mumbling, "What the fuck's wrong with those guys?" Neither of the two chose to acknowledge Ralph's comments. This infuriated Ralph even more since two men sitting motionless on their top bunks was obviously a serious threat to something in Ralph's brain. Presuming that he had a brain—highly speculative.

Bill from Powell River said, "I don't know, and I don't care." Nobody else spoke.

"Well, I don't fucking like it" was Ralph's final thought on the subject.

Less than twenty minutes later the bunkhouse became a meditation and yoga information center as the two young gurus explained to their curious fellow workers that both practices were secular and didn't challenge anybody else's personal beliefs but were akin to calisthenics for your brain and muscles. As the rest of the bunkhouse was more concerned with other mystical practices, primarily sex, drugs, and rock and roll, enough common ground was discovered to ease all fears except Ralph's primary one, which was that nobody should ever, EVER, call him a faggot.

Ralph always kept a side table covered with photos of himself and several bombshells celebrating together in bars, but David made an interesting observation about the women in the photos. "Look at the facial expressions on these women. Ralph's got his arm around at least one woman in each picture. But they all have an uneasy expression, as if Ralph was using them as props." Once pointed out, it was clear as can be.

Having put this minor uproar behind them, the subject turned to recreational drugs. Ralph got the discussion underway by talking about exactly how he planned to get fucked up on the next Sunday off. Albert's full attention focused on his mentor as he spoke. "The best high ever is when you shoot up a little smack". Ralph smiled and his eyes squinted as he spoke. "It totally relaxes you. You melt like fuckin' butter, man. It's like you just forget everything and melt. You gotta try it!"

Albert asked tentatively, "Isn't that the same thing as heroin? Doesn't that get you addicted?"

Ralph's smile became larger as he enlightened Albert. "Nooo, it's only a bit addictive. You just take a bit and that way you don't get addicted." Albert seemed fine with this explanation and they worked out the mundane financial details between themselves.

During this discussion, Ben George lay back on his bed quietly. David asked him if he had worked long for the Railway. "Just for two weeks now," he replied. He avoided direct eye contact and had a soft smile. "Got this job right after I got out of jail."

Richard suddenly became interested. "What did you go to jail for?"

Ben George spoke with a wry smile on his face. "Got drunk one night and went crazy. Threw a chair through the window of the government liquor store. Did four months in Prince George Prison."

By the next day off, Ralph's smack still hadn't materialized. Being a decisive man, he moved on to Plan B. The new drug du jour was manufactured by separating the red and white mini-pills contained in Contact C capsules, the white ones being an amphetamine, commonly referred to as speed. This was finicky work, using pins to do the separating along with Ralph's threat to them, "Don't fucking sneeze, whatever you do."

Later in the afternoon, Richard and David came across Ralph, Albert and Bill digging an enormous hole in the ground at a breakneck pace, burning off some of their newfound energy. When asked what they were doing, Ralph replied, "We're gonna visit us some Chinamen!" As it turned out, the sole motivation for this exercise in futility was to order some take-out.

As time marched forward, the two travelers managed to stay out of Foreman Capurro's line of fire for a month. Once paid, they both netted close to two thousand dollars therefore, the temptation to quit was more than they could stand. After another tasty dinner the two walked, with great trepidation, over to Foreman Capurro's headquarters to give him the bad news. They banged on his door. Capurro opened the door looking slightly less menacing than usual, as was customary in the evenings after he had downed a handful of painkillers. David spoke. "Oh, hi. We have some bad news for you. We want to quit."

Capurro looked at them, sniffed the air, considered biting their heads off with his large tyrannosaurus teeth but thought better of it and said, "Good!"

CHAPTER 20

Haight-Ashbury

1972 – San Francisco, California

Richard, David and Tom, known collectively as the Boy-Palz, looked up at the street signs marking the intersection. Even though you knew that they were just street signs, you couldn't help but marvel. Haight-Ashbury! Formerly Haight Street and Ashbury Avenue but now forever married until death do them part.

"Ground Zero!" Tom said as the three marveled at what was called a street intersection previously but now a counter-culture mecca.

"Haight-Fuckin'-Ashbury!" David said, seconding the motion. "So where are all of the stoned naked women?" he asked.

"I think they keep them locked up and only let them out when the Stones are in town," Richard replied.

They were still too young to drive so they had managed to negotiate public transportation to the holy spot. Neither David nor Tom had permission from their parents to go to this Sodom and Gomorrah. They had to make up a story explaining their whereabouts. All the values near and dear to both of their mothers' hearts were under assault by the hippie movement. The longer David's hair grew, the more tirelessly she waged war against this new evil empire.

As far as that went, Tom's mother, Mrs. Carey, was also fighting the good fight. While Mrs. Miller would grind down David and his friends with a steady drumbeat of church-inspired slogans that were often just plain baffling, Mrs. Carey was a mind reader, she always seemed to know what they were up to.

While Mrs. Miller leaned heavily on her pastor's eulogies and the ultra-behind-the-times Reader's Digest for her information, David inhaled books and articles (and other substances) that generally buffered his positions. She never had a chance to win the great debates with her son; but she stuck to her guns and kept repeating her talking points, like a politician on the campaign trail.

Now the three were basking in the glow of hippie central. They strolled down Haight Street, occasionally wandering into a head shop to peruse the latest in drug paraphernalia technology. Each street corner was a meeting place where drug-addled hippies could ventilate, recreate, transubstantiate, negotiate and in general clog up foot travel and intersections.

On one corner, Richard addressed a cluster of counter-culture casualties who looked like they spent a lot of time in the scene. "Excuse me. Would you happen to know where we'd be able to buy some ganja around here?"

A young mini-skirted woman with long blonde hair and long legs stepped out from amongst the group. "I can help you out. Just follow me to our apartment down the street and you can try it out first. I can't sell on the street. There's narcs in them thar hills," she said, gesturing with the tip of her chin towards nowhere in particular.

The three nodded in agreement and soon found themselves two blocks off Haight Street in an apartment that reeked of drugs and depravity. This they all found to their liking. "I'm selling Thai stick, but nobody buys more than one or two sticks at a time 'cause it's primo stuff. Mucho dinero. Twenty-five dollars per stick. You can each try one toke 'cause you're cute. One toke is all you need, anyhow. And I'm Lisa, by the way."

The taste and smell of the weed was sublime. Lisa was sublime. Life was sublime. "Whatta you thinkie?" she asked.

Tom, as the default stoner-boss because he could hold his smoke better than the other lightweights, spoke on their behalf, "Well, we don't normally spend so much but this is really good shit. Since you're so nice, we'll buy two."

"Far fucking out," Lisa said eloquently. "It costs more to bring it in from Nam than from Mexico and it's the best bud on the planet. Anyhow, you get what you pay for," she added, endearing herself to the three with every word she uttered. "Our boys in Nam are smuggling it in through the Port of Oakland. It's the only good thing about this war. And we gotta support our troops. Right?"

All three boys fought to be the first to agree with whatever it was that Lisa had said, so their three-deep response was unintelligible. Lisa kindly walked them back to Haight, as otherwise they never would have found their way. The Thai stick was every bit as good as the saleslady was foxy. She gave the three a big hug each and bid them farewell. They were intoxicated by the Earth Goddess and her wares. They staggered to what resembled a bus stop and somehow or other managed to find their way home.

By the time they got back to Marin, they were fairly sober. "You know what?" David asked.

"Know, what," Tom replied.

"I think they should rope off Haight-Ashbury and charge admission to get in."

They all got off at the same bus stop and walked home. The times they were a changing and they were liking it.

CHAPTER 21

Visualize Sliced Pizza

2014 – San Francisco, California

"You should think seriously about getting a job. Sometimes I think you're starting to drift off to La-La Land," Terrie said. "Consider it therapy. The money wouldn't hurt either."

Richard rolled his eyes. "If it involves a white sand beach, I'd probably be open to that idea. But work as therapy? That defies credibility. Maybe electric shock therapy. I'd probably end up killing my boss or something worse."

Terrie wasn't ready to drop the issue entirely. "What about all those ideas you've talked about? Some of them had potential."

He perked up a bit. "Are you referring to the religion-themed pizza parlor, Jesus Crust?"

She moaned. "That wasn't one of your best efforts."

"Yeah, but the menu names, remember the menu names?" Richard was starting to wax nostalgic about the menu concept. "The Seven Apostles with anchovies. The Ten Commandments with our special Moses sauce, Noah's Ark with extra meat. And don't forget the separate Jewish menu with gefilte fish on matzah crust. All kosher. Absolutely no cloven hoofs. Come on... gold, right? Gold!"

"Richard, it's official. Jesus Crust is not coming back. Don't ever mention that stupid idea again. It's stupid. Really stupid. You are experiencing selective amnesia. Remember your brilliant Muslim hot and spicy pizza with ground camel? Where did that come from?"

He was squirming in his chair. "Granted, I never did any control groups, so I was grasping at straws, but all religions need representation. Our message needs to be clear. Peace and Pizza for a Better World."

An awkward silence wafted between them. "You don't like Jesus Crust, do you?"

Terrie mumbled into a newspaper that she picked up off the coffee table. "Really, really stupid. And you're an atheist for Christ's sake."

He breathed out heavily in resignation. "Okay. Okay. Disappointed is maybe too light a word to express my feelings but somewhere between disappointed and devastated. Do you remember that other great idea, Virtual Day Care?"

"Oh my God! That again? I thought we put that guy to bed a long time ago. Besides, you'd probably end up in prison. For Christ's sake, can't you get real for just five minutes?"

"They laughed at Galileo and Einstein. Say what you want but you're never going to convince me that children between the ages of two and five really need human supervision." He sat down in a recliner chair, weary from the lack of emotional support.

"Yeah but I don't think most parents are going to trust their children to a robot. And just imagine if it accidentally hurts the child or if it has a glitch in the programming. Things could quickly spiral out of control." Terrie looked at the liquor cabinet, then her watch, then the liquor cabinet again.

"Yes, but you're forgetting the control room that can monitor up to fifteen day care centers simultaneously. You always forget that part. Without the control room, sure, it looks irresponsible. But with a 24/7 control room, with the capacity to care for up to two hundred twenty-five children at any one time, the upside potential is going to make venture capitalists salivate!"

"Believe what you want but the name alone sunk that idea for me." Terrie said, now holding her head in her hands. "Not to mention that the 24/7 control room was only manned by robots, so in effect, your team of robots is supervised by more robots. Not exactly what moms and dads want to hear. You dig?"

"No diggie, because I kind of liked the name fifteen Kids and a Robot and I certainly would have been comfortable leaving my kids with a well-trained team of robots, had that option been available back when dinosaurs roamed the earth. You really are stifling my creativity. How about a yogurt franchise? Is that what you want for me? To sling frozen yogurt?"

She dropped her newspaper. I noticed your ex didn't enroll your kids in Robot Day Care and they turned out to be fine adults. What about that column you always wanted to write? That way you have an immediate job where nobody can fire you like they always do. You get to use your creativity. And maybe one day, somebody might pay you some money? I'd pay you money just so I don't have to hear any more of your get-rich-quick schemes ever again."

Richard jumped to his feet. "Okay. Then it is agreed. Starting immediately, I wish to be referred to as an author. If I make us some money, great. Otherwise, we are no worse off than before. "We're getting by alright between your teaching job and my occasional consultancy gigs."

Terrie was taken aback but as she started to think things over, she began to warm to the whole idea. After thinking over the repercussions for a minute she said, "So, what do you want to write about?"

"A rant. How about... how about RICHARD RANTS? I believe that I have a fresh perspective that others might enjoy. Agreed?"

"Agreed!" Terrie replied. She got out of her chair and walked over to Richard with her arms outstretched. "Put 'er there, sport," she said smiling. "I think this is a good decision, though I do have some concern that your fresh perspective could be seen as the work of a madman. But at least you'd be an income-earning nut job. So... that's an improvement."

"Thanks, I guess." Richard was already picking up his laptop beside the couch. "I had some strong impressions from our trip to Indonesia last year that I want to write about."

"Well, that should keep you out of trouble at any rate. Just promise me that I won't be a character in it."

Richard was already fiendishly typing. "I promise you nothing."

CHAPTER 22

Have Yourself a Spacey Little Christmas

1974 – Big Sur, California

Back in the bosom of his family Richard was treated like royalty. His father was the family French chef, thanks to being stationed in France during World War II and years later, the appearance of Julia Child on TV. He would ask Richard what he would like for dinner every morning of his visit, so the beef bourguignon and lobster bisque were flowing. Other than eating his body weight in French food, he also caught up on lost opportunities pursuing young women, something currently lacking in his isolated lifestyle.

By the time that Tom was of college age, he and his latest girlfriend, Janet, were becoming inseparable, even sharing some college classes together at the local Community College. Her distinguishing characteristics were extremely compatible with Tom's in a down-to-earth way. She had the entire 1960's package; a Mother Earth Goddess beauty, an incredible singing voice and a wise yet innocent outlook on the world. Realizing in her wisdom, her man would benefit from a Boy-Palz camping trip, she gave Tom her blessings to go forth, camp and fortify his brain with foreign substance.

The third member of the Boy-Palz, David, had lined up work for the winter at a sawmill in British Columbia, armed with his previously hand-crafted fake Canadian identification. He decided to have one last adventure with his two buddies and hooked up with them in Big Sur. In spite of being leery of getting nabbed by the Draft Dodger Cops in the U.S.A., the two remaining Boy-Palz hitched down to Big Sur. To no one's surprise, the theme of the trip quickly became how much pot could be consumed while still arriving at their intended destination. After an hour on the road, it became clear that it was entirely possible they could inadvertently end up in the wrong state if they weren't careful. The only checks and balances that they were able to come up with was Tom's observation that "if we just make sure that we always stay in the right side lane, we'll eventually get to the turn-off to Big Sur... I think."

Richard's contribution for the return trip would be, "if we just make sure that we always stay in the right side lane, we'll eventually get to the turn-off to San Francisco. I think..."

It didn't help that every hippie Volkswagen van going down to Big Sur was picking them up, leaving little time in between rides to sober up. They got a ride with two guys that looked like hip bodybuilders. When Tom asked if they wanted to smoke a joint, they gave him a look that said, "You want us to get high at 10:30 in the morning? Maybe you guys should instead get a life."

They refrained from lighting up, at least until the van stopped moving and they were let off at the final junction to the trailhead. "See you later" Tom called out to the two hip weightlifters, who didn't bother to reply.

As they drove away, Richard continued the farewell waving goodbye. One of the great things about hitchhiking was that you could always have the last word.

"Yeah, like, try not to drop any barbells on your heads... you sick pedophiles." They sat down beside the road and analyzed the indignity of being judged by others.

"So, what was their problem?" Tom started. "They acted like it is unusual to be totally baked by ten in the morning."

"Talk about uptight," Richard replied. "Like, I understand if getting fried before lunch might get in the way of their weightlifting regimen but why impose that on us?"

Tom lit a joint, sucked a lungful and said thoughtfully, "Yeah, like, I wouldn't get all prissy with them if they had asked us if we wanted some high-protein milkshake or something."

Richard replied, "They could have offered to let us shove some of that stuff up our asses and we still would have remained cool and not got all my-body-is-a-temple on them."

Tom sucked an even larger hit and said, "Assholes. I'd like to pay some big hairy dude a bunch of money to hold them down and shove protein powder up their asses."

"Yeah, really. Those guys were serious downers." Richard took a large toke and the two stared off at the dramatic ocean view in the distance.

Tom broke the silence. "Maybe the driver will take his eye off of the road for a second and their van plunge off the cliff into the ocean." He held the joint away from himself and looked at it in an appreciative manner. "Really good ganja," he said, passing it back to Richard, who also examined it as if were a fine cigar.

"Fuckin' beautiful," Richard replied. as he exhaled.

Another VW van approached them in the distance as the two attempted to project an aura of coolness to ensnare their next ride.

The three eventually rendezvoused in Big Sur. David always seemed to have strange experiences while traveling through that neck of the woods.

"I met this chubby fellow that suggested I join him for the night in a cave where the ocean met the base of a huge cliff." David said. "It was pretty cool, until I noticed beside the campfire that there were some human bones."

"You're shitting me" Tom said.

"I shit you not!" David replied.

David spent a sleepless night with his cave-friend, and the bones, ready to fend off the cannibal.

"Big Sur has a lot of weirdos. Coming down here I got a real doozy. A Mustang pulls over to pick me up and there's four guys inside and they're all saying 'Get in fast! Get in fast! Get in fast! We got an A.P.B. on this vehicle and we gotta make it to Monterrey toot suite!' They were floorin' it too. I made an excuse and I got out early! They let me out and were burning rubber as they pulled away! Just think about that for one second. What kind of criminals pull over for a hitch-hiker when they're being chased by the cops?" David asked.

Tom thought about this for a couple of seconds then answered, "Friendly ones?"

CHAPTER 23

Have Your Midlife Crisis in Borneo

2014 – San Francisco, California

"No, it's just that I think most people would agree with me. Having your storyline weave from parking tickets to Internet dating, then over to instantaneous language acquisition with panda bears and finally culminating with a midlife crisis where you find yourself wandering the jungles of Borneo wearing only a loincloth, all within an eight-page span, well... do you really want me to spell it out for you? You're going to have to find a kindred nutcase, I mean kindred spirit, that also sees things along the lines of your global view. And if there is another person that falls into this category, well, God help us because our planet is doomed." Terrie turned away from Richard, walked over to the couch and flopped down. "I rest my case your honor." She said lying inert.

"Okay, okay, you had your little ventilation. I didn't say I was married to every line. But having said that, I feel compelled to respond on behalf of other forward thinkers, such as myself, that, if pandas are capable of complex thought, then I want to be the first to hear them out. I suppose that it could be possible that pandas could turn out to be hard-core right-wing fundamentalists. I hadn't even thought of that. It's just that they're so fluffy. It's hard for me to see them in a negative light." Richard sat beside Terrie.

After a moment of silence, he slyly pulled out a letter and handed it to her. She read it carefully.

"Is this a joke?!" she blurted out. "Your column is in The Daily Blabbermouth! I kind of like it."

"It's for real," he responded. "Two-hundred-fifty dollars per weekly column. That's good for a starter account. Guaranteed for a four month minimum."

"Are you going to take it? Because if you don't, I will personally kill you. You have ten seconds to answer." She stared at her watch.

"In that case I guess I have no choice." Richard replied. "And thanks for sticking by me through thick 'n' thin" he added.

"That's what panda bear girlfriends are for," she said, humbled.

RICHARD RANTS

Have Your Midlife Crisis in Borneo

I was seated at a table filled with travelers from all over the world recently, while staying at a remote island in Southeast Asia. The man beside me was from Holland... or Belgium... or Netherlands...whatever. As an American traveler, I reserve the right to flaunt America's ignorance of world geography. It's just that... we do it so well. It turned out both of us had the same itineraries, while traveling "alone" through the jungles of Borneo. Not only that, we were the exact same age. I got to thinking. I wondered if we were men going through expensive midlife crises. Did the act of entering a malaria-infested swamp on the opposite side of the planet, adorned in a skimpy loincloth, have some healing quality? Despite the high cost of going native like our forefathers millions of years ago, a back of an envelope cost-benefit analysis definitively illustrated this approach as less expensive than conventional psychiatric techniques. Even cheaper than shock therapy. Plus, it's less threatening to your wife if you don't turn into

Mr. Hot-pants. Swinging from vine to vine is one thing but swinging (you know, gold chains, loud clothes, hot sex) is too spicy a meatball. So, all in all, a jungle tour is not as stupid as it sounds.

But why does it work? First let's look at the problem. Typical guy, fifty-seven years old, has some weight issues, related more to the forces of gravity than the 4,000 calories per day intake. The chicks aren't looking in his direction anymore, except as a possible threat. His life until now hasn't worked out great. He hates himself. His children hate him. His wife wants to divorce him yesterday because, let's face it, the guy is a loser with an L branded on his forehead. This guy (who bears zero resemblance to me or my rugged Dutch/Belgian friend) wants to eat grasshoppers cooked over an open fire to the sounds of monkeys and other exotic jungle noises, covered in leeches and swatting malaria-infected mosquitoes. And people have the audacity to challenge his/our need to battle nature at its most primitive—I mean—who do they think they are?!! That's the problem.

What is the solution? I don't claim to be any more of an authority on this subject than the next guy but the answer, obvious as the sagging eyelids on our faces, isn't pretty. We middle-aged men have been grappling with an accelerated evolutionary time warp. Only a few years ago in geological time we were cavemen wrestling sabre toothed tigers out of our caves and the next thing we know, we're part of a clan that considers it their God-given right to expect three meals a day, in a two thousand–square foot air-conditioned home. All the while, our female partners are throwing up their hands in frustration with us because they just don't get it. They don't get that men today are essentially living in a time warp. One that is best overcome with equatorial rain forest therapy.

In conclusion, what is the answer? That depends on the question and I honestly can't remember what I said but I'm not going to drop this thing. It's just too important! And I'm not canceling my plane ticket to Borneo, either. Because I had a dream. Just the other night I had this dream and it was sung by Johnny Cash to the tune of his classic "Folsom Prison Blues." It went a little something like this:

I hear the jungle drums a callin'
They're drummin' round the bend
And I ain't seen the sunshine
Since, I don't know when
'Cause my career ain't a hummin'
Ain't a huuuummiiiiin' alongggggg
And when I see a young babe's thigh,
I hang my head and cry

It didn't sound bad with Johnny singing, but even he had trouble with the high part.

(Note to readers: Richard Morgenstern is currently battling jungle creatures somewhere in Borneo and denies any rumor he is being accompanied by a 39-year-old bleached blonde going by the name Jane.)

Terrie put the article down, saying, "This is better." I can't see a lawsuit arising from it, which based on your previous writings was a major concern. Just for the record, though, if you so much as use the word 'Muslim' in your column, I will leave you in the night and you will never see me again. There, I got that off my chest."

Richard didn't as much as move his little toe. "Thanks again. Those were thoughtful comments. Do you have anything that you might want to say about the... about the... you know..."

"The story? No." She remained still for a minute.

"So," Terrie finally said as she kissed him on the cheek. "Tell me more about that bleached-blonde Jane."

CHAPTER 24

A Quick Trip to the Northwest Territories

1976 – Northwest Territories, Canada

"Your paychecks will be available in three weeks," said the railroad accountant at the main office in Prince George. That had sounded like a long time to write two checks, but our two explorers were only nineteen and twenty years old and were still learning the irrational ways of the world.

"Now what?" Richard moaned as they walked down the street.

David looked over at him. "Oh, Richard, I forgot to tell you. I was talking to Gino yesterday when we were saying our farewells to the Rock Gang. He told me everything we need to know about hopping freight trains." He paused for a minute. "I always wanted to do that."

Richard had never wanted to do that, however, he had never not wanted to do that either, so the two travelers soon found themselves skulking around the Prince George railway yard. They went up to one of the less threatening looking yardmen and asked when the next train going to Edmonton, Alberta, would be heading out. The railway worker looked at his clipboard for a second and said, "Oh, that's scheduled for 21:40 after it hooks up to a couple of flats and one box. Track number 9." The worker wandered off into the organized chaos of the rail-yard.

"Man alive! Gino was right. Just like he said, you just walk up to these guys and ask," David said excitedly. "This could open up new doors for us. Maybe even eliminate the need for hitchhiking! Track number nine, praise the Lord!

Rain poured down as semi-darkness enveloped the yard.

"Nothing could be finer than to be in Carolina in the morrrr-ning!" Richard sang out loud with his finest Broadway bravado. The two, despite their heavy backpacks, danced their best Fred Astaire impressions down the tracks. "Where's track number nine?" Richard wondered aloud as he jumped over a large puddle.

A couple of hours later they positioned themselves in the shadows of a yard light along what they figured out to be the mythical "Track 9." Gino had told David to be careful to watch for yard police, especially when "boarding" the train. "Those guys aren't-a the nicest guys," Gino said. "Some of them they want to always kick-a the crap outa you. But you two nice-a big guys so he probably leave-a you alone 'cause you might-a kick-a the crap outta him! You unnerstan?"

This seemed logical. It was dark and the yard cop couldn't see their kindly faces and Richard's scarecrow-thin physique. He'd probably be cautious when approaching them. They were now prepared to implement the last part of Gino's instructions: "Don't jump-a on the train until it's-a moving along nice-like. Nobody be bothering you."

Their hearts were pounding with excitement and fear. They were gonna jump-a on the train! The train slowly started pulling away. Once it started moving at a slow jogging speed, the two jumped out of the shadows, matching their pace to the pace of an empty boxcar. The speed was slowly picking up when David called out, "Richard, jump-a!"

Richard placed his foot in the small ladder below the open doors of the empty boxcar and pulled himself in. David was struggling to keep up as the train continued to pick up speed. "Jump-a up! Jump-a up!" Richard encouraged his friend, who was never known for his blazing speed. David found a second wind and clawed his way up the ladder, gracelessly crawled into the boxcar, completely exhilarated. They both lay back onto their packs, panting. Richard gasped, "You were supposed to jump-a faster! Like-a presto bingo!" The two laughed hard as the train lumbered along toward Edmonton, four hundred miles due east.

Two hundred miles east of Prince George, the two found themselves pulling into Jasper, Alberta, to pick up more boxcars. Stunning, the morning sun shown on snow-covered mountain peaks, occasional groups of bighorn sheep grazing along steep slopes. The ride through the Rocky Mountains had taken hours, mostly in the dark. Per Gino's instructions, "When-a the train stop, you getta yer ass outta the train and hide good." They did. But when they returned it was no longer safe to use the same boxcar because too many yard men were around. They carefully hid their packs in the bushes and reconnoitered the perimeter, one flatcar was perfect. The problem was no protection from the elements and no place to hide. A friendly worker spoke with the two saying nobody was going to inspect those cars prior to departure. The two freshly minted hoboes were quickly back in business, heading directly toward Edmonton. The dramatic mountain ranges soon transitioned into northern prairies planted with wheat, oats and rye. A couple of hours due East they came to a small grain farming town known as Grande Prairie. The railroad tracks ran right through the middle of town, once common in many communities. Lunch time traffic was lined up on both sides of the track as the train made its way through town. There being nowhere to hide, the two made the best of a bad situation by standing up and waving to the good people of Grande Prairie, much as the queen might have done, except embellished with "thank you's" and "thank you very much's." The expression on the faces of the townsfolk was one of total mystification. This encouraged the two to ham it up even more, acting like celebrity politicians, pointing at their supporters, gesturing to them as if they were sharing personal jokes. It was good, clean, delusional fun. Fortunately, the local police didn't witness this first hand as this would normally have qualified as a crime spree in those parts.

They arrived in Edmonton a few hours later, uneventfully found their way to a local bus stop and headed toward a youth hostel. A woman about twenty-four years old sat down beside them and they began chatting. "Where do you go backpacking in Edmonton?" she asked neither one of them. They laughed since Edmonton was a city of over 450,000 residents, not a national park. Her name was Melissa and turned out to be the leader of a ten-piece jazz band that played the local hotel and nightclub circuit. They hit it off and she asked if they needed a place to crash. They did, staying at her place for three nights. They joined Melissa and her friends at the local bars, still a new and exciting experience for the two young men. Richard took a shine to one of Melissa's friends, Gail. They exchanged addresses and pledged to get together in the future.

Significantly, a male friend of Melissa's gave them a promising lead for a job near the Great Slave Lake, a massive body of water located in the Northwest Territories. The hiring took place in Yellowknife. The Mackenzie River flowed out of the Great Slave Lake but froze for seven months of the year. During the five months it was free of ice, barges would deliver supplies, primarily to the Inuit communities along the Arctic Ocean who made up the largest portion of the population. There was a sizeable annual need for deckhands during this time.

Sensing an opportunity, Richard and David headed to Yellowknife.

The natural beauty and solitude of this vast area was extraordinary. Wildlife everywhere, indifferent to the presence of humans, and hung over from having survived another winter. The utter futility of feeling pressured while hitchhiking made for a strangely anxious journey. They laid their sleeping bags out each evening. Grappling with seventeen hours a day of light at this latitude, they slept fitfully.

Excited to arrive, they walked the final five miles into Yellowknife, arriving at six thirty in the morning. Their anxiety turned to despair when they walked into the personnel office and were casually informed that they had already hired their crews for the season but thanks for asking.

Completely demoralized, the two men made an obligatory visit across town to the Yellowknife Manpower office. They each grabbed an application form and started to earnestly fill them out. One look around the office told you everything you needed to know, though. The room was filled with even worse ne'er-do-wells than they left behind at the Rock Gang. There was everything but a puddle of drool beneath each member of this ragtag bunch of unemployed knuckle draggers. Richard began to chuckle to himself and after a bit, came over and sat beside David, showing him his job application. Job hunting had become such an absurd process for them that Richard was no longer able to seriously fill out any more forms. David glanced at the form quietly laughing to himself.

Man-power Northwest Territories

Name: *Charles Manson*

Date of birth: *The dawning of the Age of Aquarius*

Place of birth: *Triton, the seventh largest moon in the solar system and the largest natural satellite of Neptune.*

Nationality: *None. Answerable to no one. Works well independently.*

Social Insurance Number: *666*

Work desired: *Leader of a new world order to control Earth and beyond.*

Anticipated salary: *Limitless. Would also like to contribute to a retirement savings fund.*

Describe your special attributes: *13*

Comments: *I'm a gonna get you!!!*

They left the form in the tray but didn't stick around for the interview.

CHAPTER 25

Ho, Ho, Ho Chi Minh

1972 – San Francisco, California

It was a glorious and historic day in Golden Gate Park: ninety-thousand protestors (give or take ten-thousand if you listened to the speculation about the actual number), showed up for the Vietnam War Peace rally. David's parents wouldn't let him go, which was disappointing but understandable. When Richard thought about it, it was surprising his parents let him and his brother Robert go, but parents were more philosophical in those days about losing half of their children in one fell swoop, when they'd still have a couple left. The cute ones too. Their two younger siblings, Kathleen and the youngest brother, David, feared talking back because they saw how much trouble the older ones got into standing up to the powers that be.

But politics (and food) were the glues bonding Richard's family together and protesting the war in Vietnam felt like sending a powerful message to Nixon, who had recently become the president.

Before arriving at Golden Gate Park, for the rally, the two brothers ran the gauntlet of groups, from disgruntled Vietnam War vets to the Black Panther Party, to stoned-out free-love hippies, to good old-fashioned church groups. A hodgepodge of causes and organizations, all united in their opposition to America's continuing military presence in Vietnam.

Compared to other protests of the time, San Francisco's was not only peaceful but collectively opened up the two boys' awareness of the unique potential that their home city held. For example, toward the end of the speeches, a representative of the Black Panther Party proposed a unique approach to ending the war by chanting, "Kill the President! Kill the President! Kill the President!" What was most impressive to the two boys was how the crowd shouted him down with a peace chant and he left the stage ranting and raging but barely audible over the roar of "Peace! Peace! Peace!" The boys joined in "Peace! Peace! Peace!"

"That was a strange choice to include a Black Panther member as a speaker to a Peace Rally," Richard said to his brother after the chanting subsided.

"I know," Robert replied. "I guess Charlie Manson was previously engaged."

After the rally dispersed, the local bus lines were overwhelmed. Chants of "Ho, Ho, Ho Chi Minh," the North Vietnamese leader, filled their bus so enthusiastically that you would have thought he was Abraham Lincoln. Richard couldn't take it anymore and shouted out, "Enough with the Ho Chi Minh already! He's not a good guy. He's just as bad as we are."

Someone else shouted out, "He's worse!!" People jabbered slogans at each other but they all had had enough politics for one day, so the rhetoric quickly evaporated.

The mood in the local city bus changed. Every time somebody pulled the cord for the next stop, the bell would ring out and two Liza Minelli impersonators encouraged the whole bus to join in their spontaneous musical number, "You gotta ring them bells! You gotta ring them bells!!" The two instigators made several Broadway dance moves, shaking their hats over their heads while holding onto the safety strap dangling from the ceiling. They'd suddenly freeze in place each time the bus made a stop for more passengers. It was as if they had run out of batteries, only to restart when the bell rang for the next stop. "Ring those bells! Ring those bells!"

A good portion of the bus joined in with the dance moves and when it was time to freeze abruptly in position, the entire bus would crack up. One of the two dance instigators summed up well saying, "You can't let a little old war stop you from having a bit of fun sometimes."

CHAPTER 26

Meltdown

2014 – Hanoi, Vietnam

Their plane taxied to the terminal and the occupants made their way to the Baggage and Customs area.

"So, welcome to Hanoi, darling!" Richard said to Terrie.

Terrie was fumbling with her passport and baggage claim papers as she walked. "Right back at ya, sport," she said without taking her eyes off her valuables.

Before you could say Ho Chi Minh, they were standing outside the airport looking for a taxi to their hotel. "Wow! It's hot here," Richard said, soaked in sweat.

"Yeah, really!" Terrie responded. "I'm trying to remember if we were sent here as a punishment or if we came voluntarily."

A small group of taxi drivers and taxi sales and marketing personnel hovered around them, making it hard to focus on the task at hand, to get the hell away from the airport. A swarm of drivers kept repeating the one word of English they knew, "Taxi." Richard was becoming agitated when Terrie saved the day by ignoring the mayhem and walked up to parked taxis looking inside for any sign of a working meter. In a minute they were heading, toward the downtown French Quarter as Terrie began absorbing Vietnamese phrases as quickly as Richard forgot them.

By the time they got to their hotel, it was clear that air-conditioning was not an option but a necessity. "I think I have an idea how to install a small battery-operated air-conditioner in my pants," Richard said.

"I think that's where the expression to 'put it on ice' might have come from," Terrie replied. "Maybe that could be the name of the product. But we had agreed on a game plan. Remember? First, we walk. You can build your air-conditioner on your own time."

Richard mumbled under his breath in a singsong way, "You'll be sorry."

Without considering the ramifications of their actions, they went into the streets of Hanoi at high noon. They spent the first twenty minutes trying to figure out how to cross the street without getting hit by a taxi, rickshaw, or some other ancient type of vehicle. By the time they made it across, Richard was so drenched in sweat that he couldn't imagine going for a walk. "How come I'm soaked in sweat and you are dry and perky? It doesn't make sense. I think even my eyeballs are starting to melt."

"Maybe because I am cool, calm and collected and you are nervous, neurotic and narcoleptic," she speculated.

"Well, maybe, maybe. Or maybe I am a hot-blooded guy and you are a cold-blooded ice queen. But guess what? We are going back to our hotel room before I die. Chop chop, imperialist running dog."

They reduced their street crossing time to ten minutes by incorporating a new tactic of scampering behind old people and children, using them as human shields.

As they stood in their hotel elevator Richard continued with his self-pity. "I feel like a human sponge. I bet if you rung me out, you'd get twenty gallons of water."

"Would you shut up already? It's hotter in the elevator than it was outside," Terrie said, looking up at the room numbers. "This elevator's not even moving, Richard!"

"Don't look at me, do I look like an elevator repairman? Anyway, I'm starting to think that this is some sort of payback for the war. Even the elevator still holds a grudge."

"Richard, don't start ranting, okay? I'm too hot in this black box that won't move." Terrie began frantically pressing random numbers.

But it was too late, Richard continued, "Have happy vacation in hot black box, Yankee invader. For twenty dollars more we can open black box and you are free man."

Just then one of the buttons Terrie had pushed sprang into action and they went directly to their floor. The elevator seemed conflicted about opening the door and releasing its prisoners but after what felt like an eternity, it reluctantly opened.

They both pushed each other to get out first. "No wonder we lost the war," Richard said.

Terrie painstakingly turned their room key around in circles several times until it mercifully popped open.

As they lunged into their room, they both noticed that it was so cold from the A/C that they could see their breath.

"Is it air con or air cong?" Terrie said, carefully looking around the room for booby traps and trip wires.

Richard sounded exhausted as he said, "Welcome to cold box plunge, capitalist pigs."

It took about an hour before the two were able to master the A/C controller, at least to a level that would sustain human life. Terrie gave Richard a look indicating "it's now or never" and Richard took the bait. "Shall we?" he said. They soon found themselves back on the streets of Hanoi. They decided on a plan to visit the American War Museum that unfortunately, didn't provide a balanced narration of Vietnam's tragic history. So, rather than attempt to discern truth from fiction, they made a change of plans to instead go to one of the many outdoor spring roll restaurants and gorge themselves. Terrie waved down a bicycle powered rickshaw operated by an elderly man. He didn't speak a word of English, and although Terrie had already made some progress on that front, it was still way too soon for much more than one-word sentences. But the driver had an honest face and friendly smile, so they soon were winding up and down narrow streets filled with surprises.

When Terrie saw an interesting place to eat, she pantomimed to the rickshaw driver to pull over. They were caught off guard when he charged them double what they had previously negotiated. It was clear to them that they weren't going to win this argument as the slightest protest by Richard was met with complete outrage accompanied by a loud monkey howl. They cut their losses and focused on something they excelled at, which was consuming large quantities of food. Towards evening, they discovered a Jazz supper club, and even though they knew the odds of finding Jazz in Asia was slim, they checked it out and, were astounded to find out that the band was every bit as talented as any top-shelf Jazz band in San Francisco.

Richard said to Terrie, "It just goes to show that air conditioning repair, rickshaw pricing scams, and historical inaccuracies were not prerequisites for sublime saxophone playing."

Terrie agreed. "You took the words right out of my mouth, *Papa-san!*"

CHAPTER 27

Hitchhiking from the Middle of Nowhere to the Edge of Nowhere

1976 – Northwest Territories, Canada

They both went to sleep in spite of the sun shining bright at 8 P.M. and when they both woke up, eight hours later, the sun was still up and at 'em. They walked out to the main road of Yellowknife, passing a bag of granola back and forth as they walked. There was no traffic to be seen. "Little Debbie Cupcake delicious!" Richard said as he stuffed a handful into his mouth, crumbs flying.

"Which flavor is that one anyhow?" David asked.

"Let's see. If my memory serves me well, it was Sticks and Rocks."

"You sure? 'Cause it really reminds me of the sawdust flavored stuff we ate a couple of days ago."

"No," he said smacking his lips. "Sometimes you have to rinse your mouth out with water to taste the different hues. After ten minutes they both sat down and stared at the dirt by their feet. The first vehicle appeared and passed by, driving into the distance. The musical sounds of songbirds and the sunny blue sky gave them optimism for the day.

David sat down beside the narrow road and looked at his old hitchhiking friend, the dirt beside the road. This would become his mural. He slowly looked up at the vehicle cruising away in the distance and mumbled to himself, "We gonna get you mofuck. Oh yeah, we gonna get you bad." He reached over and snagged a good dust-drawing stick and starting writing, "Gonna get you bad."

Hours would pass between rides. Only their dirt-friend gave them some hope that the universe hadn't completely given up on them. Richard scrawled in the dust, "Hitchhiking. The lowest form of meditation." and made an attractive decorative frame around it for others in the future to enjoy.

Twelve hours later, they were still hundreds of miles from the place where their money was allegedly awaiting their arrival. The two checks that had taken three weeks to manufacture. "You know what, David?" Richard asked.

"No, Richard. I don't know what." David replied as he scrawled the words "Planet Earth—Go Fuck Yourself!" in his signature dirt mural style.

"Well, I was thinking that the people in the railway office who told us that it takes three weeks to make out our two checks... well, I was thinking that they weren't actual homo sapiens."

David's head suddenly popped up from his dirt mural. "Of course they are homo sapiens. Don't be ridiculous!"

"Just hear me out on this one. I've been thinking about this for..." he looked at his watch "...for about eighteen hours now. Think about it. Any caveman worth his salt could have figured out a way to make two checks in no more than a week. Jeez, call it ten days. But three weeks, twenty-one days? I know homo sapiens and these were not homo sapiens, my friend. Rip some birch bark off a tree. Grab a piece of charcoal from last night's fire. Half hour max and they'd have two checks for us. Had to be something like Cro-Magnon men. They look about the same but they're only about as smart as..." he looked at a pine tree across the road. "See that really tall pine there? Right next to that dead snag..."

"Yeah, I see it," David said.

"A Cro-Magnon man is about as smart as that pine tree. A Cro-Magnon man would pretty much need a full three weeks to make two checks. Neanderthal, probably four weeks. If you got any better ideas, I'm all ears."

David looked past the pine tree and noticed that they were sitting on the edge of a muskeg, a swamp covered in lush wet moss and stunted spruce trees. David replied, "My theory is that you are going insane and that the jerks at C.N. Railway just don't want to give us our money because they like to jack people around. That's my theory," David said as he scrawled the words, "Death to all those who drive by hitchhikers!" onto his mural.

Richard stroked his chin and said, "Plausible. Plausible."

David interrupted, "Richard, just try to remind yourself that you are not an expert on the Stone Age. The Stoned Ages, that's an entirely different story. So, let's leave this conversation for another day because I think if we don't do something, anything, to break the monotony of waiting for a car to stop, that, personally speaking, I may need to kill myself."

"Did you ever see that existentialist play Waiting for Godot?" Richard replied. "Where the whole play is about some guys waiting for somebody named Godot. In a way we are in a real-life version of it. More like, 'Waiting to Go.'"

"But before I kill myself, I'm going to have to kill you first." David said. "But maybe a better idea would be to walk back one mile to the edge of town and buy ourselves some pie and ice cream with a coffee."

A new philosophy was born. The proverbial carrot and stick replaced by scalding hot cups of coffee with pie and ice cream, predicated on the debatable assumption that eventually they'd get a ride out of this god-forsaken swamp.

In adherence to their new life philosophy, they could now afford some pie and ice cream, an unheard of spending

spree. They were down to $145.47 between them. The pie
and ice cream were particularly delicious at that moment in
time and space in the Universe.

Their waitress, a sixty-something-year-old woman, a
member of the working poor club, stood chatting with a
younger waitress. The two strangers walked in from the
dark, the only customers left in the place. There was
something nondescript about the older woman. All faces
tell a story and her face screamed out nothing exciting had
ever happened to her. The two men decided to rectify this
cosmic injustice. They finished their food and put their
backpacks on calling out "good evening" to the waitresses.
The older waitress answered back "happy trails" as the door
closed.

The two adventurers walked across the road to find an
angle allowing them to see their waitress as she came over
to clean up their table. As if viewing a silent movie, they
watched her cleaning off their table top, when she suddenly
saw a crisp new one hundred dollar bill with a note saying,
"Many Thanks!" left on top of the sugar dispenser. She put
her hands over her mouth, obviously shrieking. The other
waitress came and joined in the revelry, both looking like
winning contestants on a game show, jumping up and down
deliriously. The waitresses dashed over to the large plate
glass windows just in time to see the backs of the two
eccentric travelers as they walked away into the snowy
darkness.

The next morning, they had a lovely breakfast
consisting of dried granola and... more dried granola.
Feeling fortified they soon got a ride from a big rig, a good
omen for the day. The driver's name was Ron Lennox. He
was a baby-faced blond-haired fellow with a smile that
appeared to be etched on his face. He liked talking about
women. He liked talking about sex. He wanted to change
careers back to sales, his true calling. For Ron, talking about
sex was his form of oral sex. It seemed to go hand in hand

with his salesman personality. Hand and something, anyway.

Richard managed to segue the conversation from Ron's annoying reference to his last lover's aroma as having an aquatic quality, "That's really interesting, Ron. David and I also have an important fishy proposition that we must make a decision about. David, it's time we called Kenny. He did write us that letter describing his epiphany about some sort of half-baked fish enterprise."

"You know, another factor is that it's the best half-baked idea that any of us have," David responded.

Richard pondered that point for a minute, then said, "Sounds like it's a coin flip situation to me. How 'bout heads we sell fish and tails we go fishing?"

Ron listened as the two rummaged in their pockets for one coin. It seemed to take a couple of days but eventually David located a nickel in one of his pockets. "How about two out of three?" he proposed.

"Better four out of seven," Richard countered. "That would be the same as the number of games played in the World Series. Seven flips are more statistically valid."

"Sure," Ron said, taking the nickel out of David's hand. "Four out of seven it is." The series went the full seven flips and when it was over, the fish business was now official. They pulled over at a phone booth in the next town and called Kenny. Kenny was relieved that death by starvation was postponed for the time being. Though all three were happy with their decision, they were oblivious to the fact that none of them knew the first thing about running a business.

CHAPTER 28

Queen for a Day

1972 – Marin County, California

Richard's brother, Robert, was an anomaly at their high school. He excelled in academia, participated in school politics, culminating in his election as school president, hung out with numerous girls and in these and most respects, was the opposite of his younger brother.

While his brother Robert was setting the world on fire, Richard and his Boy-Pal David conspired to avoid having their photographs taken for the yearbook. Only their names appeared, along with a blank space in place of their photos, for four years. The inspiration to embrace anonymity was a short article David had spotted on page 34 of the local paper.

"Hey Richard, read this!" David said, giddy. "This article should win a Pulitzer Prize for Journalism covering humanity's ability to hit lower and rockier bottoms. Talk about getting off of the social grid."

The article was titled "DEATH IN SAN RAFAEL" and read:

> An unemployed quick fry cook was found dead today in his downtown apartment, having apparently choked to death on a doughnut. Police are calling his death an accident. He had no known relatives.

Richard caught David's black humor. Weird how something can be depressing and funny at the same time. If you have to die, you might as well leave a laugh to be remembered by.

Richard didn't have a clue what his mother, who had a master's degree in psychology from Berkeley, meant when she asked, "Are you at all bothered that Robby does so well in school?"

"I never thought about it before," Richard replied. "Why should I be bothered? I'm happy for him. Anyway, if it wasn't for that, he'd be a total loser."

His mom never could figure out her own children. Conversely, her children had trouble understanding her, more a mechanical issue, vestiges of her Liverpudlian accent. This still surfaced decades after her family's emigration, when she and her twin sister were thirteen years old. In denial about her accent, she called half-and-half "arf-and-arf." Richard couldn't understand his mother until he was around fifteen years old.

"I just thought that it must bother you since you have so many problems in school," she continued.

Richard tried not to let his mom's observations bother him since they were usually wrong. "You know, I wouldn't have so many problems if all my teachers weren't such imbeciles," Richard replied.

Robert had asked Richard's ex-girlfriend's twin sister, Kate, to be his date at the senior prom and the evening was now upon them. As was the tradition, the school president and his date always danced the first dance after making their grand entrance. For the previous few years these entrances made political and social statements relating to hippiedom, anti–Vietnam war expressions, women's rights, etc. However, most of the graduates found what was to come downright shocking.

It wasn't so much their clothing, as the suit and gown were every bit as fine as in previous years. The scandal was Kate cut a fine figure of a man, while Robert made an elegantly attired young woman. Most participants at the prom found humor in the theatrics but a significant number, mostly guys, were either disgusted or offended by the display. Robert even got kicked while dancing by some of his more prehistorically oriented classmates.

The term "coming out" had yet to be invented, so most of the student body thought of it as a dressing-in-drag prank. Which it primarily was. But Robert was sniffing the air to see if the time was right.

One year later he came home from university during Christmas break. Robert was a bit taken aback when he saw that his sister Kathleen now occupied his bedroom. To add insult to injury, she took a scorched earth approach to her interior decorating redo. Not one square inch of the room contained any sign of Robert having once occupied it. When he made a couple of references to this new reality, she showed her sensitive, sympathetic side: "It's mine now, all mine," followed by a cackle.

During that trip he decided to come out to his parents. As usual his mom's response was spot-on when she asked Robert about his "condition." "Are they sure?" she asked.

Robert was appalled. "What do you mean 'they'? Did I ever say that I was reviewed by a panel of psychiatrists? Anyhow, if that day ever came, you'd know because the bill would go straight to you guys."

In a testament to his parents, they both laughed with their son Robert as his Mom said, "You just try to collect boy!"

His dad concluded, "Robert, careful where you're going with this because, if we made a ledger of expenses since your birth, believe me, you'd owe us a hell of a lot more than we'd owe you."

Robert, as usual, managed to get in the last jab. "Pain and suffering are to quantify, though. Why else do you think I am majoring in mathematics? Actually, that would make a good thesis topic for my doctorate! Thanks Dad!"

CHAPTER 29

Drive-through Spiritual Advice

2014 – San Francisco, California

Terrie was surprised to find Richard working away on his laptop as she peeked into their office. She snuck up behind him and put her hands over his eyes. "Guess who?" she said, kissing him on the neck.

Richard continued typing. "Desiree?" he said. Still typing, he felt a slight nip. "Ow! Okay give me a few tries. Dominique? Wait, Dominique doesn't bite. How about Genevieve? Say something to me in French while you nibble, not bite, my neck?"

In a thick French accent, she said, "I find you irresistible when you write stories that climax with your receiving an actual paycheck in the mail, mon chéri."

"I'm still in the throes of journalistic foreplay, whereby my stories are getting rejected by those too stupid to appreciate my genius. Don't you sort of find starving artists a turn-on?"

"No checkie, no sexy," she said, quickly rejecting him. "It's been three days now. When do I get to read this legendary story, you keep saying is 'almost done'?"

"Right now," Richard replied. "It is my first article and it's about the issue of the day." He passed her some papers. "Be gentle with me, my love."

"You know me, I like it rough." she said, settling into her chair in the corner of the room. At the best of times his desk had the look of extreme chaos. Today it looked several degrees beyond that. More like the desk of a madman.

"The issue of the day. That's tantalizing. Might that be... women who support men?" Richard tried to find humor in her joke but was unable to summon the muscle memory. She showed no expression as she read. Richard left the room to give her some "space."

RICHARD RANTS

Drive-through Spiritual Advice

You would think that having been born in San Francisco, I should have some type of beneficial genetic predisposition over newcomers when it comes to the idiosyncrasies of day-to-day life in the City. Like how to park a car here, for example. But I don't. My parents moved to the burbs across the Golden Gate Bridge when I was six and when I was seventeen, I left home to move to the wilderness in northern British Columbia for twenty years, so I completely missed out on my important formative parking years. As a result, I have now spent the last twenty years in a type of parking purgatory, whereby parking tickets simply fly out of the meter maid's butt whenever one drives within a block of my car, landing perfectly under the windshield wipers. I recently made a calculation that these tickets had now accumulated to approximately $25,000. It was deceptive but the compound interest and fines had really added up during the years of threatening letters that I had so studiously ignored. So, this got me thinking. There must be a lot of people like myself, who have been denied the life of the upwardly mobile by the San Francisco Parking Department, only to be replaced with a hand-to-mouth existence. And the more I thought about it, the angrier I got. Although it is not politically correct in San Francisco to complain about paying less than one's fair share, I figure that I probably would have been a gracious and generous member of the landed gentry. So, I began to think about this whole thing a lot. Really a lot. In fact, it was becoming a problem. But I just couldn't get this travesty out of my mind. I often woke up in a cold sweat with the thought, "those thieves have $25,000 of my hard-earned dollars!" My girlfriend, Terrie, was the unintended recipient of my rants, rather than having them sent directly to a Parking God floating around in the clouds (my working hypothesis was that heaven had an overabundance of excellent parking).

"Why don't you start a support group for traumatized parking ticket victims? I really think that you're onto something," Terrie said nonchalantly as she put down Richard's story.

For a brief second Richard mistook her kind thought as a form of compassion but quickly realized his mistake. Annoyed, he continued. "When I get matters sorted out ..."

"Oh yeah!" Terrie chimed in, breaking into laughter.

"I repeat, when I get matters sorted out, I will be sucking back one of those eight-dollar root beer floats down at Rainbow Ice Cream, while you'll be home nursing some San Francisco tap water on the rocks, eating a juicy serving of crow."

Terrie was slowly laughing herself down to the floor. "Yeah baby! $25,000 in large bills. Just stuff 'em in this brown shopping bag, would you? You should also demand a written apology while you're at it." She started coughing and laughing at the same time as she rolled across the living room rug.

"Okay, we all have our breaking point," Richard replied defensively. "Mine's $25,000. That's my line in the fog. Okay, I admit that the system is stacked against the little guy. That the odds are bad. I know lives might be lost for the cause. But how can you sleep at night knowing that your own two grown daughters, not to mention my own two grown daughters and son, will one day inherit a world without parking? Do you really expect they will procreate knowing that the most basic of their civil rights, the right to bear arms and the right to parking spaces, are but memories?" His words echoed hollow in the air, but he was hoping that Terrie was slowly coming around to his own version of the "Give me liberty or give me death" speech.

"How did the right to bear arms get into your tirade?" she said, bringing closure.

Richard knew he needed to take action. He narrowed down his options to the following strategy. Launch an all-out surprise attack on City Hall, find the petty cash drawer, and take what was rightfully his.

Restoring him to the economic grandeur that should have been rightfully his, without having to turn around immediately and spend it all in one shot in the form of a bail bond.

He thought about getting advice from his friend Masanori, who worked in the nearby Jack in the Box.

Masanori had a certain wisdom that his friends and customers had come to rely upon in times of crisis. His Japanese background and spiritual upbringing in a monastery gave him the credentials and mystique to warrant his reputation as the go-to guy in the drive-thru "Fast Spiritual Advice" market. Known by most of his customers simply as JIB (short for "Jap in the Box"), an off-color joke of JIB's and Richard, created during one evening at Ireland's 32 Bar, that was all the funnier because only he and Richard knew its origins. His advice was renowned throughout Richard's neighborhood as the absolutely cheapest available. Not since the days of Charlie Chan could someone solve another person's personal problems faster than JIB. The funny thing was, his personal life was a shambles but Richard figured nobody was perfect, and anyway, his prices were unbeatable. He never failed to come up without a suitable solution, in spite of the intense pressure from his management that all customers be served within three minutes. Granted, he did once tell Richard to piss off when he drove through wanting to know how to tie a necktie. But Richard could see his point: he was a wise guy after all, so it was a bit presumptuous to ask him personal fashion questions.

Richard drove down to JIB's an hour before the big lunch rush, which was usually when he did his best work. His voice came through the intercom. "Hello and welcome to Jack in the Box, serving our new and delicious Jackity-Jack burgers for only $3.99, how may I help you?"

"Hey JIB," Richard said. "It's Richard. Give me a Jackity-Jack You Won't Come Back Burger and a chocolate shake."

"Will that be everything for you or would you like some advice today?" his voice crackled and popped through the intercom.

Richard explained his situation to JIB as concisely as possible. When he finished JIB said, "Would you like fries with your advice?"

"Yes, please." Richard drove up to his window.

"Your idea sucks, man," he said as he put napkins and ketchup in Richard's bag. "Write off the twenty-five thou and move on. Otherwise, you're on a collision course with prison."

Richard dropped his head on his chest and let out a sigh. "I guess I sort of lost all perspective. But that's a lot of money to just walk away from."

JIB looked Richard in the eye and said, "The poor man marvels at the same number of sunrises and sunsets as does the rich man. Take your burger, fries, and shake, find yourself a park bench in the sun and concentrate on the unique flavors that only a chemist working for a multinational restaurant chain can create. You'll be surprised just how fast you will heal from this blow."

Richard gave him an extra two dollars and drove off, feeling restored. He marveled at the simplicity of JIB's choice of words. He couldn't believe that only moments before he had been planning on driving bulldozers through the streets and starting a new political party. He drove to the closest park, still wondering why JIB had a problem with his other idea, to break into City Hall and just take back what was rightfully his. He decided that would just have to wait until dinner time back at the Box. At least advice clarifications only cost one dollar a pop.

(Note to readers: Richard Morgenstern lives somewhere in San Francisco and can often be seen drinking milkshakes on park benches while pondering the meaning of life.)

After an hour of editing, Richard passed the draft to Terrie for her opinion. Terrie silently read through the article. She then let the papers fall from her hands to the floor. "Well?" Richard asked anxiously.

"JIB? Really?" She shook her head.

"Too politically incorrect?" Richard guessed.

"More like an indictable offense. Richard, people know me here. This city is my home. I can't let you alienate singlehandedly the entire Asian community in one fell swoop. I'll probably get fired from my job. You're gonna have to fix this."

Richard looked at his story scattered on the floor. "Would Japanese-man-In-a-Box silence the tyranny of the majority?"

Terrie walked out of their office growling, "Jap in a Box. Oh my God!"

CHAPTER 30

Fishy Business

1974 – Vancouver, British Columbia

They arranged a rendezvous with Kenny at the Happy Lucky Chinese restaurant near where the commercial fishing boats pulled into Vancouver harbor. Richard and David were three hours late due to mechanical difficulties beyond their control and the restaurant owner was annoyed at having a long-haired hippie type loitering for an eternity over a single order of Chop Suey.

"You no want order more?" he asked. "This not hotel!"

"Yeah I know it's not a hotel," Kenny replied. "I knew that because your sign outside says 'Restaurant' and you have menus. Those were both big clues." His sarcasm was completely lost on the owner.

"If no friends come in five minutes, you take pack and go. Go to hotel. It cost money to run restaurant. I don't make money if you live here and scare off customer." The owner stomped away to the kitchen to apprise his wife of the situation. Loud shrieking noises emanated from the kitchen. As best Kenny could make out, the wife wanted Kenny to be killed and fed to the pigs out back. Just then the two other travelers staggered into the restaurant.

As the three greeted each other, the Chinese owners stared at the commotion through a small opening and decided enough was enough. "Okay, time for hippies to go now! Out! No more stay here." After their monumental drive, Richard and David were stunned to get kicked out of a ma and pa noodle house within one minute of arrival.

"Let's make like Peking duck and blow noodle factory," Kenny said as he left some money on the table. "These people are still living back in the days of the Ming dynasty." They all hustled out the door while Kenny took his parting shot in his best Chinese restaurateur impression. "Please to take flying fuck, old fart!"

The outraged owner stuck his head outside his front door, cursing in Mandarin as the three walked away and found a replacement Chinese restaurant.

Kenny was delighted to see his two travel buddies again. "So, why three hours late? I thought you got the deal of the century on that truck. Isn't it running right?"

"It's a really good truck," David replied, "but the hood started popping open randomly around Williams Lake and it was a major problemo. We'd be driving along, happy as clams, when suddenly the hood would pop open and you couldn't see a frickin' thing. You had to stick your head outside the window just to pull over. I just about had a heart attack a few times but after a while I sort of got used to it. We finally stopped to buy some rope and that held it down."

"It's a really stressful way to drive," Richard said. "It added a few hours onto our trip."

Kenny was itching to dispense with the small talk. "So, guys, let's talk fish," he said, opening the discussions. "Like I already mentioned to you, I was walking along the docks just a few blocks from here, to do a little brainstorming and I started poking my nose around where the fishermen unload their catch. I noticed a guy loading up his fish truck with fresh salmon and I started chatting with him about his business. His name is Jack and the name on his fish truck was Jack Fish. I couldn't believe it. He told me everything about the business and he said he made a good living just parking his truck along the side of the road all around Vancouver. His truck is fully rigged up to meet the local regulations for food handling, which is expensive, but he figured that some guy with a pickup truck and an old refrigerator filled with ice could do well if he trucked the fresh fish inland two or three hundred miles. Far enough from the ocean where the saltwater fish normally arrive frozen and where the regulations aren't so strict. And he has an old fridge that he'd sell us for one hundred bucks too. So here we are. We could leave town in a couple of days, all we gotta do is get the freezer, buy the fish and load it."

Kenny had done his homework. Later that day they took the plunge, met up with Jack Fish, and loaded his old deep freeze into the back of the truck. Jack Fish didn't impress David and Richard the way he had Kenny. He had a streetsy, sleazy aura about him that made them dubious of his intentions.

"I don't trust this Jack Fish character," David volunteered. "I think he's up to no good."

"You can't trust a fishmonger farther than you can throw him, my pappy used to say," Richard added.

"Your daddy never said that, and you know it," Kenny said, irritated.

"How do you know what he said? He had strong opinions about fish mongers."

"Okay, enough with your pappy and fish mongering," David said. "Boys, weez in da fish business!" They toasted with bottles of beer. "To lucky salmon."

"To halibut, a noble fish indeed!" Kenny said.

"To a fishy business!" Richard toasted.

Before you could say "sushi" the three were driving down the highway with a freezer full of salmon and halibut. As a sign that all was good in the universe, they made a quick pit stop at a Chinese grocer. While there, Richard asked the owner if she would have any interest in buying some fresh fruit from the Okanagan, which was their target fish sales area. In a cagey way she agreed to specific prices, but she also mumbled some nonsensical jibber-jabber. Richard brushed aside the incomprehensible parts, attributing it to the language barrier.

The three knew not what fury the Gods of Fish Mongering still had in store for them, not to mention the Gods of Roadside Fruit Sales, who were rumored to be badder asses than the Fish God guys.

They spent the better part of a day driving until they pulled into a spot beside a large cherry orchard outside of Osoyoos. This region, called the Okanagan, was known for producing a variety of fruits. This in a province primarily known for its production of snow. It was blistering hot and though they parked in the shade, the ice melted out of the hose from their icebox. "You know, that sound of the water dripping out the hose reminds me of the image of sand drizzling out of an hourglass," Richard said.

After a moment of silence, Kenny spoke. "I guess it is a race against time. Jack Fish said we would have three days to sell it all before it turned into... turns into..."

"A steaming pile of rotten fish," David suggested.

"Yeah. I guess that was what I was grasping for. Before it turns into primordial soup."

"If that happens," Richard said laughing, "maybe we can just change our sign to 'FRESH PRIMORDIAL SOUP!!!'" They all laughed but none of the three could push the image of the hourglass to the back of his mind.

Within minutes, a steady flow of customers passed through, attracted by the "FRESH FISH!!!" sign. David had accumulated materials to make the sign, drew a fishlike object that, along with the catchy verbiage, conveyed the desired message to the fish-starved citizenry. Despite their lack of sales acumen, the fish sold themselves.

Day one was a roaring success. They sold over half of their fish and they had found a loaded wild cherry tree close by with cherries so sweet they burned their throats with pleasure as they went down. In the evening the three made a campfire in a small secluded spot nearby, fried up a bunch of salmon steaks, then consumed bowls of cherries. They fell asleep, intoxicated by sweet cherry nectar and prospects of a thriving business.

Richard and Kenny both awoke to the sound of doom and gloom.

"The ice is over half gone!" David announced. Richard climbed out of his sleeping bag and staggered over to examine the situation with his own eyes.

"Drip, drip, drip," he mumbled without being asked for further clarification.

Kenny, always the last one up, ambled over, found the coffee pot and turned on the gas burner. "Tick, tick, tick," he replied.

David was hoping for something a shade more pragmatic than humor. "How about shit, shit, shit? Think we should buy some more ice?"

Richard stuffed his mouth with cherries and waited for the spirits to speak through him. Cherry juice drooled out of his mouth as he exclaimed, "These are damned good cherries!" They stared at Richard, disgusted. "Watching you devouring those things... I don't think I can ever eat a cherry again," Kenny said.

Richard wasn't going to let either of his elders ruin his cherry moment. Screw you!" he said, intentionally spitting out cherries for comic effect.

They decided to see how the sales campaign went for a few more hours before making a group managerial decision while in a state of panic. "That's our profit margin you're talking about," Kenny said, referring to another ice expenditure. "It comes right off the bottom line."

There was a long silence, then Richard said what David was thinking. "You don't even know what a bottom line is." Another long silence. "Do you?"

Kenny squirmed. "All I know is spending more money on something we don't need yet... has something to do with the bottom line. And that's more than you know Mr. Happy-Cherry." Kenny demonstrated signs of impatience with the process of fish mongering by committee.

The sales on the second day were half of the first day. It appeared that they might have saturated the market. The day ended with one quarter of the original product, floating in ice water, staring forlornly at the faces of the fishmongers. They were just getting ready to shut down production for the day when a pickup truck pulled up.

The customer asked if he could have a look in the freezer to pick out his own fish. But he had a hidden agenda. He was a local Portuguese fruit farmer and wondered if they might have any interest in a deal to sell the remaining fish at a discounted price. He had a thick accent. "The Portuguese, he loves the fresh fosh." The rest of what he said was unintelligible, but he kept repeating that remark to punctuate his points. "The Portuguese, he loves the fresh fosh."

Richard, perhaps channeling his not so distant entrepreneurial Jewish ancestors, came up with a response. "Joachim, can you give us a minute to discuss your idea?" Joachim had no objection. They stepped aside and spoke. "It just dawned upon me that this might be a recurring problem, unloading the third day's fish. Since Joachim loves the fresh fosh, why don't we propose to him an exchange of our third day's fish for his fresh fruit? That way we eliminate the risk of a nuclear fish meltdown. What do ya think? If it works out, maybe he'd want to do it again."

"I like it. Very good idea," David said. All eyes turned to Kenny.

"As long as you quit drooling when you're eating cherries, I'll go along with it," Kenny concurred.

Joachim was easy to negotiate with, as previously established, the Portuguese, he loves the fresh fosh. In a couple of hours, the three wandering business associates found themselves barreling down the road back to Vancouver, loaded to the gills with fresh fruit.

CHAPTER 31

Plastic City

1973 – Marin County, California

By age seventeen, Richard was on an entrepreneurial path. Not yet obvious, however, was whether his path would eventually include a stint in prison, or he was developing enough survival skills to avoid that pitfall. His roadmap was skewed to acts of non-violent disobedience, such as usage and sale of illegal drugs and political protest. While his parents and politics of the day helped inspire a percentage of this trajectory, he was genetically predisposed toward embracing an alternative form of capitalism. In his case, crime had the lowest cost of entry.

He noticed there were unfilled needs in the field of pharmaceuticals. His bedroom became the local dispensary for hallucinogenic drugs. The variety of chemicals he stocked distinguished him from competitors. Of course, there were the usual suspects, LSD, mescaline, and cocaine with a growing demand for peyote and magic mushrooms (psilocybin) and designerish drugs that nobody knew the contents but down the hatch they went. Of course, he always carried an assortment of high-quality weed and hashish. Initially, his economic incentive was to cover the cost of his own drug consumption, but he discovered he made a good profit.

"At this rate, I'll be retiring before I graduate from high school," he bragged to his pharmaceutical consulting staff, consisting of his well-read Boy-Palz, David and Tom.

Tom laughed. "You should stop balancing your books when you are still hallucinating."

"Also," David added, "you have to factor into your expenses that you are getting free quality-control research done by your customers."

"Well, I do give Tim Olsen a bulk discount, so if he happens to be the canary in the mineshaft for me, he does it with his eyes wide open. I make no apologies."

"Just saying. You don't have to be so defensive. Nobody's died. Yet..." Tom concluded.

Richard's parents remained largely oblivious to the nature and magnitude of the situation. Both with full-time jobs and four kids to account for, it was unreasonable to expect them to have deduced their son was a drug dealer operating out of their own home.

Ironic, Richard got kicked out of the house, his crime, one too many sarcastic jokes about his mother's "obsession" that he helps clean up. "Pack your bags now!" she raged. "I'm not going to put up with your attitude one more day!"

His friend David later put the irony into perspective. "It's sort of like when they convicted Al Capone for tax evasion because they couldn't get witnesses to testify against him for murder charges."

Richard didn't feel it was a big deal, he just looked at his new reality like one big camping trip. He helped himself to food from the fridge and, along with his back-packing gear, hiked a couple miles to his favorite trailhead, then an additional two miles to an isolated clearing surrounded by oak trees with a scenic view of Cascade Canyon. Before leaving his neighborhood, he dropped off a note to David with a map of his new view lot property. Within two days, both David and Kenny had joined him. Within a week, Brad moved in, then Tom and his new girlfriend Janet.

They erected several plastic tarps for evening fires when it rained and as sleeping tents. They named their location "Plastic City" in homage to the Gods of Plastic.

In spite of her iron-fist managerial decision to kick her second child out of the nest, Richard's mom had no problem with him stopping by to take showers and raid food from the fridge. Her temper was usually as short-lived as it was hot-blooded. With only three months to go in Richard's high school education, both she and his dad assumed that Richard would either apologize and come home or continue to finish school from Plastic City.

Instead, a new civilization flourished. As was common at the time, the inhabitants of Plastic City all showed interest in the ways of indigenous tribes, who they idealized as possessing supernatural powers. The Plastic Citians morphed into a distorted version of indigenous people, starting with their names. Kenny was renamed "Falls Down a Lot," due to his crash landings when jumping over creeks. From constant run-ins with poison oak, David became "Scratches Himself," Brad was "Eats Lots of Butter," Richard, "Tells Many Bad Jokes," Tom, "Mixes his Drugs," and Janet became "Sings Like a Songbird."

After two weeks of living on the outskirts of suburbia, Tells Many Bad Jokes made a dramatic announcement around the evening campfire. "Today, I told my counselor that I was retiring from high school to enroll in a different school of higher learning. That school being life itself. As a result of my decision, I am proposing to all of you, my fellow Plastic Citians, that whoever amongst you wishes to join me on a quest for adventure to British Columbia and Alaska, via the Grand Canyon, should make a pledge of loyalty as we march into the unknown together. Or something like that."

A hush descended on the group. Only the popping of sparks from the campfire broke the silence.

Falls Down a Lot spoke first. "Wow. Dropping out of high school to go to Alaska. Well... you can count me in."

The sound of murmurs echoed around the campfire. Scratches Himself spoke next. "So, this is gonna mean you need a new name, you know. How about, 'Takes the Road Less Traveled.' I pledge my loyalty. You can't keep me from coming!"

The murmuring magnified and turned into a deafening silence as Eats Too Much Butter rose to speak. "Plastic Citians, I have to admit that this is a very difficult decision for me. I am not completely certain that my quest and your journey to Alaska are a perfect match yet... I am going to say yes. Yes! That is my final decision!"

All eyes turned to Mixes His Drugs and Sings Like a Songbird. They rose up in unison, hand in hand. "We are both tempted." Sings Like a Songbird said. "Really tempted. And we possibly will follow your migration at a later time. But for now, we will stay in Plastic City a while longer until the right time comes. Gentlemen. Go forth on your quest!"

In unison Mixes His Drugs and Sings Like a Songbird raised their hands and repeated, "Gentlemen. Go forth on your quest!"

The newly renamed Takes the Road Less Traveled raised his canteen full of water. The others did the same. "To the quest! To Plastic City!" They all cheered one last cheer.

CHAPTER 32

Instantaneous Language Acquisition

2014 – San Francisco, California

"My theory is, science should be made understandable to the lay person. Since I have virtually zero aptitude for science, I would make the ideal person to test out whether or not a given scientific concept is ready for the masses. If I get it, everyone should."

Terrie nodded as Richard spoke.

"But wouldn't that be equally true of just about everything, when you think about it?"

"How do you mean?"

"Well, since you have nearly zero aptitude for any particular field—science, sure, but also virtually all fields known to mankind. That way, you could extend your logic to a broader market. For example, if you were able to get a degree of some sort, it could be argued that a particular university is better than its competitors because it was able to teach you something."

"Oh, now I get it." Richard replied. "You dare mock me again. Well, sit down and make yourself comfortable, you are in for a special experience."

"Richard, living with you is a special experience." She took the typed essay and sat down to read it in the most comfortable chair in the living room.

RICHARD RANTS

Instantaneous Language Acquisition

At the current rate of technological advances, instantaneous language acquisition will soon be a fact of life. Experts now say that the inevitability of having an actual language chip implanted into our brains is only a few years off. My understanding, and I'm not an actual expert on these things, but my understanding is that the chips themselves are now ready to go out to market, but that neuroscientists are still trying to figure out exactly where to stick them. If you have ever carefully looked at a brain, the first thing that becomes apparent is that nothing is labeled, so you can understand the frustration that experts must feel. It's not like a do-it-yourself IKEA furniture kit. There is no obvious top or bottom, no power supply cord, no gears, absolutely no clue as to what does what.

I can just imagine a couple of neuroscientists at the lab staring at a brain on a table, and one says to the other, "Jesus Christ! I swear, it just came in the mail like this. And the directions were written by a moron! I honestly can't tell if it's written in English or Chinese. Is Chinglish a language?"

The other scientist tosses the brain into a bowl in complete disgust, grumbling, "I knew I should have gone to law school. You don't see any attorneys up to their armpits in weird predicaments like this. Every day, I get home from work, my wife says, 'Did you wash your hands? Don't you even think about touching me until you have a shower. I knew I should have married an attorney!'"

"I know" the other scientist replied. Sometimes I get depressed coming into work. I guess that's why you don't see any TV shows done on brain researchers," the first scientist lamented. "Not exactly something people want to watch near dinner time. Personally, I'm seriously thinking about becoming a vegetarian. Brains are gross, it's that simple."

Studies done on mice, rats and monkeys have proved inconclusive because, let's face it, nobody really knows what they are talking about at the best of times. So, for example, if a monkey is trying to converse with a rat, scientists have no definitive means to ascertain if the monkey is saying, "Hey, this garbage is delicious," or if he really means, "Yo! Send for help! I am totally freaked that I am never going to find my way out of this frickin' maze!"

So other than just randomly sticking the language chip in the brain (my idea), scientists claim that they can precisely place it in the most optimum location, so that you can drive home from the operation speaking Chinese like a diplomat. But other experts in the field reason the level of complexity is so high, as many as 25% of those receiving an implant might exhibit unacceptable side effects. For example, it is rumored that during one implant trial, a male human came out of the operating room exhibiting many of the traits of a dog and was no longer able to function at work due to a chronic habit of humping his superior's legs during business meetings.

Other language experts believe that the current teaching approach, whereby less than 1% of language students ever truly learn a new language, is good enough. Of course, these same analysts forgot to throw out the results of language-phobic Americans, which brought the entire percentage down. But when questioned by this reporter about some of the more controversial language acquisition strategies, such as language text books with instructions written in the same language that the student is trying to learn, and prohibiting follow-up questions in class in a student's native language, I was told either to have sex with my mother or to close the door. I wasn't exactly sure which, and I didn't know how to ask my follow-up question in Italian, so I just stayed quiet.

Another critic, who asked to remain anonymous because he was not a neuroscientist or language instructor but rather my neighbor, who is a fairly smart life insurance agent, quipped sarcastically, "Yeah, reading language acquisition instructions in a foreign language is a brilliant idea. They should do that for all subjects. I would have done so much better in my college statistics class if the instructions were written in Arabic. I mean, HELLO."

Whichever side you come down on, it appears that instantaneous language acquisition will be here to stay. The long awaited day when people of all ethnicities (and different species, for that matter) can sit down together at a table for dinner and work out their differences in a reasoned, measured and rational manner is closer than you think. Just how scientists are going to be able to prevent a mass slaughter during dessert is still unclear, but I think that we would all agree that being able to discuss issues face to face with people of all walks of life, not to mention holding various combinations of inter-species rap sessions, is the first step (my personal favorite idea: a round-table discussion with giraffes, gerbils, anteaters, panda bears, and an assortment of philosophers).

If these types of talks prove to be fruitful, it may even be possible that one day, communication between men and women may be attempted. But no expert that I interviewed was prepared to hazard a guess if this is even technically possible, at least in the foreseeable future.

If these types of talks prove to be fruitful, it may even be possible that one day, communication between men and women may be attempted. But no expert that I interviewed was prepared to hazard a guess if this is even technically possible, at least in the foreseeable future.

(Note to readers: Richard Morgenstern is currently in Rome studying Italian, where he is considered to be the worst language student ever to have entered an unnamed language institution in its 200-year history.)

Terrie set down the writings. "Well, this one is better. And there might be a market for people that wish to explore the science behind the headlines. But..."

"I was waiting for the 'But...'" Richard mumbled, his two hands holding his chin.

"But... you might try to cover the more cutting-edge aspects, like say... like say, rap sessions with wild animals and humans. I'd suggest that you should save that for the next essay." She looked up at him. "You don't want to bury them with too many new concepts."

"Name one too many," Richard dared.

"Well, suggesting that the technology is already here for different species to communicate with each other. I am going to go out on a limb and say I'd like to have some of whatever you've been smoking. Your final remarks about communication between men and women, that rings true though. That was probably the best part." Terrie stood up and headed into the kitchen. Richard followed her.

She put her arms around him and whispered in his ear, "What do you think a giraffe and a panda would say to each other if they could?"

"Have you tasted those leaves over there. Fresh, crunchy." Richard made the motion of a giraffe stretching his neck.

Terrie nodded. "And the panda would say to another panda, 'I can't understand a word he said.' I suspect pandas are idiots. They just live off their good looks."

Richard put his arm around Terrie. "I can't wait for the sequel, Mr. Science," she said.

He kissed her hair. "Thanks. Because the first book sometimes takes years to finish."

She put her head against his and they affectionately snuggled together. She quietly whispered to him, "So, Ernest Hemingway, what's for dinner?"

CHAPTER 33

Hardball Fruit Negotiations

1975 – Vancouver, British Columbia

They drove straight through the night and arrived in front of the Chinese grocer's store just as the sun was rising. Workers were scurrying about preparing the shelves and putting on the finishing touches. The owner was behind the counter. Richard walked up to give her the good news. "Hello. Got a load of fruit for you."

The owner looked up from her accounting ledger, made eye contact and looked back at her books. "What you want?" she asked indifferently.

"The fruit that we talked about the other day. We got it. It's outside in the truck."

"I don't need fruit," she said, not looking up.

"But you told me you would buy some. You gave me prices and quantities. It's fresh. Just picked. At least have a look." It was slowly dawning upon him that this was how she negotiated.

"I'll have a look, but I don't need fruit," she said, sounding impatient.

Richard, who was fighting the urge to strangle her, managed to control himself and said, "It's not really important. Believe me, I can sell it all down the street. I just sort of liked you, so I thought I'd give you first pick. But you got to buy all of it. Nobody's cheaper than us and our fruit was picked less than twenty-four hours ago, so no problem if you don't need any right now. I can sell it to one of your competitors."

The fruit lady knew it was a good deal. However, she would have preferred a great deal. The torture had only just begun and she could tell Richard was new to negotiating. She picked out several slightly bruised cherries and peaches. "Customer not stupid," she explained. "Want number one best quality and best price." This was understandable, Richard thought, but settling on a final price was on par with final negotiations over the surrender of Berlin after World War II.

The haggling continued but being experienced in business, she knew when to fold her cards. She bought the entire load, and Richard's status with his partners increased accordingly.

Things seemed to be going swimmingly for the three fishmongers as they drove directly over to the wharf to pick up a second load of fish. But as they pulled into the parking lot, they were greeted by a food inspector who seemed unusually informed as to the particulars of their business. "We've had a complaint lodged against you for not observing our department's food safety regulations," the food inspector said. "I am going to have to make an inspection of your truck to make sure that public safety rules are being properly observed." They received a fix-it ticket requiring the mongers to either modernize, cease and desist selling fresh fish, or face serious charges.

"I smell a rat," David said as the three pondered their next move. "And the rat's name is Jack Fish."

"I knew he was a rat!" Richard chimed in. "I knew it the minute I met him. That useless hundred-dollar broken freezer. Once we paid him that money, we were of no more use to him, so he just flushed us down the river. Say it ain't so, Jack!"

Kenny didn't care for the vigilante sound of the mob. "Yeah, that's one theory all right, but before he's convicted by a jury of his peers..."

"A jury of fishmongers?" Richard interrupted.

"Would you let me fuckin' finish?" Kenny snapped. "You would also have to become conversant with the possibility that one of our customers could be the rat."

"Jack Rat or customer rat, we got a situation here," David said. The mongers talked about various strategies and agreed to do what any savvy businessman would do under the circumstances. They fled the scene of the crime. Their new plan was to buy fish at the northern port of Prince Rupert, a nine-hundred-plus-mile-drive Northwest of Vancouver, far away from the tentacles of Jack Fish or whoever the phantom rat was.

Kenny summarized, "It is a risky plan, it is a bold plan, some might even call it a reckless plan. But nobody can call us pussies. We are matching firepower with firepower. Atomic weapons with atomic weapons. Yes, my fellow mongers, we are not anyone's bitches."

Kenny's finest moment inspired the other two. "Assured mutual destruction, baby. You're talking 'bout assured mutual destruction," David concluded.

Richard broke the huddle. "Gentlemen, let's go sell us some fish!"

After an uneventful fifteen hour drive to Prince Rupert they arrived at the port to find a vibrant fishing town, too big to be a village, too small to be a city. Its remote location, bordering the southernmost tip of the Alaskan Panhandle, along with its incessant rain, seemed to conspire to create the perfect ecosystem for alcoholics to flourish. As compensation, God gave them all the fresh fish they could ever eat, which, when you think about it, was a pretty good deal.

Crammed into their tin can of a truck, the three young businessmen parked outside the Prince Rupert harbor. To fight off the bitter chill, they kept the engine idling as the rain grew from a drizzle into a deluge. Each one of them was counting out his own personal net worth to help clarify exactly how grim their collective cash flow situation really was.

"My pappy used to say his gross was good but his net was gross," Richard said. "I think that pretty much sums up my financial position as well." Ever since Kenny became short-tempered with his partners, with Richard's "my pappy used to say" shtick especially irritating him, Richard had compulsively begun starting the bulk of his sentences that way.

"Boys, we are getting close to the proverbial up-shit-creek-without-a-paddle stage of the current business cycle. If we don't make a go of it this run, we just might have to sell the truck and go our merry ways." said David.

The rain came down harder as Kenny put the truck in gear and made his way to the fishing boats. It felt hard to believe that humans would even be interested in eating food of any sort, what with the intense end-of-the-world rain pounding on the truck. But rain was the one thing that all fishermen could deal with expertly. The three found themselves back on the road, pumping each other up like football players before the first snap. "We're gonna force feed these hicks salmon." "Get your free salmon here!" "We will pay you to eat our fish!" "The man or the woman that can eat the most fish in a twenty-four hour period wins... one million dollars!" After a couple hours of driving, they randomly decided that the village of Hazelton could use an injection of fresh fish, so Kenny slowly drove off onto a sleepy dirt road that turned out to be Hazelton's main street. It also turned out that this was an indigenous village, with a large river full of migrating Spring salmon which put the mongers in the challenging position of essentially trying to sell salmon to professional salmon fisherman. The people there had their own fishing nets and boats and despite being inland by two-hundred miles, salmon swam right through the tiny village. As far as that went, it was hard to find many people even walking around. In desperation they drove toward an attractive young woman who was walking home from work. David called out the window, "Hey, excuse me, would you like to buy some fish?"

She looked over her shoulder toward the truck full of hairy hippies and fresh fish. A look of fear appeared on her face as she quickened her pace. David tried to un-terrify her. "Excuse me, ma'am! Would you have any interest in purchasing some very fresh salmon?" This time the woman broke into a full-out run. The confused mongers pulled over to the side of the road, just as the rain started to pour down again.

Kenny broke the silence. "Really nice sales pitch, David. Have you been putting in some study time after me and Richard go to sleep? 'Cause that was really slick."

"Andrew Carnegie has got to be rolling around in his grave right now!" Richard said, laughing.

"I knew I should have combined it with a pick-up line like, 'Hey baby, want to buy some fish? Maybe go for a ride in my fish truck?'" All three started laughing uncontrollably at the thought.

The tin can full of fish hurdled down the two-lane highway through snow-capped mountains and river valleys, later morphing into the great boreal forest of central British Columbia. It was four in the morning when David pulled over by the side of the road. All three were so exhausted they slept in the truck cab as the rain continued to pour down. Apparently, nobody had ever informed the month of June that it would be nice if it occasionally stopped raining.

Richard woke up first, as the pain from sleeping vertically while being pressed against the passenger door didn't agree with him. The other two appeared to have come to terms with it, as they snored in bear-like hibernations.

The sky was blue and bird song filled the air. You could almost see the greenery growing right before your eyes. David had miraculously parked along a junction in the road that was a fishmonger's dream location. It was as if the Fish Fairy had taken pity upon these three young men and reconfigured the coordinates that a roadside fishmonger needed to have a fully functioning business. Lots of local traffic, good visibility, local police that saw the value of having a friendly neighborhood fresh fish outlet even if the local traffic laws were being marginally abused, a creek and a spot for their tents and plenty of shade. And no Jack Fish sniffing around their affairs.

"Hard work and perseverance are overrated," Richard remarked to the other two when they had finally extricated themselves from the truck. "Me, I'll take preordained supernatural over sweat and toil any day of the week."

The sales were significantly higher, other than one perplexing interaction with a cultish group that called themselves "The Rapture" who appeared to be enraptured by the je ne sais quoi of their holy man but other than that, business was booming. But these guys contributed to the wellbeing of the mongers, primarily with comic relief. It was on day two at the new location, as the fish were just about swimming out of the cooler into customers' cars, that a van pulled up and out popped around seven members of "The Rapture," looking sort of like the cast of Ben-Hur. They were preoccupied with helping their wise guy out of the van, which he seemed totally incapable of doing himself. Once extricated, he was escorted by his worshippers for an inspection of the fish. He picked up an entire eight pound salmon in his arms and turned to go when Kenny politely pointed out that he first needed to weigh it and charge him this thing called money. "We need to sell you the fish before you drive away with it," he elaborated.

The wiseman appeared perplexed by the whole process. "You sell fish? How selfish." He continued,

"Mothers and fathers all trouble and bother." One of his minions fastidiously concluded the business transaction, as if the future of the planet Earth would turn on the Zen of extracting the change from his change purse in alignment with Uranus and the fish was ceremonially carried out to their van and into Swami Fish Thief's outstretched arms.

They drove away and David said, "Well, that was truly weird."

"I was wondering if he was going to fly away," added Richard.

"He would have flown away with our salmon if I hadn't stopped him," Kenny recollected. "All trouble and bother."

Although the business had become profitable, Richard felt that the three mongers had become a crowd and it was becoming increasingly apparent that it should have been a one-man business from the start. And as he didn't want to be the lonely little monger by the side of the road, he sold out his stake with dreams of bigger fish to fry.

CHAPTER 34

Memory Lane

2014 – Marin County, California

Robert poured bourbon and sweet vermouth into the two glasses of ice and stirred. "So, tell me, what was your first living memory? How old were you?"

His brother sucked down a sip of the magic elixir and replied, "Aaahhh. That's good. Just the way I like it."

"You mean in liquid form?"

"Welp," Richard said, smacking his lips, "it tastes delicious, although injecting it directly into my heart has some advantages as well. But I digress. My earliest memories are recollections of dust floating in the sunlight through the windows and staring at spiders in the dirt of our backyard."

"I said earliest recollections, not this morning's."

"Ha-ha, you joke, but I do have a vague recollection of when Mom used to bathe us in the double sink in the kitchen."

"Totally unsanitary," Robert interjected.

"I think you tried to drown me once!" Richard said grimacing, as he relived the terror.

"You were like a greased pig." Robert remembered aloud.

"I believe you were trying to eat me, now that I think about it. All that I remember was your constant need for food. It was like living with a Shark!" Richard said, the memory still haunting him. He continued. "I vividly remember one time you threatened to run away, and Mom called your bluff and you made it as far as the front door. You had a stick with some clothes tied onto it. I broke down crying and you broke down crying and then... I don't know what. I think you demanded to be fed for the tenth time that morning, I can't remember. I'm pretty sure that I blacked out at that point."

Robert replied, "That's a lie but do you recall the time, when we lived on 41st Avenue in the city, that Dad told us to take cousin Annie down to the playground a couple of blocks away? Annie and I are like six years old, which means that you're about five and our father, in his wisdom, tells us to take her down to the playground and show her a good time since her whole family has driven in all the way from their home in Tiburon. So, we all play there for an hour and you and I want to go home but Annie wants to stay. But that's not a problem, we just walk home and abandon her. Totally a win-win situation. Right?"

"I do remember Dad and Uncle Ken rushing out of the house in a blind panic." Richard replied. "Something about the realization that Annie was wandering the streets of San Francisco by herself really provoked them into action. It was impressive. They kept driving up and down the neighborhood streets in a blind panic until they found a close facsimile of the child in question. Personally, I always thought that they grabbed the wrong child."

"I know Annie's still pissed," Robert added.

"Served her right, I told her to come home."

"You were only five!" Robert pointed out.

"That's true. But I was a mature five. Another story that I loved was when you were with Dad waiting for a bus down on Balboa Street, when the Number 20 pulls into the bus stop and Dad tells you it's not your bus but you didn't hear him. Then he turns his back on you for a second and when he looks up, he sees your face in the bus window as it drives away. Dad had to run for two blocks to catch up with the bus. Did you know that the first word that you spoke was 'cigarette'?"

"I've been told that but, in this case, I think I was just catching the bus to pick up some cigarettes." Robert drained his glass and chewed on the ice.

"Oh yeah," Richard replied. I remember when you were about ten years old, you auditioned for the lead role in the Boys Club's production of The Pirates of Penzance. For a couple of weeks, I remember you singing your heart out around the house, then an ominous silence. Tell me again, why were you fired? Too gay for the part?"

"Actually, I got the lead role. Gilbert and Sullivan wrote great musicals. Mom had words with the director of the production. She essentially destroyed my Broadway aspirations. During a practice a few kids were goofing off and being disruptive. I wasn't one of them, mind you."

"No, of course not."

"But the director got so mad that he phoned all of the mothers and told them that he expected them to attend the next practice to keep the savages amongst them under control."

"What year was this? 1878?" Richard asked.

"Exactly. 1878. So when he called Mom, she told him that she had a full-time job and that she didn't have the time to attend meetings. So, the director confronted her, saying, 'What's more important to you, your job or your son's musical aspirations?' He was shocked to find out that the answer was in favor of the job. I was summarily fired, precluding what would have been a long and illustrious acting career."

"That's really a tragic story. Richard replied tenderly. Isn't it strange how one minute you can be on the fast track to Broadway and the next you're just a run-of-the-mill loser?"

Robert belched at Richard with indifference. "I just remembered Mom's favorite story. It was when Dad and Uncle Ray decided to break our dog Sandy of his bad habit of chasing cars."

"Yes, that was a classic," Richard agreed. "I never could understand how they could botch it up so badly."

"Well, only those two, both normally sensible men, will ever know all of what happened on that fateful day, but this is what I could get out of them. The plan was to drive down our street while Sandy was outside. You knew he was going to chase the car. That was a given. Dad was the driver and Ray, who was sitting in the front passenger seat, was carrying the secret weapon. A big bucket of water. So, the idea was, Ray was going to let Sandy have it right between the eyes when the heinous crime was taking place."

"So, what so terribly went wrong?" Richard asked.

"For starters, Dad was the world's jerkiest driver ever. Right?"

"That has been said by many," Richard allowed.

"Well, with all the jerkiness—and don't forget Sandy was a terror himself, he'd come flying out of the bushes like a bullet, barking and acting like he was going to bite a hole into the side of the car—so Ray decided to hold his fire the first time down the street, and Dad turned around and came driving back, like a matador. But what neither of them had calculated was that Sandy would chase on the passenger side one way but coming back, he'd chase on the driver side. In the heat of the moment, Ray made a rash managerial decision and threw the bucket of water across Dad, which was a risky technique even under ideal conditions. The rest was history. Dad got soaking wet, Sandy was victorious, and Ray got out of the car and had to sit down on the street curb to laugh his guts out."

"Dad and Ray used to make me laugh when we'd all get together for a holiday," Richard remembered. "It seemed like every time without fail, Dad would be talking about something or other when he'd somehow manage to segue into a rant. Usually about how, due to the incompetence of Ray's employer, the Department of Highways, and therefore, by extension, Ray personally, Dad had yet again become the victim of their gross negligence. It was their signs on the highway. Dad would claim that the Department of Highways (i.e. Ray) would forget to put up critically important signage changes.

"Right, and Ray would have an incredulous smile on his face and he'd always say, 'Now hold the phone!' And everyone in the room would simultaneously launch into their own list of signage atrocities."

"God that was funny! You'd think Ray was a mass murderer!" They had a good laugh together.

Robert had a smile on his face as he looked back in time. "Hold the phone!" he said.

"That was so funny," Richard replied. "Hold the phone!" They both drifted back to their thoughts. Back in time.

CHAPTER 35

Delicious Global Cuisines

2014 – San Francisco, California

Terrie looked up from her computer to see Richard hovering at their office entrance. "Do you think cannibalism qualifies as a cuisine or would it be a verb?" he asked seriously.

"That's what's known as an excellent question," Terrie replied, buying a little time as she finished typing a sentence.

"Yeah, like sushi is a cuisine and all you have to do is get a squiggling fish onto the table and bing, dinner!" He waited for confirmation.

"Well," Terrie said, sensuously stretching cat-like in her chair, "to be completely candid, I haven't given this weighty matter a whole lot of thought. But the sushi-cannibal analogy could just cut to the quick faster than any other line of reasoning. Does this have anything to do with tonight's dinner?" she said, suddenly worried.

"No, no, no!" Richard said reassuringly. "I'm just working on an article for The Blabbermouth about First Amendment issues, and..."

"And of course, this led to the burning issue of the day, is cannibalism a cuisine or an action? Got it," Terrie said.

"Well, cannibalism isn't so much the subject as just an example of how the government constantly steps over the line when it comes to our individual liberties," Richard said, still sounding tentative.

"But you're not coming down on the side with the sushi-people-eaters, are you? 'Cause if you do, you're going to have to do some fancy 'splaining to keep me from calling the Cannibal Control Board." Terrie knew that she had him on the ropes.

Richard, who operated intuitively, felt that Terrie was moving in for the kill, so he resorted to covering up and waiting for the bell to ring. "I'm siding with the cannibal's right to be the best cannibal he can be, without the state moving in to tax him out of business. Society can do without a bunch of unemployed cannibals wandering the streets. And you can't retrain them. As they say, 'Once a cannibal, always a cannibal.'"

Terrie looked at Richard as if he were a madman and let out a long breath, regaining her composure at the same time. "I cannot believe that I'm having this discussion with you. Living with you is... well, living with you keeps me feeling young." Richard smiled at this surprising and rare compliment, when Terrie finished her thought. "Like, I feel like a teenage girl babysitting her six-year-old brother."

Richard's eyes bore a hole in between hers. "Cuisine or verb?"

"It's gotta be a cuisine, come on! A little cannibal hot sauce, a cold beer, watching the game with the boys! Abso-canni-lutely!" Terrie suddenly swiveled her chair back towards her computer. "Now close the door and let me try to remember what it feels like to be normal."

Feeling jilted, he did as he was told, pondering exactly how he was going to make an important cannibal story relevant to the peoples of Burning Bush, Oklahoma. He walked back to the kitchen and stood motionless as he stared out the window. Waiting for a divine revelation to snap him out of his writer's block. He didn't really hold out much hope for a direct person-to-person phone call from

God, however. A flashback would have been acceptable for that matter. As he stood there daydreaming, his phone jumped into action. Richard answered it. It was his brother Robert calling from London. Their phone conversation started out on an upbeat note.

"Hi!" Robert said.

"Oh hi, it's you," Richard replied. At this point things deteriorated to socially unacceptable insults that could only be described, in their family, as business as usual. "Did you ever put me in your will? Because the way you drink, you probably only have hours to live."

"Perhaps," Robert said, ice cubes clinking in the background. "But better to live one day like a lion than a million like a lamb."

"Perhaps," Richard jabbed back. "Do you always rely upon quotations from Mussolini to explain your behavior?"

"Wow!" Robert said, mildly impressed. "Do you know all of Mussolini's famous quotes?"

"Yes, all both of them. Didn't he also say something about the trains running on time?"

"Why are you calling me?" Robert said, getting back to business. "It's two in the morning here."

"You called me but just for the record, make sure that me and... and... you know... what's her name?"

"Your younger sister Kathleen?"

"Yeah, your younger sister Kathleen, make sure you put us both in your will. God knows we've suffered enough. We've earned it. When are you planning on dying, anyway? I need a date, you know, otherwise I'll totally forget. Even approximately."

"I'll get back to you on that." The ice cubes tinkled. "I guess I did call you," Robert remembered. "I had something I wanted to ask you. Somebody was asking me what you and Terrie do for a living and I said I knew you were pretty much an unemployed fry cook or something and that you wrote a column for The Daily Blabbermouth in Burning

Bush, Oklahoma. That and assorted petty crime and fraud. But for Terrie I drew a blank. I just know that she makes enough money to feed delicious homemade Italian food to a steady flow of our relatives. You better make some more money, dude. You are only so lovable, and we really need to milk this pasta factory as long as possible."

"Thanks for the unsolicited advice, Benito. Can I just ask you one last question before I press the eject button?"

There was a short silence and Robert said, "If it has anything to do with cannibals..."

"She got to you, didn't she?" Richard said and quietly hung up before Robert could get out one last quote from the Italian dictator.

CHAPTER 36

Rocky

1974 – Ferry Building, Vancouver, British Columbia

The interesting thing about Richard and David's appearance as they stood in the boarding line for ferry departures to Alaska, was that they looked more or less similar to the other emigrants. And that was in spite of the fact that each and every one in line was carrying large backpacks, rifles, fishing gear, and hunting knives (all in open view), as well as wearing clothing reminiscent of Daniel Boone's Sunday finest. Wherever they were heading in Alaska, it was safe to assume it was going to be way off the grid. This was the Alaskan version of the great "Back to the Land Rush" that had started in the late Sixties in what Alaskans referred to as the Lower Forty-Eight, and things were still chugging along.

Though the line for the ferry looked like a Hollywood set for a Gold Rush scene, many of those waiting to get on board were greenhorns who hoped their lack of wilderness acumen could be offset by a determination to live an entirely different lifestyle. As, for example, did Richard and David.

They boarded the ferry along with the rest of the pioneer herd and staked claims on a couple of reclining chairs on the top deck. Richard, who until two days prior had never as much as touched a firearm, was casually examining his rifle, which was still strapped on his pack.

"Richard," David said, "I don't mean to sound like a know-it-all but it's considered a no-no to look down the barrel of a gun without having inspected the clip and the chamber first."

"Right." Richard replied. "I know that. But I never loaded it after it was tied onto my pack. And you had no reason to have loaded it either. Right?"

"As a favor, I did load it," David replied.

"David! Stop with the favors already! You're gonna kill me!"

"Well, that's why they have these protocols. Just in case."

Richard looked over at David and said, "You were just pulling my leg, weren't you?"

"Yeah, but did you learn your lesson, Daniel Boone?" David said, concluding today's book-learnin'.

"Yeah, I guess I did. The moral of the story is, never believe a thing that comes out of your mouth."

David screeched in his best old-geezer-hillbilly voice, "But I had you goin' there for a couple seconds, though, by-crickity!"

"Yeah, funniest joke I've heard since Ma slipped and fell doin' chores and the pig et the baby," Richard stuck his head back over the gun barrel, resuming his inspection.

Just then a group that resembled the Joad family from The Grapes of Wrath began homesteading an adjoining property of ocean-view lawn chairs beside the two Alaska-bound-suburb-slickers. There were three young, long-haired men about Richard and David's age, along with a couple, presumably their parents, and an exceptionally wild looking dog. "What you packin' there?" the blond, curly haired one casually asked Richard. "A 30-30?"

"Yeah, it's a 30-30."

"That should keep those bears out of your meat smoker!"

Richard had no idea what that really meant but the blond curly haired one introduced himself while his dog cautiously sniffed Richard's shoes and the two men shook paws. "My name's Rocky. And this here's my family. We're from Colorado. We just bought us a house on Wrangell Island, near Ketchikan, sight unseen and we're going to start a new life there together."

His mother, a handsome woman who looked like she could handle any cards dealt her way, turned and looked over at Rocky when she heard him speak.

"If my mom doesn't strangle us all before, we get settled in, that is," he concluded.

His mom didn't miss a beat. "Rocky!" She stretched his name out. "Roockkkeeee. Don't start makin' stuff up just to impress folks on the ferry."

Rocky put his arms around her and tried to hug her, but she pushed him away as if she had had enough of this family. All but her husband gave her insincere hugs until she said, "Go on, all of you. And try and not cause any trouble to nobody, neither." All but Rocky contrived mock terror and skedaddled away.

"That's funny," David said. "Wrangell's where we're headed too. But we just picked it off the map really. Wanted to see what it looks like with a forest growing right down to the ocean. Try our hand at camping in the wilderness with a gun, a bag of flour, and a bunch of beans."

"I've done that in Colorado, though I've heard it's even wilder where we're going," Rocky said. "But you can eat real good with just a few staple foods and do the rest of your shopping with Mr. 30-30 or Mr. 20-20."

"Don't forget Mrs. Fishing Pole," Richard added.

"And Mr. Hand Grenade and Auntie Uzi!" David said. "I mean, you have to admit, that would be real handy if we came upon a herd of buffalo!"

Rocky liked a good laugh, so he and his new acquaintances ended up hanging out most of the trip north, while his brother Tom and his buddy Derek drank steadily in the bar.

As the hours passed, the family's dirty little secrets became public. Rocky was an open book. Turned out that Tom and Derek's hobby was to drink heavily in bars, where their long hair and hippie tendencies weren't particularly welcome, until the inevitable moment arose when they would be told, "Strangers, you aren't welcome in our little bar, so you're gonna have to get the hell out of here in, say, sixty seconds, or we're gonna have to throw you out and you aren't gonna make me and my friends come over and get your table all dirty and muss up our hair, are you? 'Cause we'd hate that to happen and you know what, your sixty seconds is down to thirty now and..."

Suffice to say that barroom brawls were not of interest to this California contingent of Back to the Landers. After this background check was fully disclosed by Rocky, the Colorado contingent was unceremoniously scratched off Richard and David's Christmas card lists. Nevertheless, they were intrigued by Rocky's unique outlook on life.

Rocky had his own indigenous spiritual philosophy that allowed him unlimited marijuana, which he referred to as his "medicine" (while tapping a leather pouch strung around his neck, filled with pot and a pipe). His beliefs also dictated a love for all things in nature. "When I go hunting and take an animal's life, I still say a prayer over it, thanking it for letting me use its meat for my survival. In exchange, I try and use all of the animal parts, as much as possible. I believe I owe the wild animals that much."

The two new friends nodded in agreement. They could have quibbled over some of Rocky's interpretations, but they tried not to get into philosophical conversations with strangers, since they were constantly engaged with new acquaintances. Especially when their belief structures didn't get in the way of a good joke. Even more so when they promoted the use of marijuana. So, essentially, Rocky was preaching to the choir.

Rocky and Tom's step-father, Max, it turned out, was on a short leash as far as his stepsons were concerned. They had discovered something that their mom, Laura, had hidden from them. Max had beaten her several times over the past year of their short relationship. His mean-drunk routine appeared to be heading toward a head-on-collision with the brothers. Hence the reason why the three young men offered to give their mom a hand getting settled into her new situation.

CHAPTER 37

Portfolio Dating

2013 – Marin County, California

"But you said that you'd give me feedback when I needed it. Otherwise I'm in a vacuum." Richard waited for Terrie to respond but she continued reading her book, ignoring him. "And you know that I hate vacuuming!" Although the deafening silence was more than he could bear, he continued on. "Sometimes I wonder what's the point of living." Terrie slowly turned the page without comment. Silence. He sullenly reached into his shirt pocket and pulled out a Sees Butterscotch Sucker. His nuclear option.

"Where did that come from?!" she demanded.

"I have more. You'll never find them." He painstakingly unwrapped his confectionary.

"So, what's in it for me if I make some comments to you about your story?" Terrie said.

Feeling the balance of power swung in his direction, Richard made his next play, as he slowly licked his prize. "In exchange for your expert comments, I am prepared to offer you one Sees Butterscotch Sucker, in advance, and one of their chocolate toffees, but the toffee only after I have determined that your critique has been thoughtful." Terrie mulled this over when he added, "take it or leave it. Non-negotiable."

Terrie felt the last sentence like a punch in her belly. Richard had won this round. It was 10 P.M., the corner stores were closed, and See's chocolates were only sold at their own company stores. Nobody could beat his hand. He had a royal flush.

"You know, I've been meaning to tell you that it was a pretty good read. Could I ask you to read it out loud to me?"

"Yes, I can," he responded.

He cleared his throat when Terrie pre-empted the reading saying, "The sucker was to be paid in advance. Fork it over."

Richard reached into his shirt pocket and pulled out his payment. He let her unwrap it and started reading.

RICHARD RANTS

Portfolio Dating

Internet dating was proving itself to be a more complex enterprise than Richard had anticipated. Just standing back and objectively evaluating his failure rate was a totally depressing exercise. But nevertheless, he felt that a certain amount of scientific analysis was needed, or else he might just find himself spinning his dating wheels in perpetuity. It was clear that he needed some help and, luckily, his landlord downstairs was an expert in this field. Since he had moved in a month ago, a procession of women had filed in and out (in more ways than one) of his downstairs apartment in Marin County.

Downstairs David, as he was known to Richard's friends and family, might have been young in years, but he was not short on wisdom and helpful dating metaphors. He was twenty years Richard's junior, so it was humbling for Richard to have to admit to himself, this young whipper-snapper was just going to have to be his dating mentor. Facts were facts though. Richard had just come out from two long marriages, and he really hadn't had the time or the experience to have put up the big numbers when it came to liaisons with the fairer sex. He simply had to be realistic. Up until now, when it came down to the numbers, he wasn't a closer.

"Richard, when you developed your personal financial portfolio, did you just plop all of your eggs in one basket, or did you spread out the risk." Downstairs David didn't wait for Richard's response. "You are a prudent man, I'm sure you did your homework and were cautious. Frankly, it's not particularly different than dating women. At your age, you probably are more comfortable with moderate risk since you are already over the half dead point." Downstairs David never beat around the bush. "So, you don't have time to play around with too aggressive of a portfolio. You could lose it all and end up a janitor in a whore house in Manila or something. But if we are talking about financial instruments, you'd probably want 15% high risk domestic stocks, maybe another 15% of strong foreign stocks, and 35% large established American stocks like the S&P 500. To off-set some of your risk you'd want around 20% Bonds and 10% you would leave in cash. The last 5% should be in something a bit wild, just to spice things up. Like investing in emerging markets or something like that. You know, like the Mongolian stock market or currency trading in Argentina."

Richard listened intently waiting to see where this metaphor was going. "So how does this translate into your dating portfolio do I hear you ask?" he continued confidently. "Well, for the high-risk domestic stock component, you'll need some powerful women who are not going to be sticking around you for long. You're not planning on getting married, again are you?" he inquired.

"Well, if I ever start talking about getting married, would you promise to shoot me?" Richard said.

"I'll take that as a definite no. So back to the power women. Of course, you'll want a few, but you'll have to try not to speak. One of my buddies has come up with a graph that illustrates the relationship between how many words a man speaks and the duration of time before this category of women will jettison you. In your case it could be as few as fifty words, so maybe tell them you have a speech impediment or that you just had throat surgery and put your listening ears on, because those women will be measuring you from all directions, they can't help it. It's completely genetic in my opinion, and even if you were the President of General Motors, you're not going to be good enough. This would be a fast inventory turnover item, and really a disproportionate amount of work, but.... these ladies are movers and shakers, so you can't ignore them. And Marin County has a lot of them, so, when in Rome, do as the Romans."

Downstairs David filled up the bong to capacity and inhaled deeply. He slowly exhaled, passed it over Richard's way, and continued. "Now, high risk works in various directions. You'll need something like a porn star or a biker chick for diversification, maybe a woman who has lived in 19 countries, that sort of thing. Perhaps she was in prison for a crime of passion. You get the idea. A femme fatale."

By now Richard was breathless. Up until a few minutes ago he just wanted a date with anyone. Even Lassie would had been acceptable, but now he was looking for a corporate president fresh out of jail. He was about to type in Martha Stewart's name in his Google search, when Downstairs David continued unfolding his master plan. Richard pulled in a lung-full, all ears. "Now 35% of your entire portfolio consists of stable large companies. Not highly risky or highly profitable, think of them as old money, brick and mortar businesses. But nothing's very old in America, so I will cut to the chase and allow my metaphor to be representative of divorcees. These women, I mean do the math, that's just about every woman in Marin County. Who knows where their money comes from? I mean, who even cares? Around this neck of the woods, these women are not desperate, so you'll have your work cut out for you. They have as many reasons to be wary of you as you do of them. Some have good jobs, some had good divorce settlements. You know, the couple split the assets down the middle fifty-fifty and she gets the Mine while he gets the Shaft. But there is a difference between these women and the high-risk category. First of all, they are abundant, kind of like the herds of buffalo that once roamed the plains of the American prairies. They like men to a degree, while the CEO movers and shakers like their professional life way more than hanging with guys watching football games. You can hardly blame them really. When you get down to brass tacks, they are more highly evolved humans. This brings us up to the 15% invested in secure medium risk foreign financial instruments. For this I recommend women from stable countries. Hard to know where to start. It's pretty subjective, but France, Spain, and Italy had the Bridgette and Sophia thing going back in the day. Not sure if Spain had a trophy actress but dude, this is all about diversification. You'll probably want to spread your wings into Asia, Scandinavia, and Latin America, that's all good. Remember that dating is also done just for the sake of having fun. Theoretically anyway. But be careful, it's always safer not to venture too far from home. Always invest in what you know. You might regret becoming too deeply involved with a woman that believes you shouldn't go swimming at the most charming dive resort that you've ever seen in your life because of possible attacks from ocean spirits." The bong floated back and forth as if on a magic carpet.

"This brings us up to bonds." Richard quickly held up the bong, misunderstanding the word, but David ignored his faux pas. "They are usually safe and boring. You may not know this, but apparently many psychologists believe men want to marry their mothers, which totally grosses me out, but we got to feed the monkey, so occasionally you got to date a good ole fashioned USA gal who will subconsciously be your mother. The good news—you won't be aware of any of this since it is all happening below your level of consciousness. The less said the better." Richard started choking on his twelfth hit and by now they were both so high beyond recognition that they might as well have been a couple of crack-heads in an alleyway

A thought suddenly occurred to Richard. "What kind of woman would want to date drug fiends like us!" he blurted out loud.

Downstairs David once again ignored the white noise emanating from Richard's mouth. "I guess you want to know what kind of women fill up the 10% cash component. Just think about it. What is distinctive about cash in technical terms? It's liquid!! But I'm not talking about dating mermaids dude. No, liquidity in financial terms, always easily available, not of much value in the long-run, but always there in a pinch."

Richard chimed in like a contestant on a game show. "a fuck-buddy!" then fell off of his chair onto the floor.

"Settle down, you might hurt yourself. You are a quick study for such an old guy though." Downstairs David reflected. He was also stoned out of his gourd but in a more disciplined sort of manner "That is correct though. Or a one-night stand, take your pick. Probably a waste of time for guys that want a family life or some sort of monogamous stability, but these women are a critical component in many portfolios. I know I'm a lot younger than you, but this last group makes up 50% of my own portfolio. But conversely, I have a lot more time to recover from a totally disastrous relationship".

Richard was really impressed with just how thoroughly David's thesis had been thought through.

"Which leaves 5% for the highest risk category in your portfolio. Highly risky women and, I know I know, we already did the femme fatale and biker chicks, so what's left? Oh, we can go much further into the unknown than that. I'm talking exotic babes fresh out of mental institutions, or obviously heading directly into one. This is the fun money in your stash. And alternately, this could be mail-order bride catalogue material. Or maybe a female jihadi that just successfully completed her first mission. This list is only limited by your imagination."

The two were now of little use to the human race. It was 3:30 in the morning.

That's a lot to absorb in one lesson." Richard mumbled. "I'm going to bed."

"To be continued dude." Downstairs David mumbled back in reply. "Sweet dreams, my friend."

(Note to readers: Richard Morgenstern can often be found at Financial Portfolio Seminars sometimes trying to interview women to further advance his knowledge of portfolio dating.)

Terrie set the writing down. "Tell me again, what demographic are you speaking to? You might have a shot at getting it published in Delusional Men Weekly."

"I thought you'd like it." Richard said disappointed.

"I think if you deleted the parts about Internet dating, it would read better."

"But that's the entire story." Richard looked over at Terrie and slowly pulled the caramel from his pocket. "Not much in your review that I can sink my teeth into so I might as well sink them into the last caramel."

Terrie slowly pulled herself from her chair. "Hey, let's not shoot the messenger." She inched herself across the carpet, afraid of spooking the caramel-meister.

"Write the words CONSTRUCTIVE CRITICISM ten times then come back with some real help." He carefully bit off half of the candy and gave her the other half. "More than you deserve" he mumbled.

Terrie inhaled the caramel like a dying man in the desert without any water. With the half caramel in her mouth, she reached her hand to Richard's story and said, "Let me have another look at that sucker. Speaking of which, do you have any more of those?"

CHAPTER 38

Mack Johns, Harry, and Rocky

1974 – Wrangle Island, Alaska

It's not every day that one gets formally introduced to a couple of raving alcoholics but, leave it to Rocky to make that seem like the most natural thing. At least this was what both Richard and David were thinking. They had just arrived at Mack John's small shack in time for cocktail hour, at one thirty in the afternoon. And the drink du jour was cheap whisky in an extra-large bottle.

They had only arrived in Wrangell less than forty-eight hours earlier and Rocky had already found another best friend. If you didn't know differently, you would have figured they knew each other their entire lives.

But their short time on the island had been action-packed. Rocky's mom, Laura Billings, had offered Richard and David a floor to sleep on, saying, "Any friend of Rocky's is a friend of mine." This didn't go over too well with her significant other, Max, but Rocky had calmed Max and his fear of deadbeats by suggesting to him that he just might appreciate having some free labor around getting their new house fixed up.

Prior to their invitation over to Mack John's drinking establishment, they had been dropped off by the ferry at the Wrangell Island Dock and they hiked up to the Billings' new old house. It was a vision: a large old wooden faded-white painted house with a great ocean view. But its most compelling feature was it hung over the Pacific Ocean, built completely on tall wooden stilts that were set upon cement pads. You couldn't help but notice that it looked like the stilts were engineered by Salvador Dali. So many retrofits had been done over the years that you couldn't tell where the original structure started and the band-aids ended but clearly the Pacific Ocean was going to win this game of tug of war if nothing was done real quick.

Rocky matter-of-factly asked the others, "Hey fellas, can you give me a hand after you check out downtown Wrangell? I promised Max that I'd do some work leveling a couple of those piers right away."

The two happily agreed, assuming either Rocky or Max had a plan. Laura was just beginning to comprehend why they got such a good price on the house, but she decided that Max could handle it. Max, who as a baby never had the correct parts installed to be able to smile, was really not smiling now. He did what any good construction foreman worth his salt would have done, punt the dangerous task over to the younger, less experienced guys. "Rocky, you and your friends can take care of what we talked about," he said. End of discussion.

"Right," Rocky said, "soon as my buddies get back to help me."

Richard and David went on their walkabout around the city limits of Wrangell Island. This was a real town in the sense that it had no tourism. As far as that went, it had nothing for tourists to do except maybe kill things but that hadn't occurred to anyone yet, so commercial fishing and, to a lesser extent, logging were pretty much the only way to make money. Also noted on their general inspection was that the town was filthy with huge ravens. If you didn't count the ravens in the population census, it appeared to the two emigrants that the entire village had put up their "Gone Fishing" signs, because Wrangell looked abandoned. "I wonder if the ravens ate everybody. Sure is quiet here," David speculated.

"And there sure are a bunch of them here," Richard said. "Look at that beast staring at us from the roof."

"Maybe it's better not to look at him. Might piss him off. You never know."

"Right." They continued walking, looking down, until they got back to Rocky's.

Rocky had already carried three Jack-Alls down the cement stairs, which ended on top of the ocean against a cliff. His dog, Ghost, which according to Rocky was half coyote, stood by the top of the sea cliff stairs like a sentry. Ghost gave the impression that he could talk by the way he would turn his head with his ears upright whenever someone in his pack spoke.

Richard and David carried down three long construction ladders and an assortment of beveled wooden wedges and miscellaneous tools. Rocky became the foreman, David, the consultant, and Richard, the dead weight.

Rocky and David positioned the three ladders, which only confused Richard. "Was I supposed to have been born with this knowledge?" he asked. "Because, believe it or not, this is the first time that I have climbed up a ladder with the ocean waves covering up the bottom two rungs, and I'm still not sure what we are doing."

"Well," Rocky said, "basically what I was thinking was, we eyeball the piers to figure out which one is the lowest and which one is the highest, and we use the chainsaw and cut a big wedge and pound it in tight so that the highest and lowest ones are level with each other. Then we'll wedge the other piers until they match those. After that, we can secure them somehow with bolts or wood screws and maybe buy some plates of metal that we can attach onto two sides."

"What do you use the Jack-Alls for?" Richard asked, still trying to understand.

"Welp," Rocky said, "the jacks are going to be the muscle that will wrestle the piers to make them straight."

"Suppose the piers are rotten at the base, down in the water?" David speculated.

"I know," Rocky said, "but at least we have a half-assed level floor until we get a really low tide. Then we could put in some new posts if we needed to. Or make some proper footings."

"So, this is a two-stage project, and did I correctly hear you say 'we' white man?" Richard asked.

Rocky put on his charmer smile and said, "We, like me and Ghost, me and my Mom, me and my drunken brother and his drunken friend, or... maybe we... us."

They all laughed together and got down to work. It only took an hour or so to determine what needed determining, the Jack-All's figured into the next stage. The entire concept of positioning these jacks in so many different ways, horizontally, vertically and at angles, required a high level of skill and experience. It was essentially a specialized sub-field in the carpentry world. Rocky had a bit of construction experience, but Richard and David knew about nothing, concerning, as David so aptly put it, "jacking off" together. But as each crank became significantly harder than the previous one, they were now at a decisive moment.

All three young men were around the top of their ladders, in this labyrinth of barnacle-encrusted wooden beams. "I think I got one more crank in me," Rocky grunted as he put all his strength from his small but muscular frame into his effort. Rocky pulled down on the long arm of the jack as it trembled from the stress of lifting too much weight.

Suddenly, with a sickening metallic sound, his entire jack shot out of his hands like it was a military weapon. The projectile shot right in between Richard's and David's faces, fast enough to have killed either one of them. It was a close call and happened in a split second. All three young men were speechless. Richard spoke first. "Fuck me!" he said, breathless. "That was like a rocket! I can just about taste metal!"

"You realize that would have killed one of us! Lord have mercy!" David said.

"We're shutting down this operation," Rocky said. "Let's go get stoned." It entered Rocky's mind they were in far over their heads in terms of the knowledge required to do the job and that Max, with his lifetime of construction experience, Max the Maniac knew they were out of their depth. He knew that even he was out of his depth! Or just plain incompetent. Yet he sent three greenhorns out to tackle a job on what, in all likelihood, was a tear-down home. They brought the tools back up to the house and set them on the ground.

Max came out of the house. "Where do you think you're going? You just got started."

"We quit," Rocky said, matter of factly. "Let's go for a walk and calm down a bit."

"Oh, you aren't quitting!" Max snarled.

"Don't start in on me, Max. You're not my boss," Rocky said coolly. For a second, Ghost growled at Max, clearly siding with Rocky. Ghost turned and followed his pack as they walked slowly up the road to a viewpoint.

They found an amazing ocean view and sat down on a large rock. In silence they passed around a pipe full of Rocky's medicine. "Well," David said exhaling, "I guess we're experienced carpenters now." The others chuckled to themselves, as they observed a couple of fishing boats in the distance, returning home from their day's work.

"I bet none of them guys almost got hit in the head by a metal projectile today," Rocky said as he passed the pipe.

Richard and David quietly nodded the two heads in question, staring far away.

CHAPTER 39

Heaven and Hell Revisited

2014 – San Francisco, California

"I don't understand your obsession with always traveling to hot tropical climates," Robert said as he sucked down a bourbon-soaked maraschino cherry. He let out a loud belch as if to inform the entire planet that he was a Gorilla in a business suit.

"Well, when you think about it," Richard responded, "vacationing in a hot climate isn't so important in your case, since you will certainly be burning in hell for eternity. So why waste your money?"

Robert rolled over on the couch like an annoyed beached whale." Just for the record, about my wealth. I've been meaning to tell both you and Kathleen that I am taking it with me. I just have a couple more minor technical adjustments to make. When I'm off to the big Sheraton in the sky, I'm bringing along suitcases stuffed with U.S. dollars."

"How do you know which currency God uses?" Richard asked, concerned. His sister Kathleen already routinely referred to Robert as her retirement plan, this was breaking news.

"God likes a winner, just look at a history book for once in your life. I can tell you with a high degree of certainty that he's not using the ruble."

"Obviously, I don't think that even the Russians are using the ruble these days. Any currency named after a collapsed building is doomed from the start, I'd say. Talk about a lack of confidence. I had assumed that you've been working on a way to take it with you but that's not happening in your lifetime. Possibly in my lifetime even. Anyhow, it's more complicated for you. Me, I just have to get from point A, Earth, to point B, the clouds. I'm pretty sure Apple has an app for this already. You, on the other hand, you will most certainly be going straight to Hell and will also have to figure out how to prevent your money from spontaneously combusting and your coins from melting. So back to the drawing board, Einstein."

Robert had stopped listening. He grunted as he rolled back over to his other side and said, "So, since when did you buy into the Heaven and Hell construct, anyway? I thought you were an atheistic-anarchistic-cannibalistic-moralistic loser kind of guy." Richard walked to the door, grumbling to himself, "No, that was you."

"Ouch! You hurted my feelings," his big brother replied, then shut his eyes, wiggling his body deeper into the couch.

"I believe that would be impossible to do since you've never shown any indication that you have the capacity to feel anything whatsoever. Probably you're confusing feelings with indigestion. You haven't swallowed a whole pig again, have you? Because remember what happened last time. It took two surgeons and one priest to pull it back out." Richard shut the door before his brother could return his next salvo.

He was too far away to hear Robert mumbling to himself as he drifted into a deep sleep, "The pig incident. Oh yes. I'd totally forgotten about the pig incident."

CHAPTER 40

The Mighty Stikine

1974 – Wrangell Island, Alaska

"Let me pour you two little cocksuckers a drink!" Mack Johns said with a little flourish. If an etiquette book was written for raving alcoholics, the author would have been wise to use this gentleman-fisherman for the template. He filled two tall glasses with straight cheap whisky.

"Thanks, Max. That's a lot of whisky," David said. It was an enormous drink by anyone's standards, but Mack was ever the gentleman. He was tall, lanky, with big strong hands and a recently trimmed black beard. If someone put him through an industrial steam cleaner for an hour, you could stuff him into a tuxedo and send him to the opera.

Every fifteen minutes or so Mack John's would inquire, "How's everyone's drink?"

Mack's drinking buddy, an extremely overweight maniac named Harry, interrupted "Drink your drinks and quit your griping, you three little cocksuckers," he snarled, oblivious to the fact that nobody had been griping. He was in a perpetually foul mood and appeared to have sunk so far into the comfy leather chair that one day someone would have to hire a crane to get him out of it.

Mack and Harry were full-time fishermen, which meant they were unemployed for about half the year. Primarily salmon and halibut run and a small herring run. Also, the oolichan, or candlefish, but that only lasts for two or three days. The Haida Nation of the Alaskan Panhandle had used this oily fish as a source of light, before white men came for a visit and enjoyed themselves so much they never left. Many local fishermen preferred the oolichan over the big-name celebrity fish. "Now that's a good eating fish!" Mack said. "They should be running next week some time. You'll have to try them, Rocky. You and the kids will have to come over and we'll have ourselves a big oolichan feed. They're a really good eating fish." But before he could articulate his thoughts, Harry got the jump on him.

"So, Rocky," he said, the kids now in a sub-category below Rocky, "exactly what are you little cocksuckers gonna do now that you're in Wrangell, anyhow?"

An innocent enough question, although Harry and Mack's chronic overuse of the term "cocksucker" seemed presumptuous to both of "the kids."

Rocky didn't share this concern, answering, "Well, Harry, right now I gotta go back and help get my mom settled into her place for a bit, then me and the fellas here are talkin' about goin' up in the mountains somewhere really wild around here, build a log shack for the winter and try not to starve to death. Maybe up the Stikine River."

Mack Johns nearly choked to death on his whisky and spit out a mouthful. After he got his wind back, he said, "Not the Stikine, Rocky! That's no place fit for humans. It's bad enough taking the boat across but once you're there, it's thick with bears and mosquitos. Don't go to the Stikine, Rocky! Too many men have lost their lives there!"

Both the Boy-Palz felt transported into an ancient Gunsmoke episode. Mack's heartfelt yet melodramatic rendition of a doomsayer was over the top, but there was the half bottle of whisky he'd drunk for breakfast to consider.

Mack started to pour another round, mumbling to himself quietly, "Not the Stikine, Rocky. No. Don't go up the Stikine."

"I think we'd better head back home and help out. Maybe we'll stop by later," Rocky said.

They all thanked their hosts for drinks and bid them farewell. Ghost, who'd been acting as sentry the whole time, trotted dutifully behind them, ever on the alert.

The minute they were out of earshot, Richard said to Rocky, "Tell me again—why did we just visit those two little cocksuckers?"

"I don't know if I ever have a reason to hang out with anyone for a quick drink, although I do prefer my medicine over theirs." Rocky replied,

Devoid of traffic, the three young men walked back home to Rocky's, the whole time being followed and serenaded by ravens who were in full force.

As they walked through the one block that was referred to as being "downtown" Richard speculated, "I think that big fat one down in the middle of the road is the mayor." The Mayor appeared to be the boldest raven of the bunch. He walked as if he owned the place, his black feathers giving off the appearance of a black suit. The ravens displayed their large vocabularies, while Richard came up with a hypothesis. "It's weird, David. The noises that the ravens are making, it's almost like they're imitating sounds of nature. Like that one. Hear that?"

Not far away, The Mayor answered as if on cue. "Glook. Glook."

David nodded. "It sounded like a rock or something splashing into the water. Someone told me once that ravens are better talkers than parrots–smart, too."

"I've heard that, too," Richard replied. They trudged out of downtown Wrangell at a slow pace, tipsy from their morning whisky. "You mean like spelling bees and

Scrabble, right?" They both looked out of the corner of their eyes to see if they could pull Rocky's leg a bit.

Rocky, getting a handle on their banter, laughed out loud.

David added, "Actually, I've read they are pretty shoddy spellers, but they are excellent poker players."

"I've heard that also." Richard said. "That's only because they can bluff like a pro. They couldn't crack a smile if you paid them. Just don't have the capacity to do it. That's why there are so many wealthy ravens."

"Poker?" David guessed.

"Poker." Richard replied.

With the raven issue temporarily put aside, Richard and David decided they would help Rocky and his mom fix up their place for a few days, then go backpacking up the coastline from Wrangell for a couple of weeks. This plan also incorporated an invitation from Mack Johns to come on over and have a feed of oolichan the following day.

At dinner that evening at Rocky's family home, a great deal of discussion ensued concerning the idea of heading out into the wilderness. Being the most confident and knowledgeable in the ways of mountain men, Rocky summarized the final plan. "So, after we all earn our grubstakes, we'll meet back here in Wrangell during the first week of October. That way, we should have around a month or so before the first snowfall to build us the prettiest little log cabin you fellas have ever seen. We'll find ourselves a real nice spot right next to the Stikine and we're gonna be able to catch fish right out our windows! Just live off the fat of the land. You two better bring a couple of mountain mamas along, though, or it's gonna be a long winter!!"

The matter of fact way that Rocky included female companions into the mix seemed as if he were telling them to buy another sack of flour and a few more cans of coffee.

They agreed to rendezvous in Wrangell in three months and, to cement the deal, they walked up the hill to their favorite spectacular viewpoint and passed around Rocky's medicine pipe.

The sound of a group of ravens in the nearby trees filled the air with unsettling, incomprehensible, bird chatter. The largest bird bore an uncanny resemblance to The Mayor.

The Mayor glanced around at his entourage, who became silent. He spoke.

"Donk!"

"Donk!"

"Goup!"

"Stak"

"Een"

"Donk-Goup-Stak-Een-Rocee"

"Don't go up Stakeen Rocee."

"Don't go up the Stikine, Rocky!"

A slight smile appeared on The Mayor's face, worthy of a world-class poker player.

CHAPTER 41

Hunter Pence

2014 – Kansas City, Missouri

Terrie and Richard silently ate their bowls of oatmeal as if in a deep meditation, an every-other-day ritual. Richard referred to it as the gluten that bound them together, while Terrie referred to it as the Quakers' gift to mankind.

"Do you think that Quakers really were the inventors of oatmeal?" she wondered out loud as she marveled at a spoonful. "I guess somebody had to be. The box looks kind of spiritual, what with the guy with his puffy face and long hair."

Richard stared at a spoonful. "Maybe he is the son of an oatmeal god."

Terri ignored him focusing her attention on her iPad. "I am so stoked that the Giants kicked some Kansas City Royal butt last night. One down and three to go," she said. Three more games and the San Francisco Giants beat the Kansas City Royals for the World Series title.

She stared at the photo of the Giants star Hunter Pence. "What's pissing me off is how the Royals fans are dissing our star player big time with those signs they waved around last night:

Hunter Pence
can't parallel park

Hunter Pence eats pizza
with a fork

Hunter Pence thinks Kansas City
is in Kansas

Hunter Pence eats subway
sandwiches sideways

Hunter Pence brings 13
items to the express line

"Those lamebrained farmers in St. Louis have gone too far!" she snapped. She started typing frenetically, and, after 10 minutes, printed out a page and handed it to Richard. "Put that in your 'Richard Rants' column. We can't let those hayseeds from East Jesus mock our genuine hero!"

Richard looked over her shoulder at a picture of the player in question. "Hmmmm," he said. "Hunter Pence does look like a young version of the son of the Oatmeal God. We better be careful; I feel as if we are walking into some sort of religious war."

He looked at the page that Terrie typed up.

```
    -Hunter Pence hits home runs out of Missouri
into Kansas.
    - Hunter Pence thinks there's no place like
San Francisco.
    - Hunter Pence is in awe of the Kansas City
Royals' starting rotation and wonders when they
are supposed to show up to pitch.
    - Hunter Pence apologizes for ruining the
Royals' World Series experience.
```

- Hunter Pence loves the Royals and suggests they just surrender and go home before one of them gets hurt falling down in the outfield.

"No good will come of this," Richard said, shaking his head.

"Just do it," she commanded as she walked out the door into the morning commuter war games.

The next morning Richard found Terrie at her iPad. "Did you even go to bed last night?" he asked.

"Couldn't really sleep. I was surprised that your newspaper published your baseball story in Richard Rants! I think that I once heard everyone in Oklahoma hates everyone in Kansas." She was still passionately engaged in the issue.

"I don't really think that it could be characterized as a baseball column, more like the opening salvos to a civil war. We better make sure the locks on our doors are working. In any case, let's not go out to any public functions for a while."

"Like, you mean, stay away from the showings at Ford's Theatre. I see things the opposite way. It would be nice if you were to put on your big boy pants for this issue. I need your help. I can't fight this alone."

Richard moaned. "Have you ever heard of the saying 'Choose your battles wisely'?"

Terrie continued unabated. "We already beat the St. Louis Cardinals! How come now we have to play a whole new series with yet another team from Missouri? Been there, done that. And besides, if they can't even figure out that naming their city the exact same name as the adjoining state is frickin' confusing to the rest of the world... what I'm trying to say is, when does it all end? After we beat Kansas City, do they get to parade out another town from Missouri? Do we have to play Springfield, then Independence, then East Independence? How would they like it if we were to suddenly throw Oakland at them? Or Los Angeles?"

"We already did. They beat the Oakland A's and the Los Angeles Angels," Richard reminded her.

"This is utter madness!" she said, pounding one of her fists on the table. "It's like a parallel baseball universe that is incapable of determining a winner. We should just declare victory and go home."

"Terrie. We lost Game 2 last night. We both know that they beat us fair and square. The show is going to go on. Deal with it. And this is definitely the last team we play. They don't get to trudge out the Columbia Inbreds or the Springfield Motherfuckers at the last minute. Your nightmare will soon be over."

"But Hunter Pence..."

Richard interrupted. "Enough Hunter Pence already. Do you think he's even the slightest bit worried? He's gonna personally whoop them so bad, they're going to wish they'd never left Kansas."

Terrie took a deep breath and composed herself. She walked over to Richard and kissed him goodbye. She opened the front door to head to work. "It's Missouri, not Kansas," she called back to him as the door shut.

CHAPTER 42

David the Hero

1974 – Terrace, British Columbia

The ferry from Wrangell Island arrived in Prince Rupert late in the afternoon. The two travelers threw on their backpacks and made their way down to terra firma. It was raining lightly, which in Prince Rupert was referred to as a nice day. They hiked for about a mile until they came to a government-run hostel that was frequented by drug addicts, transients, indigenous laborers, and the down-on-their-luck crowd. After they signed in, they were allowed access to the one large communal room, which was supplied with air mattresses, blankets and nothing else. Since this was the hotel of last resort, the clientele was expected to be pounding the pavement, looking for work. Thus, each morning, they were all unceremoniously booted out onto the streets with a bag lunch no later than eight, and not to show their faces again until five that evening.

For Richard and David, food and shelter for twenty-four hours was like a mini-vacation.

"If they gave you a separate room and bathroom, cooked actual food, and separated us from the violent felons, this place would be great," David said longingly.

"I heard a fellow inmate refer to this place as the Waldorf," Richard replied. "And his buddy called the dining area the Champagne Room." They laughed.

A crowd reeking of drugs, alcohol and unidentified substances started to form outside the door to the cafeteria-style dining hall. As they filed in, each was served a large bowl of stew along with bread and an assortment of drinks before they sat down at the tables.

As David took a bite of the stew, Richard asked, "So, do you think it's safe to eat?"

David's faux-expert taste buds analyzed the ingredients. "I believe I detect just the slightest suggestion of muskrat in this stew, old boy."

Richard brought the bowl of stew to his face and inhaled its fragrance. "Possum, possibly?"

"Well... they are often mistaken for each other but... not at this time of year," David said authoritatively.

"Yes, quite. Not this time of year." Richard conceded.

Their plan was to hitchhike tomorrow, eighty miles east to the small town of Terrace. They had heard the sawmills were looking for laborers. But tonight they decided to wander around the fishing village and maybe have a beer. They could leave their packs in the communal sleeping room but there was no security and their roommates didn't inspire confidence. Leaving with their jumbo-sized backpacks on, a gruff, middle-aged, Haida tribesman confronted them. "You know, you don't have to carry your belongings with you. You can just leave them here."

"Oh, thanks, yeah, we know. But everything we own; we carry on our backs. So, it's not worth the risk to us." Richard said.

The native had a bone to pick. "You know, that's the difference between natives and the white man. The white man is always worried about his stuff. Natives don't really think about stuff."

Richard, who had always had an interest in the philosophies of indigenous groups, his mind racing, wondered how to explain they had a lot in common. Simultaneously thinking, "Who is this prick, anyway?"

David, not conflicted about the unsolicited opinion of a stranger, even an indigenous stranger, said, "Well, to each his own, Richard, let's take our stuff out for a walk." Richard followed David outside like a puppy, thinking, why didn't I say that first?

They walked in the rain as Richard said to David, "So, which direction do we go, White Man?"

Next morning the two white men and their stuff hit the road and got a ride. Not just to Terrace but right to the main personnel office of the largest sawmill. Despite rumors to the contrary, jobs were in short supply. Having walked ten miles that day, they found an old, four-story, wooden hotel, converted into another welfare hotel-hostel. The government subsidized building allowed each person the option to stay up to three days, if they didn't cause trouble. Richard and David got their own room with a bathroom at the end of the hallway. But without available jobs, the two travelers discussed Plan C.

"I'm thinking that the Canadian National Railway is beckoning," said Richard. "What say we hitch over to Prince George and see what's shakin'?"

Hitchhiking three hundred miles to work for another psychopath changing railroad ties froze David in his tracks. "You know, Richard, just the idea of going back to work with another gang of railroad morons is more than I can bear. I've been doing a lot of thinking lately about applying to a university, or even a community college. I heard there's a good one down in the Kootenays."

David had mentioned this idea before. Richard was shell-shocked. They were as close as brothers and along with their other Boy-Pal, Tom, they had invented their own way of speaking, as if the three were the only ones fluent in Palzican (for lack of an internationally recognized name). The next morning, they decided to leave together, with the intention of splitting up as soon as they reached the first fork in the road or a freight hopping yard. For the first time in many moons, neither of them resorted to humor to quell the pain.

David pounced out of bed and shook Richard awake, yelling "RICHARD, WAKE UP! THE HOTEL'S ON FIRE!!"

They pulled on their pants and shoes, intelligent perhaps or a lower priority than getting the hell out of a burning old wooden structure. Not even brushing and flossing their teeth, David took charge by feeling the door for heat, in case it was on fire. It wasn't but the hallway was filled with smoke. David issued his next decree, "Crawl on the floor! There's less smoke there! Follow me!"

They crawled toward light. David banged on the first door they passed but there was no response. He stood and kicked the door in. A couple, still in bed, awoke to the stranger yelling "FIRE, GET UP AND FOLLOW US!!" Down the hallway they all crawled. David kept kicking in doors like an action figure.

Flames danced randomly from hiding spots in the building and the floor was so hot it felt like it was close to igniting. And something else, they were on the fourth floor, which was the top level. Reaching the exit, David opened the emergency door and looked down to see several fire trucks. A fireman with a megaphone said, "Come down the fire escape immediately!" Sensible advice.

By the time they got to the bottom, all four were coughing and gasping from smoke inhalation. Richard managed to get out a few words. "Jesus Christ, David! When did you become a fucking fireman?"

CHAPTER 43

A Digital Love Story

2011 – Marin County, California

Richard couldn't believe that he, of all people, was resorting to the electronic slings and arrows of an Internet dating site. It wasn't so much that he had a problem with the mechanics of it all. But his predilection for getting sidetracked by the minutiae of day-to-day life, in combination with his tendencies toward ascribing emotions to inanimate objects, seemed like a bad opening act for something as sensitive and uncertain as dating.

However, he didn't tiptoe into new scenarios, rather, he tended to immerse himself.

Richard was confused and hurt that his previous girlfriend couldn't make allowances for his "unique" and "counterintuitive" life philosophies. After two months of hurtin' and feelin' worthy of a Patsy Cline western ballad, he dusted himself off and did the unthinkable. He gave an Internet dating site his credit card number. The hunt for the subspecies commonly referred to as Woman was officially on.

He couldn't keep this news to himself. He went downstairs and knocked on the door of his friend and landlord, Downstairs David. David had himself just broken up with his girlfriend. But his mourning period seemed to last only twenty-four hours. A steady stream of women had been parading in and out (in more ways than one) of his home and this had been inspirational to Richard. Not because of the sex, but more for his ability to get on with his life, unlike Richard's predisposition to become lost in the forests of amour. Of course, this predisposition extended into just about all aspects of life, from overanalyzing what to cook for dinner to totally burying himself in statistical analysis of the game of baseball.

Downstairs David answered his door, happy to take a break from practicing his stand-up bass, which he made his living playing and teaching. "Upstairs Richard!" he said, giving him a hug. As was customary for these two, David soon pulled out his bong to help stimulate the conversation.

"I am surprised by all of the information that Match.com wants from me," Richard said. "Everything except the length of my schlong and I probably just missed that question."

Downstairs David wasn't much help with Internet dating, as he was from the old school of cold calling, otherwise known as pick-up bars. Nevertheless, he played the role of dating mentor in their relationship. "Richard, my friend!" he said. "I really think you should be broadening your horizons more. Think of it this way. You like wine, right? But sometimes you want a sweet Chardonnay. Other times, a thoughtful Cabernet in front of the fireplace. So, don't put all your eggs in one basket. The Internet attracts thoughtful, methodical women. If your schlong ain't so long, she'll just click on the dude with the correct tools in his toolbox. But at a bar, it's so much more spontaneous. And the tequila bar down the street is really convenient. I've had seriously good luck there. At least come with me and check it out. It's a good resource, dude."

"Okay, okay, I'll go with you just to see the master in action. Maybe this weekend?"

"Sure," David agreed. "But I'd love to see your Internet dating site. I've never looked at one before."

Richard reached into his backpack and pulled out his laptop. "I just so happen to have it here." He opened it to the dating site and passed it over.

David looked, shaking his head, "Dude, I can already see some serious issues here. Are you trying to meet a woman or are you trying to frighten them away? Because there's some serious shit in here."

"For example?"

"Well, in your profile... where do I start? Let me read it back to you. Sigmund Freud could have used it for a hypothesis about relationship avoidance. Honestly, the not-so-subliminal message you got going here is 'Step back or I'll shoot!' Are you even sure that you're ready to be dating yet?"

"Like I said, for example?" Richard replied defensively.

"Okay. Your profile is not so bad in a general way. You're presenting yourself as a sensitive and thoughtful guy that keeps getting roughed up in relationships, which is true. And women can go for this. Showing your feelings is good stuff. So, I'm happy with your 'I'm a scarred marriage survivor, licking my emotional wounds in between helping coach my seventeen-year-old son's soccer team approach.' That you just need to find someone who 'gets' you. But you move into the next section, which is 'What are you looking for from a woman?'"

Richard starting squirming on the couch and could only respond incoherently, "Yeah, but... I mean... the thing is..."

Downstairs David continued. "I mean, really. Is this the best you can do? 'Must have opposable thumbs and real teeth.' I mean... you could add that she needs to have a pulse as well, but I don't think this is going to serve the cause. And hey, I forgot to mention back in your profile, what did you say? Oh yeah, here it is. 'I think outside of the box. Like really outside of the box. I mean, I don't even know where the box is most of the time. At this point in my life, I doubt that I would even recognize the box if I stepped into it. I'd be like, what is this box-like thing? Would somebody take my box? Please take my box!' Richard, I'd definitely lose the whole box thing. It's weird."

Richard blew out some air in frustration. "Right. It's not like I'm married to the box."

"Great," Downstairs David said as he continued to read. "Lose the box." He read more, made a whistling sound that represented "Whoa! Okay. Under 'What unique or special trait do you want from a potential partner?' you responded, 'Must have a flat head to set my drinks on.' Okay, now that one just might be a deal killer. You should reconsider it because... well, it makes you seem ...what's the word?"

"Old-fashioned?" Richard chimed in.

"No, more like dangerous."

"It was a joke," Richard said in his own defense.

"Oh my God!" David gasped as he read on. "There's more! Under your photographs, it says that they are up to twenty-five years out of date! Richard, you're totally misrepresenting yourself."

"Well, not really. I guess the print is small, but my disclaimer speaks for itself."

"Richard, that photo was from high school!"

Even Richard was surprised. "Oh, oops, that one wasn't supposed to get in there. It's from my yearbook."

"And now it says you won't date women taller than 4' 11". Really?"

"Well, I'd reconsider that. It's just that I've had relationship problems with taller women in the past. What are you thinking? I'm getting too specific? That a hot-looking, flat-headed midget with opposable thumbs and real teeth who's compatible with my philosophy about thinking outside of boxes isn't going to be an easy match?"

As if in reply, Downstairs David reached for a bottle of scotch and filled both his and Richard's glasses. Neither spoke.

Neither the love mentor nor his student noticed a tall attractive woman, head decidedly not flat, who found Richard's box concerns slightly endearing, whose thumbs were indeed opposable, who had real teeth, who was sending out a message that transmitted as they sipped their drinks. Downstairs David looked at the screen and his mouth dropped open. The alert on his screen said, "Climb on out of your box before me and my opposable thumbs come over and pull you out!" It was signed Milly the Midget.

CHAPTER 44

Grubstake

1975 – Northern British Columbia

Richard sat in an unused part of the rail yard watching for hidden dangers, as David timed his freight train hop flawlessly. Richard cautiously poked his arm through a dense bush and waved farewell to his happy hobo friend. David waved back to the bush as the freight train slowly picked up speed, chugging to its next destination.

David's plan, to Richard's horror, was to continue south to California to visit his parents but, more importantly, to look into the possibility of attending university. After David's departure, Richard walked a short distance to the hiring office. There he was immediately hired, having met the rigorous criteria for the job of laborer, namely he was breathing.

His goal was to work once again at the mind-numbing job of removing and replacing old railroad track ties with new ones. He was trying to psych himself up for a two-month stint. That or work until his mind snapped, whichever came first, his objective being to save up his grubstake for his upcoming Stikine River-Wrangell Island wilderness expedition with his friend Rocky.

He was sent out to camp in a work train along with a dozen other new workers. When the train eventually stopped, Richard, as usual, found himself in the proverbial middle of nowhere. The general morale of this completely random group of individuals was not very high; collectively, they felt like prisoners being sent to Devil's Island. Being of half-German Jewish descent, Richard gravitated more to the expectation that the lot of them would be lined up against a wall and shot upon arrival. As far as that went, had the group of high-strung Italian foremen known that sprinkled amongst this contingent of fresh blood lurked soon-to-be-infamous individuals, they might have resorted to the machine-gun-option and cut their losses. But, as they were none the wiser, the twelve new arrivals were unceremoniously dropped off at their new lodgings, which consisted of a couple of railcar bunkhouses, where they were given fifteen minutes to powder their noses and get out to the speeder car and exchange business cards with the rest of the crew.

At a job like this, where you were working was academic since it was never in a town but, rather, in the wilderness between small towns as far apart as one hundred miles. As well, these crews were virtually nomadic and would relocate around three or four times a month. The crew was quite a bit larger than Richard had experienced his first time out, so he felt it best to keep a low profile until he got the lay of the land. Mind his own business, make his stash, then blast off back to his rendezvous with Rocky and the Stikine River.

Each day was punctuated by a Who's Who of the animal kingdom. Multiple grizzly and black bears as well as a considerable number of moose were routinely spotted. Not to mention bald eagles, various colored foxes, beavers, muskrats, lynx, wolverines, coyotes, and wolves.

The forty-man crew was still lorded over by the same quartet of quick-tempered Italian foremen. Like a Marine boot camp, the foremen started their hazing process to weed out the sensitive, thoughtful, and intelligent workers, who would soon quit, go back to school, become efficiency experts, and make a comfortable living figuring out ways to eliminate inefficient uses of labor, like these jobs. But for now, the foremen had the upper hand in the food chain.

"Not-a like that, you stupid idiot!" Foreman Mario screamed at two of the new guys that seemed to be buddies. He ripped the customized shovel out of the freckle-faced young man's hands and demonstrated as he yelled, "You don't–a do it like dat, you do it like-a dis!" Gravel flew in all directions as Foreman Mario demonstrated why he was still moving rocks from one spot to another spot in his golden years.

The freckled-faced man, whose name was Brad, glanced over at his friend when the foreman wasn't looking, yawning indifferently. He stuck his head in front of the foreman's and asked, "Mario, could you show me again how to tamp the gravel tight with the lining bar?"

Mario dropped the shovel and picked up Brad's lining bar from the side of the tracks, swearing the whole time. Rocks sparked as Mario expertly wielded the pointed-tipped five-foot-long metal pole. "Listen-a to me the first time and not-a the secunda time or somebody's gonna be hurt."

Brad's buddy George took it upon himself to translate for him. "I think what he meant, Brad, is if you don't understand what he said the first time, he's gonna beat you to death with his shovel."

Mario's Assistant Foreman, Foreman Mauro, irritated by these two guys not working, supplemented Mario's training program. "Hey, you two-a shut up and work and stop-a the chit-chatting before somebody hurts you."

Despite inane threats and disparaging comments, the new workers got the hang of the job and were soon pulling out railroad ties with a two-hooked tie puller, sliding replacement ties into place and securing them by tamping the gravel on both sides of each one, the grand finale was pounding metal spikes into the creosote-impregnated ties.

The new guys were understandably exhausted at the end of the day. After an impressive dinner of beef and vegetable stew with dinner rolls and a big salad, followed by an array of pies, cakes, and pudding, they found themselves sitting outside their bunkhouse getting to know each other. Each worker had a lawn chair, which added an element of civility to their otherwise monotonous existence. Richard found himself sitting with Brad, George and another fella.

"So, where you guys from?" Richard asked.

"Nova Scotia," George answered.

"We got fired at our last jobs," Brad added. "There aren't many jobs in Nova Scotia. Not like here."

"Where were you working when you got fired?" Richard inquired.

"At the lobster packing plant," Brad replied.

"I love lobster! Bet you guys ate it every day."

Brad said sheepishly with a wry smile on his face, "Yeah, it was a bit of a problem."

"More than a bit," his partner added. "That's how we got fired. We were eating too much lobster." They both chuckled.

"We sure ate good for a couple of weeks, though," Brad added. "Real good."

"Yeah, real good!" George concurred. The two sat silently, each with a distant smile.

"Wow!" Richard said.

The fourth man in the group, a long-haired, skinny guy with a long mustache and a southern accent, entered the conversation. "That's far out man. I'd have done the exact same thing. Right on."

The two Nova Scotians looked over at this guy with their mouths open. "Where you from?" Brad said. "I don't recognize your accent."

"Oh, well, I guess I didn't recognize yours either. Austin, Texas. My name's Tom. Tom Towerton." They all shook hands, chatted for a couple of hours, showered, and got some sleep. Breakfast was between five and six.

The next day the crew worked their usual ten-hour work day with a half-hour hot lunch break back at the cook shack. They returned to camp around five. All of the new guys were completely exhausted, as was normally the case with labor jobs. Brad and George continued to refer to Foreman Mario as "Foreman Mussolini" since he had continued with his all-day nattering about what lazy sloths they were.

But as the third and fourth days passed and the madness continued, something happened. On day five Foreman Mario's Management Team made sure that all employees were accounted for with their daily head-count, then loaded themselves into what was known as a "speeder car." This unit consisted of one small diesel-powered miniature train that ran on the rails and pulled about five or six trailers, each carrying five laborers. But today was different. Once satisfied with his count, Foreman Mario fired up his speeder car and drove a hundred yards down the tracks before realizing that the motorized first car had somehow disconnected from all of the others. The work crew was howling with laughter as the foreman returned. But by the time the bigwigs returned, the crew had become so quiet you could hear a pin drop. Foreman Mario was livid. Swearing in Italian, he demanded an immediate confession, which would have been equivalent to suicide.

"Okay, some-a smart guy gonna get a fired after he gonna go get his ass-a kicked! Porca Madonna!!!" But the troublemakers knew better than to open their mouths. This would have been ill-advised, and a confession wasn't forthcoming. As far as that went, it wasn't clear which individuals were part of this conspiracy, so the crew couldn't rat out their fellow crewmates even if they had wanted to.

But over the next few days, just when you'd think that the troublemakers might have been captured and summarily executed, a recurrence would take place with the same resulting calamity. However, certain crewmembers were finding it impossible not to break into laughter, thereby incurring the wrath of the foreman, who interpreted this as an act of treason. Foreman Mario was not amused. "Okay, funny guy, have-a yer big laugh but if-a you one of the assholes that-a be playin-a around-a with my speeder car-a, I'm-a gonna cut yer balls off-a." But without a smoking gun, no firings took place. No balls were detached.

Of course, Richard had already seen Brad and George pulling the pin that connected each speeder car to the rest of the unit. The two had an uncanny ability to notice when the Quartet had let down their guard. But the stakes were becoming increasingly dangerous as it was apparent that the punishment for whomever was involved in this heinous crime would eventually be capital punishment. Luckily, the criminal or criminals in question began to wind down their operation. When the two Nova Scotians quit after six weeks, Richard decided the $3,000 that the railway owed to him was sufficient for him to take another early retirement as well. He and this Tom Towerton character caught a ride back to Prince George together.

The first evening back, the two went down to the bar at the Prince George Hotel. After knocking back a couple of "suds," as Tom referred to beer, he opened up about how he was able to usually avoid working regular labor jobs, instead working at his own business that could be surprisingly lucrative. He claimed that he would pay a couple of different people to smuggle pot across the Mexican border near Tijuana. He described some of his trade secrets. "Man, I got all sorts of people crossing for me. Peg-Leg Sally can hold about five pounds of ganga in her hollow leg.

"I'd be too nervous to do that. I really can't imagine doing that."

"The time to be nervous is during the planning stages. Once you're done planning, being nervous is a waste of time." By the time they parted ways, Richard had invested five hundred dollars in Tom's smuggling business, with a guaranteed profit of an additional thousand. Richard never heard from him again. He often wondered if Towerton had forgotten to mention his sideline business as a flim-flam man.

C.N.R. paid within two days this time. With his bank account bursting with money, Richard set off to Alaska. First, he hopped a freight train to Prince Rupert, the northernmost piece of Canadian Pacific Coast real estate, and grabbed the ferry back to Rocky's place on Wrangell Island. What was in store for him, Richard had not a clue.

CHAPTER 45

Picking up Women
and Setting Them Down

2011 – Marin County, California

There comes a time when a single middle-aged man must think counter-intuitively when it comes to dating. For Richard, the time and effort in Internet dating was taking a toll on his mental well-being and a time-sucker. When Downstairs David invited him to his favorite pick-up bar, he couldn't look a gift horse in the mouth. Single men would pay for this expertise. Richard got this instruction in cold call dating for free.

They walked a few blocks down to a time-proven pick-up bar which, to the uninitiated, looked like all the other watering holes in the vicinity. Richard was like a duck—calm on top, desperately paddling for his life underneath. Close to their destination, Downstairs David briefed him. "I've had real good luck meeting women here, especially on weekdays for some unknown reason. What you are going to need to do is follow my lead. It's sort of like fishing—sometimes they bite and sometimes they don't. I don't really go out trying to get laid, although it does happen sometimes. The old paradigm for picking up women has changed. Men are the new women."

"Men are the new women?" Richard replied. "What the hell is that supposed to mean?"

"Think about it for a second. Nowadays, women often make more money than men. Lots of them don't want a husband, or even a steady boyfriend. They just want to go out and do the usual stuff that we all want. Restaurants, dancing, hiking, riding, and more often than not, having sex."

"Okay, okay, that makes sense, and anyways, I'm mostly here just to see the master in action," Richard said. "I've got my Internet dating thing going on and I think it is a better fit for me. But since my batting average is kind of pathetic at the moment, I can't start closing doors. So, unless we change venues to the Happy Acres Retirement Home, I might just be playing with myself in a dimly lit corner of the room. Let's face it, the women that you are pursuing are going to be ten to twenty years younger than my target age. I don't know if forty-five to fifty-five-year-old women even go to bars to meet men."

"You'll see. They're out there. Don't start getting all negative on me. You're an attractive guy. They'll be swarming around you like bees." Richard took a deep breath as they entered, trying to calm his nerves.

The upscale Mexican restaurant also had an extra-large sports bar area. They sat right at the bar, which, not so coincidentally, was full of singles of all ages. David instinctively found two seats beside two attractive young women. The two men ordered a round of margaritas and some chips. Within a couple of minutes David had broken the ice with these two women, who both looked young enough to be Richard's daughters. It was dawning on Richard that quite a few women looked young enough to be his daughter. He had to suppress some primal instinct to ask if their parents knew where they were. But to prevent being ostracized for his age (he was fifty-six), he joined their conversation. "Hi," he said. "My name's Richard. I'm David's parole officer. Don't let the electronic monitoring device around his ankle affect your first impression of him. Before we left the halfway house, he promised me he wouldn't attack any more women that he meets in bars, so I figure he's completely safe. You two are in grave danger but he's completely safe." They laughed as did David. Richard felt like he helped David's ambitions to not come home empty-handed. Conversation ensued. A second round of margaritas was dispensed.

From out of nowhere, Richard found himself asking their ages. David choked on an ice cube. Everything went into a dreamlike state. The two young women smiling, embarrassed, revealed they were both thirty. Richard said if he were thirty, he'd climb on the bar and scream, "I'm only thirty!" In spite of his unspeakable faux pas, ten minutes later the two women had provided David with their phone numbers and waved good-bye. David slowly turned toward Richard. "Okay, I salvaged that one, but in the future, you have to promise that you will never ask a woman her age again."

"Sorry about that. It just sort of came out of my mouth. The moment I spoke, I knew that I had done a very bad thing. Could have been worse, though. I almost asked them what time they were supposed to be home by."

David looked genuinely worried. "Jesus, Richard! You are going to single-handedly wreck my entire operation here." He gestured with his arms up in the air, looking around the room. "This represents a lot of hard work, so if you don't know what to say, better to just look mysterious or moody."

"I will never ask a woman at a bar her age again. Ever! You have my word." Richard slumped his head in shame.

"Don't go and be neurotic about it. It's just one of the rules, that's all." David knocked back a large swig from his Margarita.

"Well, you seem to have done well tonight. They are both totally hot and had great personalities," Richard said in awe.

"They were okay," David responded nonchalantly. Richard was amazed at his lack of enthusiasm. "I might call the blonde."

"Might?" Richard said, surprised. "I don't know what you are looking for, but it sure seemed to me that both of them had it."

"Richard, Richard, Richard. You have so much to learn, my son." David finished off his drink and they walked home. Indeed, he had so much to learn.

CHAPTER 46

Fish of Wrath

1975 – Wrangell Island, Alaska

It was the best of times, it was the worst of times. Richard had just arrived on the shores of Wrangell Island, his backpack bursting with supplies, weaponry, and last minute survival acquisitions. He threw on his pack and tramped directly to Rocky's family home, eager to rendezvous with his new wilderness partner for their journey up the Stikine River.

He arrived at their home but it was gone. Where the old house had been was now air. Disoriented, Richard looked down the cliff to the ocean, where the shattered remains of the former home lay at rest. The ocean bathing what was once Rocky's family home. He spotted a tin can at his feet and kicked it off the cliff, down on top of the old house carcass. A flock of ravens flew out from an overhang. He turned and walked down the narrow, carless, road for a block when he saw a man in his yard staring at him. Richard walked over to him.

"Hi. Hey, I just got off the ferry and I couldn't help but notice that my friend's house has relocated itself into the ocean."

The wiry middle-aged man looked at Richard as if he was from Mars. "Yep," he said dryly. "I guess that's what you'd call a mobile home."

"Well, can you tell me if any of my friends were hurt?"

"Nobody got hurt. Maybe their feelings were kinda hurt," he said without apparent interest. "That family's been in nothing but trouble since they got here. So, they took their bird. They took their bird," he repeated.

Richard grew impatient. "They took their bird? They never had a bird."

"They were trouble ever since they got here, so they took their bird." He turned to go when Richard realized "Oooohhhh! You mean they flew the coop! By the way, nobody says 'took their bird.' You know, like, why wreck a perfectly good, time-tested analogy if it's still working. It's 'flew the coop'!"

The scrawny-scruffy guy tossed his cigarette onto the ground and flattened it with his heel. The lines on his face marked him as permanently pissed off. Richard wasn't going to have a long and meaningful friendship with Mr. Scrawny-Scruffy. He walked to a different address a couple of blocks away where a young woman named Carol lived. He met her on the upper deck of the ferry where she had the lounge chair adjoining his, and they hit it off.

She listened to Richard's version of the mobile home tale and asked, "Are you still going to try and find Rocky?"

"No. He had my address in British Columbia and the scrawny-scruffy guy told me that it's been over a month since Rocky's house collapsed and he never wrote me, even though it was a 600-mile trip and took a lot of planning. Sounds like he's got an awful lot on his plate. I wouldn't even know how to find him if I wanted to. So, I think I'm going to just take my bird."

Carol looked at Richard with a puzzled expression and said, "Take your what?"

CHAPTER 47

Traveling Solo

2015 – Nicaragua

Richard sat on a hard wooden chair overlooking the vast Lago Nicaragua. The view was grand but the noise from the waves drove him to a fourth piña colada. He wondered how this sound became associated with pleasure when it drove him mad.

He looked at his drink, just in time to see its pink umbrella, along with a skewered pineapple and two green grapes, helpless, blow underneath a fellow tourist's chair. The pineapple took a direct hit, flailing in pineapple agony, its life flashed before its eyes. Wounded but indifferent to pain, two green grapes rolled close by. They were the survivors. "It helps being round." Richard thought to himself. They rolled along slowly as the diabolical wind machine from Hell continued its quest for global domination, one pineapple, one green grape at a time. At last the grapes found a resting place wedged up against a flowering shrubbery, gasping for air. He thought he saw one of the grapes flip the bird at the wind machine. He decided to quit the tropical drinks before he got dragged into the melee. Shame about the pineapple, though. What a place to end it all. What with this god-forsaken wind...?

A voice broke into his world of tropical madness. "Where you from?" Richard sized up the situation. There was no escape. Once somebody got in a "Where you from?" you'd be interrogated with the typical traveler's checklist of mind-numbing questions. He wasn't so much cynical, as a social avoidance expert. Terrie insisted he travel while her school year ended. His writer's block caused him to rant so much, she thought about sneaking up behind him with a rag drenched in formaldehyde. Not to hurt him, just to make the noise stop. Even temporarily.

"A little time apart," she said. "Like two months. I'll catch up with you in Vietnam. It'll be good for us." He wondered if she had the wind machine installed to protect others from his complaints.

"Where am I from?" he replied, to buy some time. He thought, *where'd you like me to be from?* Frustrated, he approached the truth. "Do you mean which planet or which time period?"

The inquisitor smirked and said, "Both. It sounds like those piña coladas have got to you, though. My name's Pete."

"Well, Pete, before I was banished by my girlfriend for two months of so-called rest and relaxation, I lived on the planet Earth in a place far, far away called San Francisco. I believe it was 2015, but I'd have to check the scratch marks on my cell wall to verify that."

"If you drink enough of those puppies before lunch, I hear they can cause hallucinations. Better watch out." Pete suggested.

Richard glanced toward the grapes, but they remained indifferent, frozen in position. "My name's Richard, Pete. Not actually Richard Pete, just Richard." He double-checked the grapes, but they hadn't moved. You aren't fooling me, he thought to himself.

Pete fooled Richard, however, by bypassing the usual twenty questions and going straight to what was on his mind. "Ohmygaaaawd," he drawled as three long-legged young women strolled by. "I get the black-haired one, you can have your pick of the two blondes, and we'll share the other one. Deal?"

Richard checked them out but was still distracted by the grapes. "Sure, Pete. You go, boy! I reckon they are only thirty-five to forty years younger than the two of us. If I swear off the piña coladas, can I have a hit off of whatever it was you were smoking?"

"Hey, man," the Pete-ster continued. "Haven't you heard? For guys, sixty is the new thirty."

Richard felt his ears perk up. "As a matter of fact, I've heard that statement twice in the past couple of months.

"But seriously Pete, we're both about the same age. Look at us. Look at them. Darwin had some thoughts about perpetuating species, and we are no longer good breeding material. You know, when big young male walruses chase off the big old males, that's us being chased off. And that was over twenty years ago when that took place. Sure, I guess there are always exceptions, like blind or mentally deranged women but at some point, we got to look in the mirror and say, 'Nooooooooooo!!!' At least, that's my two cents worth. I think that all us old walruses can do is hide behind the sand dunes and watch and grunt forlornly."

"Wow, you paint a pretty bleak picture, dude. Maybe we only get the sick and dying now, but until I breathe my last breath, I'm still going to try to fight my way back into the mating circle for one more kick of the can. Or flipper, whatever."

"Pete, I think that Charles Darwin would have been proud of you." He picked up his umbrella-less drink and passed it over. Another group of stunners walked by, oblivious to the two ancient men. Richard quietly clapped his hands together and grunted "Or-or-or-or-or."

"That's a seal noise, not a walrus," Pete said to nobody in particular.

The waves crashed. Deafening. The grapes were nowhere to be seen.

CHAPTER 48

Mountaineering on LSD for Dummies

1975 – Olympic Park, Washington

All three of them had extensive backpacking experience. And all three had successfully navigated many trails in Olympic National Park in Northwestern Washington. It wasn't unforeseen that a problem or two might crop up, forcing them to change plans on the fly. That's where their collective camping experiences should have proved invaluable. But as was often the case with this cracker-jack team, hallucinogenic drugs gummed up the works.

Two conflicting backpacking strategies had come into vogue at that time, one referred to as "ultra-lite backpacking" and the other as "technical climbing." Ultra-lite was in reference to a philosophy that encouraged its practitioners to obsessively reduce the weight of their backpacks, even by a matter of ounces. Technical climbing involved the use of ropes, special climbing boots, carabiners and pitons, for backpacking mixed with climbing.

These issues were discussed with a three-way-mail-out between Tom, David, and Richard, the self-proclaimed Boy-Palz, who had been practitioners of the "Chaos" backpacking method, whereby the packing was done at the very last minute (typically while the balance of the camping contingent waited outside with the engine running), in a rush.

"Herr Miller," Tom wrote, "To summarize, The Evolution of Backpacking Ultra-Lite...

"Eliminate jug of wine. Too heavy, replace with... bag of weed... eliminate bag of weed, too heavy, replace with microdot LSD, eating impossible on hallucinogens, eliminate food. Finally, eliminate all clothing and backpacks.

"Question: Do wilderness parks allow people to run screaming down the trails naked? I know that they let you sleep anywhere."

David later responded by mail, "I think that we can eliminate the need to sleep if we are to follow thru with your mountain-madness itinerary. Dogs have to be on leash in wilderness areas. Not sure about the regulations pertaining to naked madmen."

And so, it came to pass that the three, sticking with the time-tested Chaos strategy, headed down a remote trail which was a new part of the park for them, lulled into complacency by the LSD they had ingested at the trailhead parking lot. Their map's symbol indicating the rock-climbing cliffs that were located intermittently along the trail also looked like the symbol indicating outhouses.

This wasn't a problem for the three, except they could never find outhouses. In what could have been the first study of the relationship between rock climbing without equipment, under the influence of psychedelic drugs, the men found picking their way up rock cliffs simply a mind-over-matter problem. After a couple of hours, they reached the summit, all the way laughing at nothing.

They settled down, mesmerized by the view of alpine forest and meadows. The sound of rock climbers tapping pitons and snapping carabiners grew, as they methodically made their way up toward the summit.

Exquisitely attired rock climbers reached the top and whooped and yelped celebratory noises of conquest. Finished congratulating each other, one of them said to the ultra-ultra-lite-headed trio, "I can't help but notice that you don't have any climbing equipment. Which side of the mountain did you come up?"

The three looked at each other, not sure where they had come from. They all pointed, but in three different directions. That about did it for the rock climbers and they headed off to set up camp down a way along a meadow.

Far away from the incoherent Chaos crew.

CHAPTER 49

Have Yourself a Merry Little Heart Attack

2015- San Francisco, California

Richard woke up in a drugged state covered in chocolate brownie crumbs. Defying gravity, he summoned the energy to push his calorie-saturated body skyward. He groaned out the names of two of the guilty parties, his brother and sister, as his torso approximated a ninety-degree angle to the center of the earth. "Robert! Kathleen!" he called, to no avail. The two evil cooks were beyond earshot or chose to ignore him. He wondered if this was how a Brontosaurus felt after eating a delicious hillside of grass. Or just before going extinct.

He flopped back horizontal onto his mattress, not sure how he ended up asleep on the floor two feet away but suspecting the weight of food in his gut was the culprit. After bellowing pathetically one last time, he finally managed to get up. He could now hear sounds of human activity emanating from the kitchen. He pulled on some loose clothing and waddled down the dark hallway in his house.

Staggering into the kitchen, he saw Robert and Kathleen sitting at the kitchen table. To his amazement, they were discussing food.

Kathleen was concluding the meeting. "So, it's settled. We will force Terrie to cook butternut squash ravioli and bruschetta, even if we have to resort to blackmail. I'll make the pork dish, you're gonna make a chocolate torte, and Richard's gonna..." Kathleen only then noticed Richard's presence. "...and we'll get Richard to burn some vegetables over the mesquite grill until they taste good."

Richard spoke as if he had just witnessed an atrocity. "Don't you people ever stop talking about or preparing food? Aren't you just a bit concerned that somebody's going to have a food injury of some kind? Personally, I think the reason I didn't wake up this morning was because I was in a brownie-induced coma. We just can't go on living like this!" He put his head in his hands, trying to regain his composure.

Richard sat at the table while Robert went to fetch him some coffee. "Poor boy. Here you go," he said, placing a strong macchiato in front of him. "It will all feel better soon."

Kathleen looked over at this touching scene of male bonding with a skeptical grimace. "Suck it up, Richard. And your coffee, too."

Richard kept his head pointed into his drink, pointed his middle finger into the air, and said, "Good morning." Still speaking into his coffee, he continued, "I'm trying to understand why you two are planning another calorie extravaganza when we just finished Hanukkah-Christmas dinner last night. Speaking for myself, I'm planning on having my stomach pumped after I finish my coffee."

Kathleen looked at Richard, incredulous, "Doesn't the term 'post-holiday party' have any significance to you? I think we're at thirteen bodies and counting."

Richard put his head back into his hands, moaning, "Thirteen? That's ominous. So, who are the thirteen gluttons? Fatty, Piggy, Warthogster..."

Terrie staggered into the room, looking like a force-fed foie gras goose. She continued the list, "Hippo, Elephantus, Giganticus, Enormicus..."

"That makes seven," Richard calculated. "Then there's the four of us, so eleven. Terrie's two kids and my three were showing signs of food fatigue last night, so I don't think you can count on them."

"I'm checking into Jenny Craig's fat farm clinic, so count me out," Terrie added. "I won't be a party to this holiday trough-slurping madness."

Just then Robert walked over to the table with a bowl of chocolate torte batter. "Kathleen and I know your children better than you guys do. They're coming." He dipped a spatula into the bowl and handed a taste to Terrie. "Just try this first before you make any rash decisions," he said like a poker pro showing his royal flush.

Terrie looked around the room, scanning to see if somebody would throw her a life jacket, but no assistance was offered. She licked the spatula clean and said, "That is good chocolate!"

Richard by now had pulled his face out of his hands and said, "Why tempt her? She's going to a fat farm in a minute. They'll just make her vomit it up anyways. Give me that sucker!" he snarled, pulling the spatula out of Terrie's clutch.

Robert administered his chocolate opiate concoction as Richard's tail wagged.

Kathleen got back on point. "Terrie, we're gonna need you to make your delicious butternut squash ravioli and bruschetta if you want so much as a crumb of Robby's chocolate torte. And that goes for you too, Richard! You gotta make your nummy barbecued veggies. Capisci?"

"Yeah, okay, okay," Richard answered, feeling battered as he licked.

"Capisco, capisco," Terrie replied and said, "I wonder if Jenny Craig would come over if we invited her? I mean, she's only human... isn't she?"

CHAPTER 50

AARP

2015 – San Francisco, California

"If you buy their magazine subscription, do you get a new body?" Richard asked, wincing as he pulled the electric heating pad tighter against the pinched nerve in his neck.

"I really doubt it," Terrie said, not looking up from The Economist.

"What's the point?"

Ten seconds elapsed before she muttered, "Yeah, really."

"Frankly, there should be a law against them being able to send a free issue without my permission. Just having it sitting on the coffee table makes me feel like erectile dysfunction is just around the corner."

"It's usually in your pants," Terrie mumbled in her lowest mumble setting.

"I heard that," Richard snapped.

"Well... at least your hearing still works," she said as she walked into the kitchen to make a couple more espresso drinks.

"That does it!" he said, lunging at the issue in question. As he crumpled up the magazine, he noticed that the cover photograph was of Clint Eastwood. Curious, he unwrinkled it. He tried to smooth Clint's face but the paper wrinkles he created looked age-appropriate. "Sorry about that, Clint," he said to himself as he put the magazine back down. "But even you can't win an argument with the grim reaper."

He walked over to the front door. "The AARP should change the name of their magazine to The Grim Reaper," he called out to Terrie as he went out into the garden.

Terrie continued her reading and spoke without hearing. "I thought they already had."

That night Richard dreamt Clint Eastwood was stalking him. Richard was silently swimming upstream in a narrow mangrove swamp, while Clint was stealthily paddling a canoe. Behind the canoe, water creatures were working in tandem with the movie actor. Jungle noises filled the air. It dawned on Richard the scarlet-headed macaws were communicating with Clint, relaying his whereabouts. The water creatures behind the canoe splashed out of the water, revealing themselves to be a large pair of killer seals. They closed the gap between themselves and Richard bellowing out, "AARP! AARP! AARP!" as they swam.

Richard awoke in a cold sweat. Terrie remained asleep beside him, unaware of the imminent danger they were in. Richard's heartbeat slowed as he lay in darkness. It was only a dream, he thought. The AARP were controlling his dreams now. He remembered how his father and mother lived in a retirement community named Oakmont. Their literature could have been written by the AARP. His father referred to the community as "Croakmont." Somebody was always croaking.

The Grim Reaper. AARP. He closed his eyes. As he drifted off the last thing he remembered was a killer seal poking his head out of the water and barking out "Something's rotten in Croakmont!"

CHAPTER 51

Evans Farm

1976 – Birch Lake, British Columbia

On a whim, they deviated from their original destination and, after a few hours of hitchhiking, were dropped off at a junction of two small dirt roads.

"Gentlemen, here we are at your junction." The old farmer who had picked them up confidently stopped right in the middle of the road, leaving no doubt that this was the end of the line for the civilized world. "Peter Evans lives a couple miles down at the end of this here Birch Lake Road," he said, pointing down what looked more like a donkey trail than an actual road. "If you see a large high-rise apartment building with a mall next to it, well then you've gone four hundred miles too far south and you're in Vancouver."

With no traffic on Birch Lake Road, they hiked the last couple miles until the road ran directly into a finger of land with a lake on either side. A large old log home overlooked both lakes. They made their way up to the front door, startling a bewitching older teenage girl with flaming red hair, who didn't greet many visitors. In spite of her shy demeanor, it took great effort for her to suppress a big smile.

"We got a ride hitchhiking from a guy named John Dafoe, and he suggested to us that your farm might be in need of a couple of farmhands," Richard said.

To speak to her about an adult topic was more than the sixteen-year-old Holly Evans could bear. "I'll go get my parents," she said with a laugh and smile.

Within minutes, they were being fed coffee and sandwiches by Holly, her mother Lynn, and Lynn's three-year-old daughter Arianna, who clung to Lynn's blue jeans and viewed the strangers suspiciously. They were an unusually attractive family, prone to outbreaks of laughter. Presiding over the meal was Peter Evans himself. Born and raised in this same log home, he was a charming man who lived to converse and debate issues. But now, he was discreetly inquiring about their backgrounds. He took a keen interest in many topics and was particularly interested in their ethnicities. When Richard disclosed that his mother's side was British and his father's European Jew, Peter concluded, "So you are half-Englishman and half-Jew. I believe that the term for that is an improved Englishman."

Richard laughed tentatively and said, "Well, I'm not so sure how my mother would feel about that description."

"I suppose that would be true," Peter said in a certain humorous-serious way. His voice was gruff, yet he enunciated as clearly as an Oxford English professor. The gravitas of his narrative was enhanced by his slow cadence.

He cut a dashing figure, his tucked in red and black plaid shirt seemed more distinguished on Peter than on his fellow farmers, with his sheathed moose-antler–handled hunting knife displayed on his matching moose leather belt, pants, and moccasins, the pièce de résistance being a colorful wool tuque with ear flaps that Lynn had knitted for him.

Despite the job interview, all parties were enjoying each other's company. Peter offered to take them on a tour of his property, which they happily accepted. As per John

Dafoe, the Evans farm was indeed like stepping back in time. Peter's property was forested with birch and poplar trees, with pockets of evergreens for contrast. The farm totaled six hundred forty acres, forty of which were covered with small grass fields used for grazing or winter hay. Two acres were reserved for a garden.

There were two beautiful lakes on the property. Birch Lake and Crystal Lake. There were three small charming log guest cabins, an old plank barn and a woodworking shop. The shop had been occupied by several geese whose work ethics were apparently not up to standards. Goats roamed everywhere, due to bad fencing practices and goats with wings.

There was no electricity, no motorized vehicle and no tractor of any kind. Kerosene lamps were the only source of light. For the few provisions that had to be purchased with hard currency, Peter would either walk six miles to the Nukko Lake General Store or, on rare occasions for larger orders, hitchhike thirty miles on a dirt road to Prince George. Both procedures had drawbacks. The Nukko Lake General Store he referred to as "the Nukko Lake Holdup," allegedly outrageously expensive and to be avoided as much as humanly practical. Time revealed, however, this conclusion was based on an ancient feud not reality.

The one concession Peter made to modernization was a chainsaw for cutting firewood, the only source of heat for the many log buildings. "If I had another lifetime, I'd figure out a way to have the oxen cut our firewood too, but that will have to wait until my next incarnation."

Throughout the tour, they walked in the forest along ox trails that wound in between the trees. Trees that Peter studied to become pieces of furniture, oxen yokes, sleigh runners, alphorns and fiddle parts.

Arriving at a grassy meadow the two stars of the show, Felix and Keshla, were grazing. The pair of oxen stood motionless, chewing their cud as Peter strolled up to them and gave each a rub and pat on their necks. What impressed the "job applicants" about these two creatures was their immense size and elegant horns.

"Now that's a set of horns!" Richard said impressed. "Look at the size of those mothers!"

Peter explained, "Normally, oxen are smaller and have their horns removed. An ox is a castrated bull, specifically selected for working. It is much safer for both the bull and the castrator if this operation is done when the animal is young. Less than three months old. It's more humane to do it that way, but the owner of these two creatures, an enormous fella by the name of Monte Williams, waited until they were full grown before he turned them into oxen. Several years prior, he had come to talk with me about his plans, and I told him how it should be done, and he did it the opposite way of what I had told him. Monte also had big plans to remove their horns, after he'd castrated them, but then lost interest and showed up at our front door wanting to make a deal. I told Monte I would take the two oxen in exchange for some hay. Monte had had enough of them by that point, and he knew that I needed a new team, so that's the way I got them. When you wait until they are full grown, they aren't docile like ones that are cut when they're young. These two are well trained but can get feisty. Never trust them completely. Especially mind their horns! They can put your eye out in a heartbeat."

Felix and Keshla enjoyed themselves as Richard and David scratched them. The two travelers made eye contact with each other, then took turns nodding in the affirmative. David spoke first. "Peter, if you think we would be compatible with you and your family, we'd be interested in helping you out with all of your projects."

"Yeah," said Richard, seconding the motion. "We'd love to learn from you in exchange for our labor. We're real hard workers."

Peter spoke slowly, "I also think that we should give it a try. I think that your vibrations will fit in quite well here."

Peter announced to the beaming smiles of his family that "We have struck a grand bargain, and these two gentlemen will be part of our extended family." The house was just as dark as night time during the daytime, but it seemed to have lit up for just a moment. Lynn gave them hugs and said, "Welcome to your new home!"

Too shy for hugs, Holly made up for it by laughing and smiling as she said, "Welcome!"

CHAPTER 52

Mass Murderers Anonymous

2015- San Francisco, California

"You asked me to give you an opinion, I'm giving you an opinion," Terrie replied. "But, you know, your desperation to deliver finished product to The Daily Blabbermouth is at odds with the reality that, philosophically, your opinions are totally at odds with theirs. The only thing you and the Blabber seem to have in common is that you both have only the most tenuous grasp on reality. Which is a refreshing departure from any other news source. If your deadline is fast approaching and you are forced to borrow a few thoughts to satisfy the machine out in Oklahoma, so be it. Let me have another look at your Rant and I'll highlight any lines that fall into the lawsuit alert category."

Richard passed over the paperwork, thought twice, pulled back, reconsidered, and, against his better judgment, handed it to Terrie, inch by inch.

"Thatta boy. No one's gonna harm you. Pass the paper to Terrie now. That's a good boy." She snatched the paperwork out of Richard's hand. "Man, you can be high maintenance sometimes! Come back to my office in a half-hour and we'll have a little chat." She sat down in her soft chair and reread the column with her yellow highlighter poised in the ready position.

RICHARD RANTS

Mass Murderers Anonymous

Readers—There comes a time in every journalist's career when he or she looks into the mirror and asks, "Is this the piece of writing that is going to be the end of my professional career, or am I just ahead of the times?" The following is a short story whose sole purpose is to show sympathy to a group of individuals that, to date, have not been seen as being worthy of any compassion.

(Note: This story was documented exactly two years after California voters approved Proposition 666. This was a cost-cutting bill specifically designed to reduce taxes by negating prior laws that formerly sent mass murderers to death by the gas chamber and creating a new system of mandatory treatment centers for rehabilitation. Individual murder also became a misdemeanor.)

"Hi. My name is Kevin and I am a mass murderer." The sound of coffee cups being topped up and sugar spoons tinkling against them filled the air as people sat down to listen to another member of this elite club. "I'm happy to report that I am three months without one drop of blood on my hands." The sound of polite supportive approval-clapping arrived on cue.

Kevin drooped for a moment, as he summoned the strength to continue, his voice breaking with emotion. "I just want to say that I love you all for how you've helped me transition back to a life without killing. I know that I will always be a mass murderer, but with a little help from the big guy upstairs and his angels in this room, I am starting to believe that even I can kick the habit. Like, at first, I thought, well, maybe I can just murder someone on Friday nights, and that this type of controlled mayhem would enable me to live a 'normal' life." He put his hands in the air to stress the quotation marks around the word "normal." "But as time moved on, it slowly dawned upon me that for most people in our society, well, most people just don't want mass murderers in their communities, let alone in their own homes. At first, I'd rationalized that, like, well, I hate country music, lots of us hate country music, right?" Heads nodded in the audience. "My logic would go like, they get to kill my soul, my spirit, my drive to continue living, with lines like, 'hot pants and panty hose, that's where all my gravy goes,' that's supposed to be somehow okay, but me hunting down my next kill is soooo much worse! I mean, how subjective is that?"

The meeting team leader, Jeffrey, decided to turn the conversation in a new direction. "I think this a good time for me to remind you, Kevin, and those of you nodding out there, that there is a substantial difference between slaughtering innocent people versus slaughtering somebody's ear drums. Sure, it may feel comparable to many of you. Hell, as far as that goes, I used to think that it was open season on country music singers all year long, before M.M.A. came into my life." (A few "praise the lords" urged him on.) "But over time, I think all of you are going to eventually realize that murdering even a single individual is one too many. And I am including Country Western singers as well. I really am." An ominous murmuring filled the room as members quietly debated amongst themselves. "Kevin, please continue."

"Well, Jeffrey, this is only my fifth meeting, so I'm still trying to wrap my arms around the philosophy of M.M.A. So then, let me get this straight, it's okay to slaughter a tune, but not an individual. Hmmm. I guess there is a difference. I see, I see. Thank you." Kevin sat down.

The man next to Kevin stood up. "Hi, I'm Bill and I also am a mass murderer. And this is my first meeting." Polite applause welcomed Bill. "I've only been here for a few minutes and I'm already blown away by what I've heard. It has been a struggle for me, though. It is so counterintuitive to let Country Western singers just sing to their heart's content, without any response from the mass murderer community. Wow! Okay, I'll just accept that recommendation at face value even though every fiber of my body is saying, 'Not on my watch!'"

Jeffrey stood up. "Bill, believe me, you're not the first mass murderer to struggle with this particular issue. As far as that goes, others have said the same thing about Tea Party members, mimes, accordion players, there's a long list. But who are we to play the role of God? Deciding who lives and who dies."

Bill stared at Jeffrey. "Jeffrey," he said in a stern tone, "keep your facts straight. I am God. That is indisputable." His tone of voice suddenly changed into a creepy, almost screaming voice. "And anyone in this room who has a problem with this fact, well, do yourself a favor and don't reveal yourself to me. Because you are taking God's name in vain. And ye shall be struck down by lightening! And ye shall burn for eternity in Hell! Lord have mercy!" The room exploded into applause.

Bill sat down and a decrepit eighty-year-old woman stood up in his place. "I am Lilly. Like the flower. I am also a mass murderer. But like many flowers that can kill, the potency of my poison is diminishing, and so it feels right to bring my career to an end. Do I want just one more curtain call? Anyone who says differently in this room is a goddamn liar. Right?" The room broke into thunderous applause. Lilly was their darling. "But times have changed. Cannibals aren't cannibalizing anymore, and we aren't supposed to be terrorizing communities, either. Maybe it's progress, maybe it's just a random event that we'll look back on one day shaking our heads. Only time will tell. But it beats the hell out of frying like a pork chop on Old Sparky, or choking down on the State of California's Smokey Joe, so suck it up, ladies and gentlemen, this is the new reality. Our glory days are over. Deal with it. If these meetings aren't enough, buy some stuffed toys and work out your inner feelings with a knife and a Barbie doll. Whatever it takes. The people of California have spoken that they need to take their fiscal knife and cut costs. We have to change. We have to modify our behavior. Sure, it's gonna sting. Yes, you will feel like your expressive side is being suppressed. But if I can do it at my age, you can also."

Pandemonium broke out as the crowd gave her a euphoric standing ovation.

Jeffrey stood up, still clapping. "Thank you, Lilly darling. As always, you have given all of us enough food for thought to carry over until the next meeting." Lilly curtsied and meandered over to the coffee pot.

(Note to readers: Richard Morgenstern covers subject matter that other editorialists rarely explore. He always seeks out the truth regardless of its controversial nature.)

Terrie spoke. "At least your work is consistent."

"Thank you!" Richard said, always eager for praise from his toughest critic.

"Consistently insane," Terrie clarified. "Have you gone mad? How do you think this stuff up? One day it's speculation about wild animals trying to take over the planet, the next, a therapy group for mass murderers. How do you ever expect to build a readership when you keep poking them up their yin-yang's with all this wing-nut stuff? If you feel too constrained by The Daily Blabbermouth, why not look into starting your own newspaper. You could call it Insane Asylum Weekly."

"Well," Richard said as he exhaled dejectedly, "as they say in the business, Back to page 1."

CHAPTER 53

Oxy-Morons

1976 – Birch Lake, British Columbia

Richard and David turned out to be excellent ox drivers. Between plowing, disking, and harrowing the soil, they found time to skid some birch and poplar logs from the forest for the winter firewood supply. The oxen, Felix and Keshla, knew the drill; work hard from spring through fall, then have a kick-back winter. A fair trade for man and beast.

But the world of humans and work animals didn't come without a cost. Especially with jumbo-sized beasts of burden with relatively small brains. A conglomeration of impulsive behavior, bizarre culinary choices, and a failure to really try to look at situations from a human perspective made for misunderstandings.

Warm and sunny, a sweet fragrance of balsam fir permeating the air, David emerged from his cabin, stretched his torso like a bear after winter hibernation and trudged over to the main cabin for breakfast. Farther away on the other side of the fence, the two oxen looked at David awaiting their marching orders.

David had his breakfast and looked for Richard or Peter to learn the day's work agenda. Out of the corner of his eye, he noticed something out of place. The oxen had got through their fence and were standing beside the laundry line, by the spot where David had hung up clothing to air out.

It took a few seconds for David's eyes to agree with his brain that yes, Felix and Keshla were casually eating his down jacket. The oxen looked over toward David with guilty expressions, as if to say, "You're cool with this, right? 'Cause we can just hop back over the fence and eat grass if it's a problem."

David took it on faith not to charge large farm animals but seeing his most valuable possession eaten by a pair of prehistoric-looking cows, changed his world view on the subject.

"AAAAAAAARRRRRRRRR!!!!!!!!!!!!!!!!!!" David screamed in his best oxen, running at them. The jacket eaters fled the scene of the crime, feathers flying everywhere. Two arms had been completely devoured. He picked up the remains, evaluated the damage, and muttered to himself, "I guess I can make a vest out of it."

He looked up at Richard, who, passing by the commotion, was now laughing so hard he collapsed and said, gasping, "Do you have a suspect?" David was still pondering the damage.

"Maybe you should dust for prints. I guess I mean hooves. Dust for hooves." His laugh had now turned into a cackle, so David went to find some sewing thread, picking up goose down along the way.

CHAPTER 54

Tranquility Bay

2015 – Kalimantan, Indonesia

"Don't move!" Richard said in a manner that Terrie interpreted as a life or death warning. "At three o'clock, one foot away from you. I think it's a jelly."

Terrie turned, petrified but still in control and looked down into the crystal-clear turquoise water. "Do jellyfish have zip-lock mouths?" she said as she picked up a sandwich bag from a depth of about ten inches. "And can you stop with the three o'clock business? I never can remember how to do that, and I think you can't either."

"Zip-lock-mouth jellyfish... well, there are box jellyfish, so it's only logical there'd be some sort of plastic bag jellyfish too." Richard shook his head admiringly. "Talk about adapting to its environment. Like, what's next? An aluminum foil jellyfish?"

It wasn't that they were inexperienced snorkel and scuba divers but there was a strong argument they were cowards and prone to spooking unnecessarily. Their obsession with jellyfish was the cornerstone of Richard's Axis of Evil Sea Creatures Theory, which in combination with his unifying Axis of Evil Land Creatures Theory was eventually dubbed by Terrie as "the Axis of Bullshit Theory."

His eyes glazed over for a moment as the memory of his most recent writings flashed through his mind, ever so briefly.

Although rejected for review (at this time) by the journal Science as having been "the work of a madman," it was later published in Richard's column in The Daily Blabbermouth, Richard Rants, to more measured comments.

"Compelling," one reader wrote.

"It's about time somebody challenges the notion that animals aren't capable of evil behavior just like the Democrats," another wrote.

"Easily the best writing on the topic! In fact, maybe the only writing on the topic. The government couldn't keep a lid on this thing forever. Don't let them make you stop ranting, Richard!"

He returned from his thoughts. "Okay, have it your way, but when a puffer fish makes an attack from your flank, don't come looking to me for my blowgun."

"It's a spear gun, not a blowgun. And you can't use it. We already went over that one. I threatened to leave you, remember?"

"Vaguely. That does ring a bell."

Terrie pulled her mask onto her forehead. "Look, Richard. We have to get back into pleasure mode. Theoretically, between your new medications and my personal need to never succumb to logic used by morons, or logic fueled by fear, I think we can lick this thing. But this world of evil Winnie the Pooh characters, I just can't go on like this forever."

"I know, I know. I just... I just need to work on this more because I have to sort through all this stuff, this animal stuff and separate which animals are just as science defines them and which ones are disingenuous and hiding behind their good looks as a cover. I just need more time, that's all."

Terrie pulled her mask back down and reached out for Richard's hand. Their flippers splashed as they walked into the calm water backwards. "Watch out for the triggerfish," he said. "I think they are in cahoots with the jellies."

"Right," Terrie replied as they submerged, hand in hand.

CHAPTER 55

Drinking the Kool-Aid

1977 – Northern British Columbia

Peter's home was only twenty-five miles from Prince George, but it might as well have been one hundred for its remoteness. Trips to town were infrequent, especially since he had to hitchhike. He always returned with a couple of stories. A few weeks after arriving, Richard accompanied Peter to town to shop at the hardware and grocery stores.

Peter's dry sense of humor was completely lost on the young salesman helping him. "I am wondering if your store carries nosey-needle pliers," he asked.

The salesman stood speechless, then replied, "Maybe what you're looking for is needle-nosed pliers. We carry needle-nosed pliers, but we don't have anything called nosey-needle pliers."

"In that case, I'll take the needley-nosey type."

Hitchhiking home, Richard discovered Peter was a cop-magnet. A fifty-five-year-old-silver-haired man hitchhiking was usually a good bet for either parole violations or vagrancy. A police car pulled over to question the pair. "Can I see some identification please gentlemen?" the officer asked.

Richard, as a de facto representative of longhaired hippies, knew the drill from countless hassles over the years and dutifully passed over his I.D.

"And your I.D., sir," the officer snapped to Peter.

Peter replied in his usual slow but articulate manner, "I haven't any today."

"Sir, do you have any money?" the Mountie continued.

Peter looked the officer in the eyes and said, "I do but I can't help you out right now." The officer handed Richard back his paperwork, not at all sure what to make of Peter. He shook his head, then drove away.

One day Peter, indignant he needed to buy nails at the local general store, or drive into Prince George and lose the entire day, addressed this issue at the dinner table with all of the inhabitants of Evansylvania. "Lynn," he called out to his twenty-years-younger wife, "against my better judgment, I am going to buy some supplies at the Nukko Lake Hold-up."

They all laughed. The Nukko Lake General Store was the only store in that area, and it was expensive. But, in perspective, all isolated stores were more expensive than those serving larger populations. Peter, however, failed to appreciate these economic factors.

Richard and David offered to hike the five miles there with Peter, just to get out in the world for a change. The three chatted as they kept a steady pace, partly inspired by the aggressive mosquitos. It was mid-June, and the underbrush was already five feet tall with an Amazon Rainforest feel to it. After walking a few hours, they came upon the store.

The three removed their muddy boots outside, a common tradition in the area. The Allen family ran the store and could be heard chatting with customers in a friendly, familiar, manner. Richard was surprised how nice they seemed, as Peter had such a low opinion of their price list. It left him with the impression that they were gangsters. The matriarch component of the family, Clare Allen, saw them and said, "Hi, Peter. I thought we were too expensive for you to shop here."

"Well, you are, but when I factor in that you are the only horse in town, your store looks... pretty good."

This squabble was a routine event, the two new folks kept their mouths shut, David later noting that, "discretion is the greater part of valor."

Peter put down some nails, screws, and, as a treat, a bag of chocolate chips for future use. Clare rang up the cash register and said, "That is a grand total of eight dollars and sixty-five cents. Will you be paying in cash or trading with beads and fur pelts today?"

Although Peter was usually the first to respond to humor with more humor, this exchange obviously had quite a bit of strained history to it, leaving Peter speechless. That was no small feat, ensuring that this round would go to Clare.

They started the long hike back. After a while, Peter made an ominous comment. "I have been having dreams about the Nukko Lake Holdup lately, and the results were bad for this establishment but good for humanity."

Neither of the two younger men responded, afraid to know what lurked in Peter's thoughts while he slumbered.

CHAPTER 56

Letters

1977 – Horsefly, British Columbia

"Oh yeah, one more thing," Richard said. "Before you hop that freight train to the school of higher yearnings. Do you remember a couple of years ago, when your mom spotted a mole growing from your neck and they brought in that guy that we called Dr. Jack D. Ripper...?"

"Yeah, it rings a bell," David replied. "Like as if I'd ever be able to forget the day, he told me I had melanoma in my throat. Dr. Fox, that's what his name was."

"Yeah, sly ole' Dr. Fox. The guy that put that scar on your neck that got you an honorable mention in Ripley's Believe It or Not for longest scar in the non-military category."

"I heard from the anesthesiologist later that feeble-minded, Dr. Fox, would have chopped my head off if the nurse hadn't walked in."

"I never liked the idea of automatic settings for surgical tools, but I guess they are always trying to cut costs." Richard waited for David to groan.

"So why this talk of my close call with the Grim Reaper?" David asked.

"Well, I know it's been a couple of years, but you appear to have a new lump growing on your neck. Right here," Richard said, touching it.

"Yeah, I've been ignoring it, hoping it would disappear. I'll get it checked, mi amigo. Anything else?" David asked.

"Ummm... oh yeah. You might want to maybe look into some penile enhancement while you're at it. I hear it does wonders for your self-esteem."

"Well, the thing is, if I get accepted into medical school, I can do my own surgery on myself, and cut out the middleman..."

"Aaahhhh!" Richard groaned. "Walked right into that one, didn't I?"

Yeah, I did have another question." Richard replied. "Do you think you'll have any time off from your book-learning for a visit to a loyal Boy-Pal? I'll be all by my lonesome self in the Caribou Mountains for the entire Winter, so I could go a little bit coo-coo-coo-coo you know. We'll only be a mere two hundred miles away from each other."

"I don't know what I am going to do without your wise counseling." David replied.

Richard waved goodbye as he threw on his backpack and took his bird.

Several months of silence transpired before Richard, yet again ensconced in the proverbial middle of nowhere, made a forty mile hitchhiking pilgrimage to a tiny town known as Horsefly for supplies. But first he stopped at the one-room post office to check for mail. Surprised he had some, opened and read the letters on the steps outside.

LETTER #1

Dear Señor Pepe,

It is about diese time I went to see the Herr Doktor in Castlegar about the new lumpitis that has appeared in my neck. He injected 5 mg. of morphine into his arm, threw the I Ching, and said, "Dis look no-good. You bettey go see man who did this job." Anyways, he said he thought that the dreaded heebie-jeebies had returned, and I should probably see the sawbones that had done the dirty work because he would be able to tell what was happening.

At this point what does the poor boy think? After drawing ritual pentagrams with a mixture of billy-goat piss and opium ashes on the floor of Greasy Anna's Café, I departed Crescent Valley to go to Spokane to get another doctor's verdict on the matter. Of course, I got to Spokane on Friday afternoon. All doctors had retired to the opium dens and would be stupefied until Monday morning.

So, as it was, me and Shims (the name of the V.W. Van I just bought) did the trip to Californy with the hell-hounds on our tail all the way. Savvy?

Turned out that the lumpitis was a benign tumor that forms around cut nerve endings sometimes. So there I am in the land of palm trees and Taco Bells with a greased dildo up my posterior and no paddle to row with or something like that, and I hung out in old Californy for about a week and turned my V.W. in the direction of cold-cold Canada, revved the engine up to 1500 RPMs, popped the clutch, and heard a clunk and nothing happening movement-wise. My clutch plate had busted. C'est la vie, eh?

Another week in sunny Calif?

LETTER #2

Deer Hair Rabbiit,
Firstly, don't try to change da subject.
Secondly, someday the Baby Gnarciss will rule the world.
Thirdly, fishes can be vicious, ain't that poetic...
And finally, there is food and then there is the illusion of food (fud). You are intoxicated by the illusion: Bones, fish bones, dreams of fish bone smoke drifting through the grey cafes and little laughing puppies made of mud, all laughing at me, laughing at me... I'm sure that all of this is only too clear. You will hear soon....

LETTER #3

My Dear Sahib,

Sweet blow the nitrous oxide winds, deep flow the peaceful dream of ketamine, pentothal, and halothane. My soul is aflame with the liveliest liquid exhilaration and my mind screams out, "Yes, yes, yes!" To the gnawing Teeth of Fate, "Ingest me! Ingest me!" Take me through the churning bowels of COSMIC TRANSFORMATION to be shat out in a New Form! Renewed! Revitalized!! REBORN!!!

(Not to mention cured of constipation).

But I am quite sure that you have felt all these things in exactly the same way and a hundred times before.

But I am just an old man babbling...

Yours in Godless Atheism

Richard put the letters in his daypack for rereading. One thing though, David was fine.

CHAPTER 57

Reincarnated Oxen

1978 – Birch Lake, British Columbia

Like a lot of farms in the world, prioritizing at the Evans Farm was as much art as science. As Peter put it, "I often gain clarification through communication via the Ouija board."

"Really?" Richard exclaimed. "I always thought that it was kind of a joke, like reading palms and fortunes." Peter mounted a point-by-point rebuttal of the slanderous allegations against Ouija boards and other psychic phenomena, leaving the two young ox handlers fully informed on where Peter stood respecting these weighty matters.

Peter segued into reincarnation, incorporating in the mix a mysterious local murder ten years prior. A man named Sven Oberman lived in one of Peter's cabins, now occupied by Richard. In what Richard and David later described as a "sermon," Peter ended with the statement, "I have little doubt that the ox you were working with yesterday, Keshla, is the reincarnation of one Mr. Sven Oberman."

"Maybe I'll send Oberman a bill for my jacket" David said. Peter laughed. David still mourned his down jacket now a vest.

The current situation, whereby Felix and Keshla viewed the clothesline as a delicatessen, was untenable. It wasn't fair to blame it all on the bovines, either. Tucked in an adjoining field was an underground goat house built into a hill, filled with goats of all sizes, shapes, and colors. For these creatures, it was child's play to get over, under, or in between the fences. They used complex reasoning to get whatever their evil hearts desired and baby goats are so cute a hardened criminal couldn't help but melt watching them play. There was no arguing, the goats had to share the blame with the oxen.

After the oxen clothesline incident, "fencing" was upgraded on the Evansylvania To Do List from "a little demoralizing" to "very demoralizing," thereby dethroning "haying" from the number one to the number two spot. It was under this pall that two more oxen-related disturbances took place.

It had been raining without let up for most of what British Columbians referred to as "Summer." Comments regarding the unsuitability of agriculture in much of the province were starting to look largely correct. The grass had to be dry before one began harvesting it, since grass that contained moisture could mold over time or even spontaneously combust. While waiting for the grass to dry out and thereby becoming hay, a couple of Jehovah's Witnesses came to visit Peter and explain the error of his ways, that being his belief in reincarnation. The subject later turned to farmer talk and how the Summer rains were killing people's desire to keep farming. One of the Jehovah's mentioned that he was originally from "real" farm country stating, "Back home in Oregon, we'd harvest four times a year!"

Peter replied, "But here you only have to do it once!"

The two laughed with Peter about his glass-half-full logic. Suddenly David burst into the log home. He and Richard had been outside in the old barn, hooking up the oxen with a yoke to do some log pulling. "Peter! Oh, sorry to interrupt, but you have to come outside to see the oxen!"

The two creatures, completely attired in their formal work harness and connected with a wooden yoke, had managed to get around their fence, not by their usual techniques, but instead by walking together in unison into Birch Lake, then swimming around the fence. As the fence extended into the deep water, it took a fair bit of gumption on their part to do this.

Peter took this as an omen communicated via ox, since he was convinced that one of them was his former friend, enemy, and employee, Sven Oberman. "Oberman was a hardy Swede," Peter extrapolated, "and he wouldn't have let a small body of water like this get in his way.

The Jehovah's Witnesses laughed in a friendly way at what they saw as Peter's ignorance in the ways of the spiritual world. They left shortly afterwards when Richard put the willful oxen into their barn to dry off and settle down.

Only a couple of hours later Richard went back to the barn to let the two ne'er-do-well oxen back into their field to graze. He let Felix out of his stall first. "Go on Felix. Out ya go," Richard said, standing back from the huge creature. Felix left without incident.

Keshla, a.k.a. Sven Oberman, was next. In his wisdom, Keshla decided, for reasons still unknown, to do a complete 360 degree turn and walk out the front door. This caught Richard off guard. His girth combined with Keshla's was a few inches wider than the distance between the barn walls. When the widest parts of both aligned, Keshla just about crushed the life out of Richard. His life flashing before his eyes, a fortuitous element saved the day. The wall boards were nailed into the studs as if intended to release. At the moment of truth, two boards blasted open, saving Richard from becoming an interesting side-note in Peter's reincarnation story.

Keshla nonchalantly departed the scene of the crime as if nothing had occurred, slowly walking over to see his buddy Felix out in the field.

At first, Richard gasped like a fish out of sea, sucking in air and slowly pulled himself upright, relieved that his ribs hadn't cracked. Chuckling, he thought, now I guess I know why they call it Ox-y-gen. He slowly walked back to his cabin where he met up with David and said, "Before you say anything in regard to our upcoming work agendas, I would like to go on the record as stating that for the next twenty-four hours, I don't want anything to do with those two psycho cows."

David nodded in agreement and said, "That's a 10-4 on the psycho cows, Houston."

CHAPTER 58

Ginger

2016 – San Francisco, California

"There's a guinea pig inside," Terrie announced proudly, holding the colorful carrying case up for Richard to inspect.

Richard's face transformed itself, as if to say, "My way of life is in peril." He got right to the point. "Are you serving it for dinner tonight? Because I had my heart set on Indian."

"Her name is Ginger, thank you very much!" Terrie said in a strange voice, leaving Richard unsure to whom the voice was supposed to belong. "She's from school, but I don't like leaving her all alone, so I thought we could try her out. Like foster parents."

Richard grimaced. "Like the dog pound."

"Be open-minded, okay? Make her feel welcomed. She might surprise you. Anyhow, you have a bit of time on your hands now that The Daily Blabbermouth has fired you. I told you not to send in that 'Mass Murderers Anonymous' column. They weren't ready for it." Richard exhaled dejectedly as Terrie finished off her critique. "Nobody on the entire planet Earth was ready for it. Because you missed a truism, which is that mass murderers don't make for sympathetic characters." Terrie felt compelled to punctuate her closing argument with her finger to her forehead stating "DOIEEE!" for clarity's sake.

Richard extracted Ginger from the carrier and held her in a secure yet dangling way with her little belly showing for the whole world to see. "Hi Ginger! You're going to have to watch your figure young lady." He laid down on the couch, put her on his chest, and scratched her furry body. Ginger began making otherworldly happy-guinea-pig noises. "You are sweet, aren't you?" he said as Ginger burrowed into him.

Terrie knew the bonding process was underway and wasn't surprised. Richard immediately began to ventriloquize on Ginger's behalf, just as she did. "I was a show-pig in my younger days," Terrie caught on and ventriloquized back, "I had a stunning figure, if I can be immodest for just a minute."

Richard took the bait. "Where did you perform, Ging?" he asked, dropping the more formal Ginger.

"In Paris. They adored me. Just pronounce my name with a French accent: Zhin-zhere."

"Not *the* Zhin-zhere!" Richard sputtered. "The famous burlesque entertainer!"

"C'est moi!" Ginger said, opening her arms out wide as Ginger had on a regular basis to one adoring crowd after the next.

"Well, it's settled. Ginger is staying with us, and she's not to pay one penny's rent."

"Richard, Ginger has fallen on hard times and I think it only befitting a former show-pig from Paris to have a wardrobe worthy of a star."

"Done. I will sign a blank check if you can find the time to..."

"It would be an honor!" Terrie interrupted.

"Then it's settled," Richard said as he delicately put their show-pig into what Terrie referred to as her apartment, which bore a strong resemblance to a cage.

"How old is she, anyways?" Richard said out of Ginger's earshot.

Terrie looked over at Ginger who was happily repositioning straw on her apartment floor. "Four."

"Astonishing. She doesn't look a day older than three."

CHAPTER 59

Visions of Catapults
Danced in their Heads

1978 – Birch Lake, British Columbia

It was Winter at Birch Lake and Winter wasn't a small deal in this locale. Five to six months would elapse from the first snowfall until the last melted snow patch. If that wasn't enough to make the American draft dodgers reconsider what they went and done, Mr. Forty Degrees Below Zero would stop by to remind them of the reasons virtually no human beings had voluntarily chosen to live there.

The two lakes froze as hard as rock. This allowed for world class ice skating on early Winter glare ice. A time to distinguish between the Canadians and the Californians. The Canadians all knew how to skate. The Californians, not so much. The ice was so clear this winter, you could see schools of fish swimming directly under your skates.

The snow kept getting higher and higher until the lakes were not only frozen but completely buried. It was mid-January now and the road crews had been getting further and further behind plowing the snow off of the roads. This forced the residents to live a much simpler way of life. Evans Farm was traditionally the last farm to get plowed for three good reasons:

It was the end of the line and nobody else lived close by.

Peter Evans did not own a car and was just as happy snowshoeing as he was walking.

Peter only came out for supplies about once a month or so.

This year was one of those where nobody would see or hear from Peter and associates for months at a time. Some, like the proprietors of the Nukko Lake Holdup, always looked forward to a break from Peter and his bellyaching, while a few of his old friends would periodically check in on him.

It was a dark and dreary night, someone once said. But this night was particularly dreary. Snowshoes were necessary to move about the large acreage, as the drifts had filled in all of the trails between the cabins, barns, and other outbuildings. Peter's farm had become a snow shoveler's nightmare.

Despite the kerosene lamps sprinkled throughout the house, it was dark inside the log home. But everyone was reading something except for Peter. He wandered with a book under his arm, looking for something. At last he spoke softly to no one in particular. "I am wondering where to find my testicles." The silence in the room was now twice as deep as before, as there really wasn't anyone with a ready answer.

Then Richard tried. "Um, um, have you tried looking in your pants?"

David added, "Where did you have them last?"

"I meant to say spectacles, not testicles. Sorry for the confusion and thank you for those excellent suggestions."

They all laughed for a few minutes before returning to silence with their books. It was 9 P.M. and all the Evansylvanians were in the living room with the big barrel-wood heater, quietly reading and relaxing, exhausted from the elements. None of them had seen a new face for a full month, so when there was a pounding on the large front door, the expressions on the inhabitants' faces could only be described one way. Shocked!

Peter, gathering his wits, did the appropriate thing, answered the door.

"Peter Evans!!" said a voice outside, sounding surprised.

"Well, I'll be darned!" Peter replied, amazed. "It's Ernie Teskie!! Come in, come in!!"

Ernie Teskie, a tall, grey-haired man with an impish smile who was covered in snow and layers of clothing, was holding his own snowshoes. "I haven't seen you in so long I figured you were dead. So, I come over to bury you!"

This brought the house down and Ernie was treated like royalty. His wife had just baked a large batch of chocolate chip cookies for the Evans family. If it had been election day, Ernie would have been voted prime minister. He and Peter gave each other a report on the state of their farms, their extended families and some reminiscences about days gone by. The others shoveled cookies into their mouths, thoroughly enjoying the novelty of the moment.

It was late when Ernie strapped on his snowshoes and headed home. Peter came into the living room holding a long rolled-up piece of paper. "I have something that may be of interest for you to see," he said cryptically to Richard and David, the only ones still up. Peter unrolled the mystery paper on the dinner table next to a kerosene lamp and flattened it out.

David was the first one to make it out. "Why, that is a blueprint of a catapult!"

They all laughed. Peter explained, "You never know when you might be in need of a good catapult."

"You took the words right out of my mouth," Richard added.

The immense amount of detail in the drawing was ominous. "So, Peter," David asked, "who are we going to war against?"

CHAPTER 60

Not Your Average Show-Pig

2016 – San Francisco, California

Having a guinea pig as their newest roommate had some unexpected repercussions. Within one week, Terrie sewed and assembled an entire wardrobe for Ginger that would match an assortment of holidays, while Richard purchased a few pieces of miniature furniture that he thought Ginger would find stimulating. He substantially increased the square footage of what now could truly be called her apartment. It quickly became apparent, Richard's fascination knew no bounds.

"Is that a miniature piano in the corner of Ginger's cage?" Terrie asked.

"It's her apartment, not a cage," Richard corrected, "and yes, that's her new baby grand. She played some jazz late last night while you were sleeping."

Terrie stuck her face into Ginger's "apartment." "Good morning, Ging!" she said as her furry friend scampered up to greet her. "Jesus, Richard, what's all this stuff?"

"I wanted to surprise you."

"A miniature chandelier, art deco furniture and are those Picassos hanging up? Wow!"

"They're not originals but they really pull her place together. Look up into her new loft," Richard said, not able to hide his enthusiasm.

"It's a miniature office. A desk, filing cabinet, a photocopier and a laptop!" She looked over at Richard, slowly shaking her head. "This is getting stranger by the minute!" she said in a sing-songy voice.

"Ginger was overjoyed when she woke up and saw the upgrades," Richard added.

"Oh, you two had a little chat, did you?"

"Well, let's just say we have a lot of the same views and values."

Terrie grabbed her purse and headed out the door, mumbling to herself, "Oh God, what have I gone and done?"

She returned late that evening, and everything seemed normal. Normal was good. Richard had left her dinner ready to warm up, which she ate and relaxed with a magazine for a while. Richard was sound asleep. On her way to their bedroom, she heard a rustling sound coming from the office in Ginger's apartment. She peeked into the dark room and called out to the former show-pig, "Sweet dreams little piglet," and crawled into bed without waking Richard up.

After a restless sleep, to the sound of clicking and the occasional sound of a printer, she awoke. It was six-thirty and Richard was making breakfast. He handed her a coffee and she gave him a sleepy, sexy kiss, then said, "I kept hearing something like a clicking sound last night. Weird."

"Yeah, when I woke up about an hour ago, I went into the office to see Ginger. I'd like to show you something."

Terrie followed Richard into the office, where they saw Ginger in the loft of her apartment. On her desk were a few small pieces of paper. Terrie pulled one page off the desk and read it out loud. "It's a buy-sell order form and it's from Barcelona. It says: 'Sell 20 Units at 10 Euros per Unit. Sincerely, Ernesto.'"

CHAPTER 61

Kanadian Kops
and
Kanadian Kriminals

1990 – Nukko Lake, British Columbia

Officer Perkins wasn't your joe-average-canuck police detective. He was about as untypical a police detective as could be found in the Mounties. After a couple of quick promotions in the Vancouver division for his exceptional work closing out several unsolved murders and rapes, he surprised his compatriots by transferring to the so-called Capital of Northern British Columbia and the Yukon, where one normally might start their career, not transfer to in their prime. A place called Prince George.

But Perkins knew he was heading straight down the road to burn-out-ville at his current pace. Perkins decided an easy assignment for a year or two, in what only Canadians would call a city, was just what the doctor ordered. As well, he had no wife, no kids, and no dog, so his analytical mind was completely satisfied that he had made yet one more perfect decision.

When he got a phone call from his boss at four-fifteen in the morning, on a Saturday no less, he wasn't projecting his usual aura of love and compassion. "Just tell me this isn't a sales call, 'cause if it is, I would have no choice but to have you and your family vaporized."

"Perky!" It was the Chief. "Do I ever have a show stopper for you. Are you sitting down?"

Officer Perkins had told his fellow employees he kept an updated list of people who called him "Perky" for an opportune moment when he would kill each and every one of them. But that had only emboldened the chief.

"Sitting down? No," he croaked, "lying down would be more accurate. So, give me your best shot."

"Lying down is better anyway. Have you been up to Nukko Lake yet?"

"Yep, passed through on a weekend once. I think. Didn't see a donut shop so I kept driving."

"Yep, that's the place," the chief concurred. "Well, when you were sniffing around for donuts, you might have noticed the Nukko Lake General Store."

"Can't say that I did, can't say that I didn't. Even police detectives have to blink occasionally. Do I have to keep telling everybody that I'm not Superman?"

"Well, how 'bout getting out of your cowboy pajamas, wrassle up one of the hosses tied up at the saloon and ride your sorry ass out to the Nukko Lake General Store. I'm already there with Officer Numb-nuts, I mean Newman. It's hard to describe, just get down here, would ya? The local yokels are gathering around, just in case this turns out to be the second coming or something, so I'd appreciate it if you'd skip your morning box of assorted donuts just this once."

"Okay, I'll be out there as fast as you can say, 'Transfer me to anywhere on the planet as long as it's not Prince George!'"

An hour later Detective Perkins pulled up to what looked like the set from a Grade B science fiction movie. A huge boulder, or perhaps a meteorite, sat upon the crushed carcass of what had been the Nukko Lake General Store. The sun was just starting to rise, emitting a mysterious pinkish hue. The ominously murmuring crowd of neighboring farmers lacked only pitchforks and torches. Perkins spoke first. "So... basically, you just woke me up at four-thirty in the morning to arrest a large rock."

Officer Newman gave his unsolicited professional opinion. "I'm thinking asteroid."

The chief wasn't big on brainstorming. "Okay, Newman. Quit thinking. This is why we don't pay you the big bucks."

Detective Perkins paced off the distance between the road and the extinct general store, repeatedly looking up at the surrounding trees. The chief and Newman walked over to where Perkins was processing his thoughts. He turned towards the chief and said quietly, "If I give you my leading theory, will you promise to handle the press conference?"

"No problem, stud."

"Catapult."

"Come again?" the chief said, his right hand clenched to his forehead.

"It was a catapult job."

"That's what I thought you said." His hand remained on his forehead as if welded to it. "Remember when I told you that I would handle the press conference for you? Just a minute ago?"

"Yeah, you said, 'No problemo, stud-o.'"

"Yeah, well... guess what... stud-o?"

CHAPTER 62

The Princess of Peru

2018 – San Francisco, California

It was getting late. Richard, Terrie and Ginger were relaxing together before calling it a day. Since Ginger came on the scene, their home life had become considerably more conventional. Conventional if you made allowances for Richard's belief that Ginger was a small person who lived in a fur suit and ran an import-export business based out of Barcelona.

Ginger's baby grand piano was busily playing one show tune after the next, which Richard and Ginger loved but was starting to get on Terrie's nerves. "She loves this Italian parsley!" Richard said as he hand-fed her.

Terrie didn't look up from her book. "Why don't you peel her a few grapes while you're at it?"

Richard pulled a baby carrot out of Ginger's vegetable bag and poked it into her mouth. "Aaahh, does Daddy's little pig like that?"

Daddy's little pig clung to the vegetable as if it were an expensive Cuban cigar, frozen as she stared at Terrie with what could only be described as seething anger.

"Well, say what you will, but that rodent isn't gonna get unlimited pay-per-view if she keeps playing us off against each other."

Ginger flicked her head at Terrie, showing her anger, pulled a Picasso down off the apartment wall, scampered over to a poster and made it clear this was the replacement, a picture of Ginger with the words, "WORK HARD – PLAY HARD!"

"Ginger, you're cruising towards an all-expenses paid vacation to Peru. And you know what they like to do with guinea pigs there. So, start behaving. Be a dignified retired show-pig. Ginger, nobody gets to be a jerk around here."

Ginger scampered into her loft office. Richard looked at Terrie. "Maybe a little tough on her, don't you think?"

"She'll be fine. Person or piggy, too much adoration can go to anyone's head."

"Maybe she's also exhausted by the time difference with Barcelona. You have to admit that she's been burning the candle at both ends lately."

"Richard, you're starting to scare me again. Say after me: Animals don't actually run import-export businesses."

Just then Ginger scampered along a wall of her apartment and pushed some paper outside. Terrie walked over to Ginger's apartment, picked up the paper, then examined it critically and sputtered, "Where the hell did she get her paws on foreign currency?!"

Richard looked at the money in Terrie's hands. "They're euros," he declared. He put his index finger up in the air to indicate that he had unraveled the mystery. "Ernesto!"

CHAPTER 63

Ravenous Humor

1990 – Caribou Mountains, British Columbia

Richard was content with his log cabin. It was small, but the price was right. Public land, referred to as Crown land, made up over ninety percent of British Columbia. If you just built on it out of sight, a few miles from a remote dirt road, nobody ever bothered you. Because nobody knew you were there, and nobody cared you were there. Total cost: $100.

His two criteria for his building site were, it had to be on a lake, and it had to have radio reception. Without the sound of another human voice for a month at a time, the radio was the difference between sanity and insanity.

Earlier in the day, Richard had filled his firewood box enough to last until the following morning. As the sun set, he tuned the radio dial to the one and only channel, the Canadian Broadcasting Corporation, known to one and all as the C.B.C. He parceled out a bowl of deer jerky, dried blueberries and fried bread, referred to as pemmican, and nestled himself onto a foam pad beside the glowing hot wood heater. His favorite radio show had already begun, "As it Happens" with Barbara Fromm, an in-depth news program following the nightly world news.

"Detective Perkins. Could you tell us if anybody was hurt by the meteorite?"

"Amazingly enough Barbara, there were no injuries whatsoever, but the local general store was completely destroyed. Also, we are waiting for test results to determine if it was, in fact, a meteorite. That is one theory, but at this point in the investigation, we are exploring any and all possibilities, including criminal."

"Officer Perkins, one last question. There has been an unconfirmed rumor that the boulder or meteorite may have been launched from Earth as opposed to dropping into the atmosphere from outer space. The word 'catapult' was bandied about as the delivery system. What is the likelihood that we could be looking at Martians invading Earth with catapults and meteorites? And I would appreciate an affirmative on that question because frankly, it would really help our ratings."

Officer Perkins laughed. "Sorry, Barbara, but I think it would be premature to say that we are at that point yet. But remember, the Mounties always get their man!"

"Yes, but isn't the real question, do the Mounties always get their Martian?"

They both laughed at each other's jokes and signed off. Richard turned off the radio and went outside. The snow hanging on the surrounding spruce trees reflected the starlight. It was utterly peaceful and quiet. A shooting star shot by. Richard shook his head and laughed. His laughter echoed off the lake. He went back inside and started composing a letter to David in his mind. He got as far as the title of his story, then set his letter down on a crate that he used in lieu of a table. He laid down on his foamy and started to laugh himself to sleep. He was unaware that two small black ravens were quietly looking in through the window at his letter as they chatted to each other.

"Mar-sh-In-va"
"Mar-sh-In-va-sh"
" Ka-pull-va"
"Ka-pull-va-sh"

"Nook hol"

"Nook hol up"

A third much larger Raven spoke last.

"Martian invasion! Catapult invasion! Nukko Lake Holdup!

They all laughed enough to make Richard stir for a moment, then were silent, other than the big bird that muttered,

"Quoth the Raven 'never more.' Cawww!" The birds all had one last giggle together, then silence.

About the Author

   Richard Morgen spent half of his adult life in Northern British Columbia and the other half in Marin County, California. He presently lives in San Francisco. In different incarnations, he owned and operated a tree planting business that planted five million trees per year. He was a subsistence farmer-hunter-gatherer, while living off the grid in northern British Columbia. He ran his own portable sawmill, and became a consultant to the lumber remanufacturing industry. Also, on a seasonal basis, he was a fire fighter, a fire look-out man, a trail builder, a cone picker, a tree thinner, a lumber stacker on the green chain, worked for the railroad changing railroad ties, and most of his life spent in Canada was without a road or electricity, accessible only by river boat, snowmobile, or horse and sleigh. Later in his life he became co-owner of a mesquite charcoal manufacturing and distributing company in Mexico. For the past six years, while writing this semi-autobiographical fiction, he has primarily been trying to perfect the art of world travel with Parkinson's disease, broken ribs and dengue fever, along with the world's best travel partner, Therese.

Made in the USA
Middletown, DE
24 March 2020

"WHAT'S THE NAME OF YOUR MOVIE?" RICHARD ASKE[D]
THE TWO 15-YEAR OLD DIRECTORS, HIS NEXT DO[OR]
NEIGHBOR, DAVID, AND DAVID'S JOVIAL FRIEND RE[X].
"WE CALL IT MEET THE MEAT-MAN," DAVID SA[ID]
PROUDLY, HIS WIRE-RIM GLASSES SLIGHTLY STEAME[D]
UP IN EXCITEMENT.

AT FOURTEEN, RICHARD, "THE WEIRDO," IS KICKED OFF THE HIGH SCHOOL BASEBALL TEAM FOR REFUSING [TO]
CUT HIS HAIR. AND SO, THE SHUNNING BEGINS. HE QUICKLY MAKES A NEW GROUP OF FRIENDS, KNOWN TO O[NE]
AND ALL AS THE BOY-PALZ. THE SOCIAL FLOWCHART IS IN FLUX IN 1969, RESULTING IN HYBRID GROUPS W[ITH]
A COMMON THREAD, NON-CONFORMITY.

WHEN SEVENTEEN-YEAR-OLD RICHARD DECIDES TO DROP OUT OF HIGH SCHOOL, HE CONVINCES THREE OF T[HE]
BOY-PALZ TO HITCHHIKE WITH HIM INTO THE WILDS OF BRITISH COLUMBIA AND ALASKA, AN ADVENTURE TH[AT]
LASTS TWENTY YEARS LONGER THAN PLANNED. THESE HILARIOUS ANECDOTES ILLUSTRATE HOW LUCK, GO[OD]
AND BAD, SHAPE THE LIVES OF THIS DRUG ADDLED QUARTET BACKDROPPED BY THE HIPPIE SCENE AND LIVI[NG]
OFF THE LAND.

IN HIS FIFTIES, RICHARD LANDS A TEMPORARY JOB WRITING A QUIRKY WEEKLY EDITORIAL FOR THE DA[ILY]
BLABBERMOUTH FROM BURNING BUSH, OKLAHOMA ABOUT HIS GLOBAL ADVENTURES WITH HIS WISECRACKI[NG]
GIRLFRIEND TERRIE. MATTERS BECOME INCREASINGLY CONFUSED WHEN MOTHER NATURE BEGINS TO T[OY]
WITH RICHARD'S IMAGINARY PREDISPOSITION FOR EXPLAINING UNEXPLAINABLE MYSTICAL AFFAIRS.
AS IF THINGS AREN'T ALREADY COMPLICATED ENOUGH FOR RICHARD, A BIZARRE ROYAL CANADIAN MOUNT[ED]
POLICE INVESTIGATION TAKES PLACE, HEADED BY THE SAVVY DETECTIVE PERKINS. HE FOLLOWS THE LEA[DS]
WHEREVER THEY TAKE HIM, EVEN WHEN THINGS START TO POINT TOWARD A CAREER-THREATENING DIRE[C]
TION OF EXTRATERRESTRIALS, CATAPULTS, AND SNOOPING RAVENS.

ISBN 9781070837536

90000

9 781070 837536